Books by Arthur Rosenfeld

A Cure for Gravity
Diamond Eye

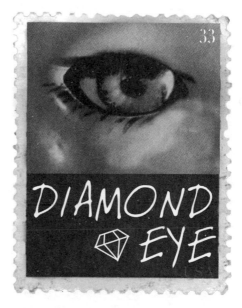

ARTHUR ROSENFELD

A Tom Doherty Associates Book
New York

DIAMOND EYE

Copyright © 2001 by Arthur Rosenfeld

Design by Heidi C. Q. Eriksen

A Forge Book
Published by Tom Doherty Associates, LLC
175 Fifth Avenue
New York, NY 10010

www.tor.com

Forge® is a registered trademark of Tom Doherty Associates, LLC.

Library of Congress Cataloging-in-Publication Data

Rosenfeld, Arthur.
    Diamond eye / Arthur Rosenfeld. — 1st ed.
        p. cm.
    "A Tom Doherty Associates book."
    ISBN 0-312-87871-0 (acid-free paper)
    1. Postal inspectors — Fiction.   2. Children in pornography —
Fiction.   3. Snuff films — Fiction.   I. Title.

    PS3568.O812 D52 2001
    813'.54 — dc21

                                        2001023204

Printed in the United States of America

0 9 8 7 6 5 4 3

For Stephen, Hildi, and Herbert,
who have taught me much of what I know about love,
loyalty, family, and children

ACKNOWLEDGMENTS

Major thanks go to professionals at the United States Postal Inspection Service — particularly the folks at the West Palm Beach, Florida, domicile, the Forensic and Technical Services Division at Dulles, Virginia, and the Career Development Division in Potomac, Maryland — for their help getting the details in this book right. Special thanks go to Inspectors J. R. Broussard, Roy Geffen, Rudolfo Guerra, Michael A. Mackert, Daniel L. Mihalko, Rafael A. Rivera, and Lieutenant Cyprian E. Jenifer. Thanks also to Lieutenant Mel Mosier and Officer Robert Manning of the Lake Worth Police Department, and to Sergeant Keith Carson of the Lantana Police Department.

Last but far from least, I owe the most special debt of all to my friend Inspector Mike Bollie, without whom there would be no Maximillian Diamond.

Sometimes our needs are most endangered
By the ones we need the most.
And there is something of the stranger
In the closest of the close.
As he kisses her forever
He is kissing her goodbye.

How the nights can fly.
And how the days can fill you.
When the chance goes by.
How the years can kill you.

FROM "HOW THE NIGHTS CAN FLY" —
A SONG BY BOB LIND

ONE

God has his thumbprint on us all, no matter if we breathe through spiracles or gills or lungs, no matter if we have two legs or four or six or eight. That's what I was thinking as I watched the courtly insect rumba of a pair of giant incandescent grasshoppers on my windowsill. Festively decked out in warning coloration, they might have been a couple of Thai dancers or mariachi players, and their stiff love ballad seemed a parody of the fantasy unfolding on my monitor. Truth was, I was more interested in their antics than the ones on my desk. I was so burned out on the low-brow porn tapes I'd been assigned to go through that I'd taken to listening to jazz or sometimes Gershwin on my lunch hour and viewing them with the fast-forward button depressed so as to force the players—today a delighted patient and his nurse, clad only in Cuban heel stockings, a white cap and stiletto shoes—into a comic scherzo of thrusts and bends.

11

The preposterous scenario broke off in the middle, leaving me with only the haunting tones of "Summertime" for entertainment. I figured the tape had snapped, but before I could eject it the blank screen was filled with the image of a candlelit restaurant; a classy joint with white tablecloths, heavy curtains, rococo chairs of scrollwork and gold leaf. The jerky, amateurish camera work was unusual, so I shed my headphones and slowed the tape. The camera panned to just inside the entrance, where a headwaiter in coat and tails greeted an opulently dressed family of three. He escorted mother, father and daughter to a four-top in the corner, and handed them menus. Then, utterly without ceremony, and in the most matter-of-fact fashion, the little girl, brown-skinned and blue-eyed, climbed up onto the table.

The waiter came back, a violin tucked under his neck, and ran his bow slowly over the strings as the child removed her clothes. First came the pinafore and then the precious blue dress. Wearing only tiny lace undies, too much lipstick, eye-liner and rouge, the little girl began a terrible, seductive dance. As the camera zoomed in, she gyrated and pirouetted on her little high heels, arms held high like a cabaret pro.

I stopped the VCR and went to the window. My shadow frightened the grasshoppers, and they leapt bravely into the sky. I let the bright Florida sunshine rinse me like a hose, and when I felt clean enough, I went back to the tape. I watched the man remove his jacket and his shirt and draw the little girl to him, kissing her lasciviously while she gazed vacantly into the distance.

The camera moved to the woman. No more than eighteen, she played to the camera, making promises with her tongue. She unbuttoned her blouse, dropped her skirt, bent backwards over the table, rubbed herself down low. The man came to her, slid between her legs and caressed her breasts. The musical waiter picked up the tempo and the little blue-eyed girl danced faster on the tabletop. Then, just as casually as if he were buttering a piece of toast, the man reached over to a silver champagne bucket, pulled out a dripping wet Colt Gold Cup .45, put the muzzle into the woman's mouth, and pulled the trigger.

Then he took a drink.

I leapt out of my chair, my breath coming in gasps. The screen went dark again, and I could hear the whir of the VCR and the high-pitched hum that TVs make. I opened the door and stepped out into the light of the hallway, bumping into my boss, Miscellaneous Team Leader Wacona Smith.

"Are you all right?" she asked, frowning at my expression. Wacona is five feet three and wears frameless glasses and her dark, straight hair in bangs. Her librarian looks are deceiving. She's a barracuda.

"No."

She glanced over my shoulder and saw the VCR on my desk. "Watching tapes?"

"Yes."

"Kiddie porn?"

"Worse."

"There *is* nothing worse."

By way of answer, I backed up the tape, turned up the volume, and started it again for her. The waiter played his violin. The blue-eyed girl danced. The murderer grunted over his victim. The sound of the shot came as a deafening roar. Wacona reached to turn off the set. I saw her hand was shaking. "It's not real," she said.

"Could have fooled me."

"Trust me, it's phony. Where did you get it?"

I pointed across the room to several cartons full of tapes. "They've been there for weeks. One of Greg's cases. I've been working my way through them."

13

Two months earlier, Greg Hunter, the fourth inspector at the Palm Beach domicile, had been shotgunned in the face during a controlled delivery of five kilos of heroin. He had been a good man to work with. He had different sensibilities than I did, but a good man nonetheless. Everyone in the office missed him.

"Well, it's a fake."

"What makes you so sure?"

"The Colt Gold Cup is an enthusiast's gun. Expensive, finicky, prone to feed failure. It's not the kind of weapon you'd use for a snuff." Her cool tone burned me.

"Not the kind of weapon *who* would use? If we have a profile on video killers, I sure haven't seen it."

"I'm telling you it's bogus," she said impatiently. "Disgusting, but bogus."

"Yeah, well, I think it's the real thing and I want to work it up."

"We'll see. Right now, I need you for backup."

Still numb, I followed her out. She walked like she was a foot taller than she was, legs and hips all going at once, eyes in the back of her head watching for stares. When we got to the parking lot she pulled out the keys to what we call a "soft" car—a chocolate-colored Porsche seized after an arrest and attached by the service in lieu of fines due. The paint glinted in the sunshine, and I touched it with my finger.

"Hands off my car," Wacona commanded.

"Wanna tell me where we're going?"

"To play Good Cop/Bad Cop."

"Some asshole mouth off to his carrier again?"

"You got it."

Wacona worked the electric door lock, but I just stood outside the car.

"Today," she said.

I got in.

"It wasn't a murder. Now put it out of your mind," she said, roaring out of the lot, keeping the transmission in first gear too long.

"See that gauge to the right of the speedometer?" I asked casually. "That's your engine speed. When the needle goes into the red, you're munching the valves."

She did a four-wheel drifting slide around the corner, skillfully staying just shy of a spin by judicious use of the throttle and clutch.

"Max?" she smiled faintly. "Don't tell me how to drive."

The United States Postal Service, despite being a branch of the federal government, is run like a corporation. The Postal Inspection Service, the oldest and least-known federal law enforcement agency in the land, is part of the postal service, and operates along similar lines. The number of postal employees is vast, and one function of the U.S.P.I.S. is to keep those employees honest. It also investigates mail fraud, letter bombs, scams, and the occasional high-profile case, like the Unabomber. Sometimes these so-called "internal" and "external" crimes intersect. This morning was one of those times.

We pulled into a West Palm Beach neighborhood of tract homes—ivory, gray, and salmon, roofs done in shake shingles, lawns immaculate, curbs numbered in white. A passing cloud dropped a few raindrops on the windshield. Wacona clucked, but resisted the temptation to smear the glass by turning on the wipers. A postal delivery van was waiting half a block up on the other side. We got out and so did the van's driver, the grin on his face saying he was glad his personal bulldogs had arrived.

"What we have here," Wacona said under her breath, "is a genuine morale-boosting mission."

It made me feel good to hear it. Postal inspectors don't

wear uniforms and swagger about in the public view, and since they are rarely portrayed on either the small or big screen, the general public is barely aware we exist. Postal employees, however, know us all too well, and generally view us as river trolls with guns.

I rang the doorbell, and we stood there for a few minutes. The sun began to burn my bald scalp. I shave the stubble every three days: more frequently than that, I get razor burn.

"Who's there?" a gruff voice finally demanded from behind the door.

"Postal inspector," I replied sternly.

"Go fuck yourself."

Like Rodney Dangerfield, we rarely get any respect. At best, most people think we are little men who examine letters to make sure the address is spelled right. Wacona reached around me and banged on the door hard enough to dent the pressboard.

"Federal agents," she bellowed.

The door swung open slowly. A middle-aged citizen with three chins shaded his gaze with his hand and took in my baggy pants and shirt.

"You're Feds like I'm the King of Siam," he smirked.

I wasn't about to explain that I didn't dress to impress, that years of t'ai chi ch'uan practice had given me a taste for loose-fitting clothing. Instead, I showed him my I.D. Wacona did the same.

"Inspectors Wacona Smith and Maximillian Diamond," she said brusquely. "Did you brandish a weapon and threaten to drop this postal carrier like a quail?"

"I don't know what you're talking about!"

"The hell you don't!" the carrier cried.

I peered inside the doorway and spied a 12-gauge Remington pump leaning against the wall. I brought it around gingerly, which was all it took for Wacona to throw the guy against the front of his house, and spread his legs with her foot.

"That's it, you're going in," Wacona enthused, pulling out her cuffs.

The citizen deflated slightly. "That's for home defense," he growled.

"Threatening a postal employee is a federal crime," I growled back.

"My social security checks keep showing up too late for my alimony payment! I'm getting hassled by my ex-wife."

"You think I control when the treasury cuts funds?" the carrier interrupted.

"I think you control when you deliver them," the citizen snapped.

"Were you inebriated when you made the threat?" I demanded.

"Of course not!"

"Because if you were, it might help explain your felonious behavior," I finished.

Holding him in a wristlock, Wacona jangled the cuffs and pulled up hard enough to bend him at the waist.

"Okay, so maybe I had one too many," he licked his lips.

"I say we take him away," Wacona groused, enjoying the part.

"My partner wants to arrest you. A little apology might help."

The man craned his head around and looked venomously at the carrier, who grinned like a schoolboy.

"I'm sorry," said the carrier. "Did you say something?"

"I'm sorry I threatened to shoot you like a quail," the citizen grumbled.

The carrier cocked his hand to his ear.

"Say what?"

17

"I'm sorry I threatened to shoot your sorry ass!" the man shouted.

"My what?" the carrier quipped. Wacona yanked again.

"You. I'm sorry I threatened to shoot you!" the man bellowed.

"How sorry?" I gave the guy a hard look.

"Very sorry."

"We all need to feel confident that you will never threaten a postal employee again," I said. "Can we do that? Can we feel confident?"

Wacona jerked the cuffs again. I could almost hear the guy's shoulder tearing. "Definitely!" he gushed. "It was the booze, that's all. And I've sworn off."

"Does Your Majesty still doubt we're federal agents?" I inquired.

"No no. Federal agents. That's you!" he cried.

I unloaded the shotgun and bowled the shells down the hall, then put the gun back where I'd found it. Wacona led the way back to the Porsche. Together we watched the carrier swagger off, smiling smugly, on top of the world.

River trolls indeed.

The last rays of sunlight fled as Seagrave Chunny stared over my shoulder at the ghastly restaurant tableau. The snuff film didn't seem to ruffle him.

"Waco is right. It's probably bogus," he said, as his big gold Rolex slid down his slender wrist.

"It's not a fake, Sea. Jesus, look at the brain soup on the kid's leg."

"You see the alien autopsy on TV a few years back? They can do that, they can fake brains."

"This isn't Hollywood. It's small-time."

"You don't know who made the tape," Sea countered mildly. "Could be it's just made to look that way just to convince hard cases like you. People pay fifty dollars a pop for the legal stuff, ten times that for kiddie porn, maybe one thousand dollars or more for a snuff. You don't have to sell many copies to make it worth going to a little extra trouble."

"The girl was murdered," I said stubbornly. "And the kid saw it all."

"If you're right, she's history, plain and simple, and she could be ancient history for all you know. You're never going to find anyone connected with that film, understand?"

"Don't say that." I put my head in my hands.

Spare, elegant, thin to the point of gaunt, Inspector Seagrave Chunny came around my desk and perched close to me.

"Max?"

"Leave me be."

"What did I tell you when you took this job?"

I shook my head.

"Hide like a rhinoceros, that's what I told you. You asked me about being a postal inspector, I told you all you needed was a hide like a rhinoceros."

My previous job had convinced me I had one. Driving around Los Angeles, breathing smoggy air and pitching the benefits of outdated arthritis pills and prescription rectal wipes will do that for anybody. Every day I'd lugged cases full of drug samples and visual aids to medical offices and talked docs into prescribing my products. Sometimes I was told that the pills were outdated and that cheap over-the-counter wipes were just as good. More often I lost sales to competing reps, as my earnestness and hard work were no match for nice lipstick and a push-up bra.

Then, suddenly, my sixty-eight-year-old paternal grandmother living in South Florida had lost her nest egg of $412,000.07 to a fraud scam and called me, desperate and crying. I'd taken the next plane east and gotten the cops involved, and the cops had brought in Seagrave Chunny, who promptly fell for Sara Diamond, even though she was ten years his senior. Working the case harder than anyone had a right to expect, he discovered that the perpetrators had fled to Brazil after gambling away nearly $4 million in a Nassau casino spree. He said he thought there was still some money left, and he was hell-bent on recovering it. It was in that crazy, magical week after he flew off to extradite the bad boys in Brazil that Chunny made up his mind to become my grandfather, and I made up my mind to become a postal inspector.

"A tough hide is one thing, Sea. Accepting that tape, that's another."

"Surrender," he advised. "The case is an orphan. You've got plenty of your own work to do. Waco shouldn't have even asked you to watch them, understand?"

"Maybe you should have accepted Sara's bad luck," I said. "Maybe you should have surrendered to that. I'm not going to stick that tape in a storage room somewhere. I can't do it. I see the kid's face in my dreams. I see that girl's body twitch. I see the guy pick up his glass and take a drink. He took a drink, Sea. You hear me?"

He looked at me sadly. I could see he was fighting it inside, judgment versus compassion, experience versus wisdom.

"Help me out here," I begged. "Where should I start?"

Chunny ejected the cassette into his hand and stared at it thoughtfully for a long moment. I'd learned not to push him. The guy had been a postal inspector forever. There was nothing he didn't know.

"Send it up to Dulles," he said, referring to the inspection service's central crime lab. "Personally I don't think the snuff's genuine, but ask them to do tight close-ups on the blood and guts and on the muzzle of the Colt,

20

just to be sure a bullet came out. Vid-caps of the actors would also be worth something. Get them to analyze the background to see where it was shot, and let them run match-ups on the tape and casing just in case they can figure out who distributed the blanks. It might take a few weeks, but if there's anything there, those guys'll find it."

Having given me those precise instructions, Seagrave Chunny ambled out. Wacona passed him on her way in. She exuded sweet chocolate, and I made a show of sniffing.

"Go ahead," she challenged. "Ask me about my love life. Give me an excuse to shoot you where you stand."

"Chunny told me to send the tape to Dulles. I'm going to scan another bunch of them tonight."

"You're on your own time then. And don't stay up all night working on it and then come crawling in at noon either. I've got audits I need your help on, and there are five fraud cases being eaten by moths in your in-box."

"You're so kind. What are you wearing, anyway? Angel?"

She narrowed her black eyes for emphasis and lowered her glasses to her nose. For months now I had suspected that she wore the frames only for effect, that she thought they made her look stern and powerful, and that they held nothing but clear, non-prescription glass. I was dying to pick them up and peek, but she never let them out of her grasp.

"I beg your pardon?"

"Your perfume. It's 'Angel,' by Thierry Mugler, isn't it? Smells terrific."

"As a matter of fact it is, Max, and you know, some women might be impressed or even flattered that you recognized it. Me, I can't help thinking you missed your calling as a department store fragrance clerk."

She pushed her glasses back up and departed, leaving

me with seventy-six tapes to scan. I borrowed two other VCRs and monitors from the other offices and set them up so I had three tapes going at once. By 9:30 that night I had still seen nothing more than what were known around the office as BSF—basic sucking and fucking—films, and I still had a stack to go.

Worse, I had no more taste for Gershwin.

         I own a one-bedroom condo in an old, mustard-colored building, in the Spanish River Land section of Boca Raton. The building isn't fancy, but it's located on a narrow barrier island sandwiched between the Atlantic Ocean and the Intracoastal Waterway. The mortgage is a stretch, but I love being surrounded by water and so close to my grandmother. What's more, the residents of Boca Raton, who worship Ferraris and plastic surgeons the way most people worship gods, provide endless entertainment.

I climbed the stairs to the second floor. There was a foul-smelling stain on the walkway carpet, and roaches were feeding on it already. Roaches and grasshoppers all in one day. Sometimes I wonder if I wasn't accidentally placed in the middle of some entomological horror show, wherein the whole of South Florida, really just a thin carpet of asphalt and dreams laid over a roiling swamp, explodes in enough centipedes, snakes, sliders, crocs and skeeters to make the plagues of Exodus feel like a night at a five-star resort.

I went inside and poured myself a glass of Hurricane Reef pale ale, rejected the impulse to pop some gourmet corn, and turned on the patio light to check on Picard, my pet Galapagos tortoise. He was huddled in the corner by the railing, and I took some broccoli out to him. I had to put my back into spinning him around to face it, as five years of loving portions of fruits and vegetables had brought him to nearly a hundred and fifty pounds. He opened his eyes and stared at me, then rose up on columnar limbs and stuck his head way out.

"Exciting day on the terrace, big fella?" I asked, scratching his leathery neck.

He yawned in response, showing me pink gums, then settled back down with a hiss.

In Darwin's day, and for perhaps fifty million years before, the Galapagos Islands were awash in these enormous brutes. People don't realize it now, as they see them lying around zoos, deprived of the volcanic terrain that causes them to forage and climb, but the giant tortoises are social, active, and intelligent. Like a dog, Picard knows what time of day to expect me home, watches through the glass door to see if I'm carrying grocery bags, and expresses preferences for certain foods — corn on the cob in particular, as well as watermelon and romaine. He has his moods, the big boy does. At times he ignores me, at other times he humps my shoes. I watched him make short work of the broccoli, promised him a tremendous repast on the weekend, and settled in front of the tube. I surfed the cable channels looking for the original Star Trek. It's usually showing somewhere in the high numbers, but this time I couldn't find it. What I came up with instead was some sort of experimental episode juxtaposing the old series with the new — Kirk there on Deep Space Nine, talking to Major Kira, Scotty and Worf in the background. The magic of video. Maybe Chunny was right. If they could do that, they could probably fake a snuff and get big money for it.

Taking my empty beer bottle back to the kitchen, I noticed that my answering machine was blinking. The machine has recorded an actual message maybe twice in three years. It's there for show, like the other relics of a past that no longer engages me: the black-and-white Berenice Abbott prints, the Bauhaus desk, and the expensive halogen floor lamp I've never even switched on. I live in a quiet, secret world now, and receive calls at home exceedingly rarely. In fact, the only reason I have a machine is to discourage sales solicitations. Everyone of any importance knows to reach me at the office or on my cell phone.

Life has been that way since I purposely stepped off the moving walkway of everyday life and entered the realm of law enforcement. After Chunny saved my grandmother's future and laid his hooks into me, I spent three months at the United States Postal Inspection Service's Career Development Center in Potomac, Maryland, learning all the sections of Title 18 of the United States Code: blackmail, threatening communications, postage stamps and meters, canceled stamps and envelopes, money orders, postmarks, desertion of mails, destruction of newspapers, obstruction of correspondence, misappropriation of postal funds, and the intimate details of lotteries, contests, swindles and frauds. I studied the Inspection Service Database Information System and how to use it, and took courses in controlled delivery, the ethics of law enforcement, electronic surveillance, interviews and interrogations, report writing, and public speaking.

At the same time that my head was being filled with all this specialized knowledge, my body and my adrenal glands were challenged by training in officer survival. As an adjunct to the Chinese arts I'd studied as a boy in New York's Chinatown, I learned how to apply pressure points to control unwilling arrestees, and, despite the fact that the closest I'd ever been to a real gun was standing beside one of NYPD's finest during the Macy's Thanksgiving Day Parade, I learned a great deal about firearms. I even learned how to drive a car when people were shooting at me, how to enter a building full of armed thugs, and how to use my voice to defuse incipient violence.

Impressive and useful as these skills were, none of them had prepared me for the tape, and none of them had prepared me for what was waiting for me on my answering machine.

"M.D., this is Phayle," the message began. "I know it's been a while. God, it's been years. More than five and less than ten, right? I wish I were calling just to catch up, but the fact is, I've got bad news. Twy Boatwright is dead. Some kind of accident. I thought you'd want to know. The funeral is tomorrow at 11:00 A.M. at a place called Graceland Memorial Park in Coral Gables. I don't know where that is, but I figure you do. I hope you're not married, M.D. Shit, I can't believe I said that. I hope you *are* married, and that you've got four beautiful children and are happy as hell. There. That better? Bye."

Phayle Tollard. I sat frozen on the couch for a good ten-count. I had known it was her the instant the tape started. That unmistakable voice, husky, slow, calling me 'M.D.' the way she had in college. She had been so smart in those days, so inside my head; one part sister, one part lover, one part shrink and one part demon. A case-study in chaos, she was as gloriously unpredictable as the growth of a galaxy, and I wondered if *she* was married, or if she'd just been teasing me.

I was saddened by news of Twy Boatwright's passing, and found it strange that he had apparently lived and died in South Florida and that I hadn't known it. We had been one half of a squad of Yale College pals, Twy and I, but the foursome had moved into dark territory and I had abandoned it after graduation. I wondered whether the other guys, Jeff Grayson and Clifton Hughes, would be at the funeral, and what I would say to them if they were. I didn't sleep for a long time, and when I did, I dreamed of Phayle's streaked, honey hair and her wide gray eyes and the way she used to be able to shut me down or fly me high as a trick kite, all with just one look.

Two

The next morning, Dade and Broward Counties were washed clean by a rapid succession of morning thunderstorms. Usually such tempests take all day to build, but overnight a heat wave had come in off the Gulf of Mexico, blown across the Everglades, and met up with a cooler Atlantic air mass. The resulting clash hosed the morning commuter rush and spattered drops the size of matchbooks on the windshield of my 1964 Porsche 356 Supercoupe. Most postal inspectors drive government cars, but I had come into a small office as a single guy and since the office was short one car at the time, I got to use my own vehicle. Just as well, since I loved the thing. I'd bought it in ratty condition on the West Coast six years earlier, and had been slowly restoring it ever since. The Bondo-free body sported a new coat of sky blue paint—the original factory color—and the red leather looked as good as it had on the showroom floor. The engine had been massaged to double the stock horsepower by a race car builder in Delray Beach, and even though on paper it put out less than a Honda Civic, the car was so light it ran like a sighthound.

The prospect of seeing Phayle Tollard had so distracted me that I had utterly botched my morning t'ai chi ch'uan practice, a routine that was close to religion for me, sparked in my callow heart by an nonagenarian Chinese man who carried a chalice of green tea everywhere he went, could still perform a full split on the floor, and was able to send energy directly into another person's liver just as easily as he brushed his still strong teeth. The rain had doused and frustrated me and I had forced myself to repeat the form over and over until I felt what I was supposed to feel deep inside, in my organs and my muscles and my joints. My compulsiveness made me late enough to miss the morning rush hour, so I didn't have to contend with commuters reading newspapers and drinking coffee while they navigated the Interstate, but I had to contend with retirees leaning over their steering wheels, pushing blindly along through the rain, heading for sales on patio furniture or volunteer jobs greeting customers at libraries and banks.

I passed the Miami Beach turnoff, crossed the Miami River, and headed west on the Tamiami Trail. The smell of old money was as heavy as the rain and as thick as the Spanish moss dripping off cypress, palms, and oaks as I slipped off onto residential streets in order to avoid traffic and wound my way west under the pulsing sky. Coral Gables, like Boca Raton, was a destination in more ways than one, a tropical, palm-lined garden brimming with flowers and secrets. I found the funeral easily, as cars were lined up for blocks near the cemetery, and slogged along the wet road, soaking my shoes, until I found myself adrift in an ocean of black umbrellas, all rising and falling ever-so-slightly with the breath of grieving souls. Had the funeral been a party I might have felt out of place, as I saw not a single familiar face, but funerals, like weddings, have a way of drawing strangers together. Professional-looking people in dark suits and dresses shared sad smiles with me. I felt too out of place to grieve with them, too nervous about seeing Phayle to do anything but nod and look quickly away.

I moved through the crowd to the grave site. The pit and the coffin were covered by a plastic tarp, and the minister had begun speaking of Twy's devotion to his community, his Christian charity, the way he smiled when he held his little boys aloft. I had trouble thinking of Twy as a father. I remembered him as a jovial youth who drank too much, studied too little, and used his pale blue eyes, ruddy complexion, and curly blond hair to draw co-eds the way a reef attracts fish. He also had a taste for the dice. I remembered a certain backgammon tournament he had organized, with me as the ringer, in order to win some money from a young professor whose class he was failing and thereby manage a passing grade. I'd pulled it off for him, but hadn't enjoyed the pressure, nor the knowledge, deep down, that the whole enterprise had been dishonest and wrong.

At the end of the eulogy, two men stepped forward and with a jump in my stomach, I recognized them as Jeff Grayson and Clifton Hughes. Funny how the past can do that to you, as if evidence of things that have gone before forces you to look at how far you've come, where you are along the timeline of life, and how the distance that remains is constantly shrinking.

Jeff was the landed WASP of the pair, gangling and earnest and laconic and shrewd, the sort who made a college drug deal with a back-slap and a wink, arranging for an ounce of Humboldt County green to be delivered to your door an hour later, tucked under a burger, alongside some fries. Like Twy Boatwright, he had a taste for aged Bourbon — Old Ezra Brooks in the old days, Maker's Mark in a pinch. He ran committees and served on task forces and was chief admiral of a social clique that could, for a price, find A-plus-garnering papers from decades past. He looked dramatically the same as he had in college, a little fuller perhaps, but not much.

Clifton Hughes was not so well preserved. The decade since college seemed to have prematurely aged him, although when I thought about it, he had *always* looked old. He wore thick glasses and carried a belly and he stooped painfully as he helped Jeff and three other men lower the mahogany casket — rain pooling on its oiled surface — into the ground. Cliff had never possessed Jeff's relaxed grace. Born into a Protestant family in Brooklyn, he had been brilliant and darkly intense at school, a social climber who ogled fine stereos in the dorm rooms of rich kids and studied Latin and French, as if by learning refined tongues he could slip sideways and unnoticed into the company of power.

The minister directed us all to bow our heads in prayer, and as I did so I felt an arm slip lightly through mine and smelled Chardonnay.

"You're handsomer without hair, Max," said Phayle, slurring slightly, "you have a smooth and beautiful head."

"Thirty-two years old, one hundred and eighty-five pounds of muscle," I replied.

She pinched me at the side of my waist.

"Okay, one hundred and seventy-five of muscle, ten soft pounds of sensitivity and caring."

She laughed at that. Like the rest of us, she had changed. Her edges were softer and her eyes seemed filled with dew, but maybe that was just the rain and the intimate company of death. All her curves were still there, and her blond hair still gleamed. Her skin had barely been touched by wrinkles. I brushed her full lips with mine.

"You still look eighteen," I whispered.

"Eye of the beholder," she whispered back.

With a thud, Twy's coffin hit bottom.

"Max boy," said Jeff Grayson, putting a big palm on my head.

"M.D.," Cliff said softly, giving my shoulders a quick squeeze.

"Hell of a place for a reunion," I said. "You guys come in from up north?"

Clifton looked uncomfortable. Jeff shifted on his feet.

"They're local," said Phayle.

"We've got a law practice in Miami," said Jeff.

For a moment I was stunned. To have them so close and not know it was both eerie and sad.

"Ah well," I said, trying to make light of it. "Sooner or later the surf and sun hook us all."

"It wasn't the sun. It was my father's firm," Jeff confessed. "Twy was in with me and Cliff."

"What do you call a hundred dead lawyers at the bottom of the sea?" interrupted Phayle, wine seeping out of her in sweat-droplets.

"Phayle," I took her arm.

"A good start," she blurted out.

"And you work in West Palm, is that right?" asked Jeff, smoothly ignoring the barb.

"Twy built his own coffin," Phayle interrupted again. "He kept it in a closet for years. Isn't that weird?"

"Here comes Nora," Cliff gestured nervously.

A thin woman clutching two little boys with Twyman Boatwright's blue eyes strode purposefully toward us.

"Thank you all for coming," said the new widow.

31

Her voice was flat. Tranquilizers. I murmured something about doing whatever I could to help, and then led Phayle away before she could say something she'd regret.

I took her to the Brown Pelican on Biscayne Bay, a restaurant and bar favored by boaters wishing to keep an eye on their yachts. A couple of million-dollar beauties were tied up a stone's throw away, all gleaming fiberglass, darkened windows, white leather deck couches and spinning radar scanners. The unstoppable South Florida sun had transformed the day, and the water was alive with craft headed for the open sea.

"I've developed a software package for matériel management," she began, stretching out as if the chair was too small to contain her limbs, her gestures, her will. "My program handles inventory at Kmart and Neimans."

"Sounds like you got most American consumers covered."

She smiled, revealing tiny, perfect teeth. The sight of her open mouth loosed a cascade of memories—brazen sex in a construction site at night in New Haven, secret rendezvous in the dining hall at night (where the fear of discovery did the trick for her), groping sweet flesh in the stall in the rest room of a local pub, fondling each other beneath a blanket at a George Thorogood concert.

I must have showed something, because she leaned forward searchingly. "Hey! Where did you slip off to?"

"Someplace nice," I smiled.

We slathered our sourdough rolls with honey butter and ate like starved peasants. Memories of old love do that to the appetite.

"How do people make that much money?" Phayle marveled, nodding at the boats. Her voice was stronger now, no more drunken wavering.

"If they were really rich, they'd be down here enjoying their toys more than just a short time each year."

"Yeah, but what a time! You and I had our times too, didn't we, M.D.?" She touched my hand.

"We sure did."

"I might have a yacht like that someday. I have the profit potential; flying solo, no boss, the pure entrepreneur. I keep what I make, and I'm trying to add the Burdine's department store chain to my client list. That's why I'm down here from Santa Barbara. I just read about Twy in the *Miami Herald*."

"Any chance you'll stay?"

"If I find a good enough reason."

Before I could take the bait, our appetizers arrived; Caesar salad for her, shrimp cocktail with extra-spicy cocktail sauce for me.

"Still with the spicy food," she shook her head.

"Makes me strong like bull," I said in a mock Russian accent.

"I remember," she smiled wickedly, wriggling out of her dark mourning jacket to reveal a sheer white blouse and a lacy bra.

"Tell me you wore that blouse just for me."

"I wore this blouse just for you."

We grinned at each other. The busboy whisked our empties away. The waitress showed up with my penne *arabbiata* and Phayle's patty melt. A man in pressed tennis shorts, a crewcut, and a Lacoste shirt emerged from the cabin of the biggest docked yacht. He stretched his arms above his head and looked about until his gaze settled on Phayle, her long legs under the table, the outline of her breasts, her high cheekbones, those eyes. Before I could stop myself, I leaned up out of my chair and kissed her possessively on the lips. The mogul withdrew.

"That was transparently territorial, Max."

"Guilty."

"I've never been kissed by a cop before."

I looked surprised. I hadn't told her I was an inspector. In fact, I hadn't told her much at all.

"I called your parents last night before I called you," she explained. "Your mother was sweet. She told me all about what you did for a living but not one word about your love life."

"Good old Mom. Always discreet."

"By the way, how's your grandmother?"

"She's the Bridge Queen of Boca. One hell of a dead-pan bluffer."

Phayle laced her fingers in mine and squeezed tightly. "I read about your father in the newspaper, Max."

I wiped my face with my napkin and pushed back from the table, thinking of my dad. Ernst Diamond had been an advertising man. Born with the gift of the gab, he was a natural networker to whom image was everything, a man who'd rather die at your feet than admit he was sick, a large, booming egomaniac who, particularly as he grew successful, required total subservience from those around him. It was natural that he should gravitate to advertising, an occupation that dealt more with perception than reality. While he wasn't creative in terms of concepts or copy, he had a definite knack for bringing bright teams together, and for overseeing the campaigns that resulted. By the time he was in his early 30s and I was in my early teens, he had hawked airlines, shampoo, vitamins, high-fidelity equipment, minivans and designer clothing, garnering every advertising award New York had to offer. His work adorned Manhattan billboards and buses and could be seen in national magazines and on network television. The toast of the town, he sold his agency for an undisclosed figure — although he talked nothing but business at home, he never mentioned specific sums — retired, and began to work real estate deals with his pals.

By the time I finished high school, things had grown palpably tense around the house. My father snapped at my mother constantly, and he grew stingier about money than he had ever been. Sometime during my college years I realized that he had been trying to apply the tactics of image to real estate, a market where image only went so far, a business dominated by such tangibles as location, condition, and price. I stayed away from home as much as possible, and on the rare occasions that I went back, his descent into dark waters was increasingly evident. He had always stayed fit, a habit I learned from him, but he began to let himself go. His breath grew sour, he drank too much wine, and he and my mother sat at opposite ends of the room. When I asked him about business, he would shake his head and say nothing more than how lucky I was that the small trust fund set up by my mother's wealthy parents — Jewish owners of a small but highly profitable jewelry casting business who perished horribly in a suspicious shop fire — meant that I would never have to swim with the sharks.

Some years later, just as I sat listening to Seagrave Chunny promise my Grandma Sara that he would do everything humanly possible to get her money back for her, those sharks finally bit off my father's legs. On an informant's tip, he was apprehended by FBI agents for perpetrating a multi-million dollar real estate scheme; the creation of a high-profile, low-income, model city within the hell-hole that was East Harlem. Sketches of his waterfront models adorned the six o'clock news, then hit again at ten and eleven. It emerged that there were no architects, the plans were bogus, and the land was not available. Local leaders were up in arms. The story dragged on for days. There were rumors of mob connections. While Sara wept and I watched numbly, the media painted the picture of a man who had climbed to the top by taking credit for the work of those beneath him, a man whose unrecognized support team had finally deserted him, a man who lost money in one investment after another until finally he was reduced to fraud.

While I was in training to become a postal inspector, my father was sentenced to fourteen months in a minimum security prison near Albany. His conviction nearly cost me my admittance to the service — perhaps it would have if not for Chunny. When he was finally released, he was not recognizably the same man he had been. He had lost two full inches in height, a function primarily of walking hunched over as if at any moment he expected to be whacked on the head from behind. My mother and I met him at the gate, and a week later he had a heart attack. When he finally got home for good, his hair had turned totally white, and though he had finally quit smoking, he coughed incessantly, as if trying to hawk up everything he had swallowed during the past five years of his life.

My father hated the fact that I had gone into law enforcement while he was in prison. He lumped all cops together as heartless bastards who had misunderstood him and ruined his life. For a long time, he refused even to talk to me, but my grandmother finally cured him of that. The best I could say was that Wacona and Sea and the rest of the men and women I worked with never mentioned him to me, pretending, no doubt, that Ernst and Maximillian Diamond were in no way related.

"Let's talk about you," I answered Phayle. "The last boyfriend I heard about wanted to turn tenement basements into fish farms and clothe the world in hemp."

"That was years ago, Max, and those dreams are no

weirder than being a postal inspector. Both of you seemed to want to duck the social spotlight."

I didn't want to admit how right she was. I had effectively bowed out of competition with my father when he was at the peak of his power. Nobody but the people I worked with knew or cared what kind of a job I did, and without having to satisfy Ernst's ambitions I was free to work on the things that mattered to me.

"Any other significant relationships in the last few years?" I inquired.

"I look like a nun to you? Of course there were significant relationships, but I don't want to talk about them any more than you want to talk about your father."

"Okay," I smiled, "then tell me how Twy Boatwright died."

"He was into woodworking—making furniture at home. He had an accident with a power tool. Jeff said that he lost so much blood so fast he probably went into shock and never felt a thing."

I had this sudden vision of Twy with a drink in his hand and a buzz saw zooming, all alone at night in the garage, just him and his tools and the wood and the bottle. I took a sip of water.

"Doesn't that shock you at all?" Phayle pressed. She seemed disappointed by my calm.

"It saddens me. He was a charming guy."

"Charming," she repeated.

"Yeah, I always thought of him that way."

She picked up her sandwich and took a bite. A cloud passed in front of the sun.

"Tell me about your job, Max. Is it like the FBI?"

"The Bureau's big, the Postal Inspection Service is small. Anything that involves mail is our bag, so sometimes we share jurisdiction on crimes."

"You do death threats?"

"With other agencies, yes."

"You carry a gun?" she asked, leaning forward and gazing at me the way a child might look at a Bushman who ate spiders. No way was I going to show her my Glock. Too cliché.

"Nah, that's a pickle in my pocket. But I *am* happy to see you."

"I'm happy to see you too, M.D., but I don't understand the mail. Why not the CIA or the Secret Service or something?"

"CIA is intelligence, not law enforcement, which to me makes it political rather than moral. As for the Postal Inspection Service, let's just say it fell into my lap and I found it damn interesting. Internet and FedEx notwithstanding, life as you know it would end without mail. One out of every three hundred and thirty working people in this country is employed by the postal service. More goes on than you would believe."

"Mail does have the hygiene of distance," she mused. "I'd say things in a letter that I'd never have the courage to say face-to-face."

"Clean way to send poison or bombs, too," I said easily.

She took my hands in hers.

"I wanted to write you for years, Max. Did you sense that? Did you feel the vibes in the air?"

"I wanted to write you too," I replied thickly.

I'd been hoping to keep things platonic for a little while longer. Emotions overcome me quickly—in that way I'm still a kid—and I wanted to keep my balance with Phayle. It was tough to do. First that terrible tape, then the funeral, and now the feel and smell of her just inches away.

"But we didn't, did we?"

"No."

"And I gather you don't keep up with Clifton and Jeff?"

"Had no idea they were even around."

"Why is that?"

"Different worlds," I turned up my palms.

"You all deal with the law."

"They make a lot more dough doing it," I smiled.

"Any guy that drives a Porsche can't be doing *too* badly."

"That, of course, is the very fiction I wish to foster. The fact is, it's a very old Porsche, and it's taken more than a couple of lumps on its way to mature elegance."

"Maybe some day you'll say the same sweet things about me," she smiled sadly.

Our waitress came by with a dessert tray. I declined, but Phayle selected Key Lime pie. When it came, she took a bite, savored it, then cut off a section for me.

"Feed it to me," I requested.

She did, and a seagull circled jealously, watching the fork travel back and forth between us until finally diving for a brazen peck of crust. Giggling, Phayle gave up on me and took on the bird.

I had seen this kind of exchange with animals before. During our sophomore year together at Yale, we had driven my second-hand Fiat convertible all the way from New Haven, Connecticut, to Prince Edward Island in the Canadian Maritime Provinces for spring break. The drive had taken much longer than we thought it would, due in no small measure to an overactive Canadian Customs officer who pretended to suspect me of drug smuggling but really just wanted to inspect nineteen-year-old Phayle. By the time we arrived on the island, having just made the last ferry, the motel we had counted on, a rickety old place with a white picket fence that seemed to go for miles, had given up on us and handed the key to our room to someone else. The result was a frigid but sexy night spent in the hayloft of an old barn, the cold Atlantic roiling not a hundred yards from us.

Just before dawn Phayle had lit the yellow plastic flashlight I kept in the trunk of the car and made her way down the ladder, alone and hastily dressed, in order to relieve herself outside. She was gone an inordinately long time, and when she came back, she was nearly frantic. She had stumbled across a group of ten puppies inside an old feeding trough. At first she had thought they were dead, but when she poked one gingerly with her finger it moved. The little dogs couldn't have been more than five weeks old, and they were emaciated, dehydrated, and covered with ticks and fleas. Their mother had doubtless been killed somewhere near the area, trapped, shot, or hit by a car, and she doubted the puppies would survive in the cold more than a few additional hours.

In the gathering light of morning, Phayle loaded them all into the Fiat, making a comfy shelf for them on the rear deck lid, under the convertible top. I turned on the heater in the car—one item in that Italian mechanical nightmare that worked properly—and we created a mobile sauna. Phayle worked to remove fleas and ticks one-by-one with her eyebrow tweezers, and when the sun rose higher and we began to see cars on the road, we found a grocery store. She purchased a dozen tins of premium, soupy, fat-laden dog food and proceeded to feed each and every puppy with her fingers, making sure that the portions were equal, and that not a single animal was left out. Then she watered them with Gatorade, dribbling it down their throats with a straw, assuring me that they would perk up once the electrolytes hit their bloodstream.

The tornado of excrement that followed didn't faze her at all, nor did the yellow river. She calmly mopped everything up, and spent the next two days of our vacation cross-examining prospective adoptive parents with a thoroughness that would have done my interrogation instructors proud, finally finding homes for every single pup. She would have kept the last one for herself if she hadn't been living in a pet-free dormitory.

"Remember the puppies?" I asked.

She looked at me all dewy-eyed.

"Are you kidding? I'll never forget them, or the way you drove them around for two days without complaining about lost vacation time. I knew right then I'd marry you if you ever asked me. You never did."

I got so flustered at that, I answered my cell phone, even though it wasn't ringing.

After lunch, I drove Phayle back to the Delano Hotel in South Beach—a trendy place with billowy fabrics in the lobby and Phillippe Starck chairs by a long, shallow pool. She invited me for a swim, but I was afraid to go too far too fast. Instead, I kissed her good-bye, left her in the lobby and headed back to my Porsche, threading my way through throngs of gay men in gold chains and statuesque models swaying for rich guys in Jaguar convertibles. I drove across MacArthur Causeway to the Interstate, at one point sniffing my sleeve where Phayle had taken my arm, hoping to get a whiff of her perfume. I got into the far left-hand HOV lane and drove ninety miles an hour, thinking about how much my life had changed in the last twenty-four hours.

Twy Boatwright had been put in the ground that morning, but at the same time other things had been unearthed; details of a past I had sought to bury. I felt a familiar disquiet, sparked by expectations of greatness, fueled by impatience, and fanned by loneliness. Like my father, I had spent the first part of my life so preoccupied with destinations that I had never even noticed I was on a journey. Yale had been a smudge, the hooks Jeff and Twy and Clifton had left in me a barely noticeable scar.

My life wasn't a sprint to the finish anymore. My Taoist studies and practices had finally taught me to smell the roses, and the U.S.P.I.S. had given me a place to dig in and belong. Thinking back, I realized that my college time with Phayle had been a way station in my mad rush toward oblivion, and seeing her in Florida, a mature, beautiful, available woman, lit up in neon the fact that the passion I felt for her hadn't been equalled since.

Bright blue lights in my rearview mirror brought my ruminations up short. An FHP pursuit car was nearly on my bumper. The trooper looked pissed. He'd probably been behind me for miles. I should have pulled over and apologized, but I didn't trust myself to be nice to anyone right then, to act my professional best. Instead I put my bubble on the dash, sending him the signal that I was in an official hurry, and watched in my mirror while he picked up his mike, ran my plates, then backed off, shaking his head.

I drove north past Delray Beach, Lantana, and Lake Worth, got off the Interstate at Southern Boulevard and headed over toward the Palm Beach International Airport thinking about the dead woman and the little dancer. The address the snuff film file linked to the tape was a small industrial complex on the southwest side of the field, almost to Military Trail. The buildings were long and low, like self-storage units. The entrance to the complex was rough and unpaved, and my tires sent clouds of crushed coral reef into the air. One of the storefronts was a speed shop specializing in competition go-carts, another an aquarium maintenance group—the sort of outfit that goes to doctors' offices and law firms once a week to keep the fish happy. There was also a company that recharged toner cartridges for computer laser printers, and a dealer who sold custom shelving featuring a patented, load-bearing bracket.

The last building in the line was unoccupied, the commercial sign torn away. I parked squarely in front and verified the numbers. Dust had adhered to the inside of the front window where adhesive letters had been, and when I cocked my head to change the angle of view, I could make out the words TWILIGHT ENTERPRISES. Twilight indeed. Purgatory would be more like it. I walked the perimeter. There was no side door, but there was a small loading dock out back. When I tried the door, I noticed a woman on a cigarette break from the cartridge company eyeing me suspiciously. I could have done everything by the book, gotten a warrant and locksmith, but instead I just used the pick gun I kept in the trunk of the Porsche. It was a surprisingly good lock, multiple tumblers, very resistant, but in the end I beat it and got inside.

The place was in shambles. The cheap metal conference table was dented, a credenza leaned on a broken leg, a couple of standing lamps looked as if they had been bent over someone's knee, and a dark brown four-drawer file cabinet had been disemboweled. I checked the bathroom and found the toilet bowl full and unflushed, clouded over with a film that looked like brown ice on a polluted pond. I peeked in the closet where there was nothing more than empty wire coat hangers.

I got down on my hands and knees and did a slow "forensic crawl" through each room, looking at knee-level for things others might have missed. The place had been cleaned with a thoroughness that belied a quick exit, and I found nothing more than seven paper clips, a Cross pen refill, and a penny wedged behind the corner of the commode. I was in the front room when I caught a glimpse of

43

a guy peering in through the window. I got up, saw him go for his gun, and went for mine. Weapons at the ready, we stared at each other through the grimy glass.

He was wearing a pretty good suit, but he was short and squat and had reddish hair that looked greasy, and a pockmarked face. He didn't look happy.

"FBI. Drop your weapon now," he said loudly.

"United States Postal Inspector. You drop yours."

He searched my face, using his eyes like fingers. "I.D.," he commanded.

"Yours first," I countered.

"Together then," he almost smiled.

Slowly, carefully, we flashed our shields. I opened the door.

"Jesus Christ," he said in disgust, holstering his Sig Sauer and snapping his badge folder shut. "I left half of a perfectly good Thai meal on the table for this."

"You get a call about me from next door?" I asked, putting away the Glock.

He shook his head, and leaned against the door frame. "We wired the place," he said.

"I didn't see anything."

"You wouldn't."

"You're full of shit. That woman next door called me in."

The smile was back, fleetingly. "Maybe."

"Maybe my ass."

"Ron Dryden," he stuck out his hand.

"Max Diamond," I took it. "So how do you figure this place?"

"Thought it was a dead lead until you showed up. I keep a general finger on the pulse of this little complex, though. I've seen dumber things than guys coming back to the scene. Like last night it was on the wire that some guy robbed a pharmacy, then went back because he forgot hypodermics. We busted him."

"I don't think these folks were dumb."

"No," he agreed. "But the john's a stinker, isn't it? I wanted to flush it three or four times but something kept holding me back, like maybe a place like this *ought* to smell bad. What are you doing out here, anyway?"

"Just checking out the joint."

"Yeah? Find anything?"

"I doubt there was much here," I shrugged. "The office is obviously a front. Probably they used the rooms in the back to warehouse product."

He nodded, and fired up an unfiltered Camel, taking in a lungful of chemicals and blowing it out noisily through his nose.

"I didn't think they made those anymore," I said.

"You gotta know where to shop."

"I'm too politically correct."

"Dressed like that?" he looked me up and down. "I don't think so."

"It's a disguise," I said. "I'm hiding from my former life. Tell me how it went down here, Dryden."

"Palm Beach Sheriff squeezed a guy who gave this address."

"What kind of a guy?"

"Courier. Smuggled goods. We raided the place."

"Moving so fast they didn't have time to flush," I interrupted.

"Yeah. But it was a bust. Tenant paid cash."

"Except for that overseas mail bag," I said.

"Coupla porn tapes, a thousand partials, no addresses on the packages, no postmarks either, not one good print."

"You peeked," I said.

"Uh huh. Before we called you."

"And since then you keep the joint covered."

"Lightly. Just in case. What brings you up here, Diamond?"

"You watched the wrong tapes."

He put his cigarette out quickly, straightening up like a monkey learning how to walk like a man.

"Yeah? Tell me what you saw."

"Gimme your card. Maybe I'll be in touch."

I could tell he didn't like that. He made a show of pulling his card out, of rubbing it between his fingers, studying it as if evaluating the paper stock.

Finally he handed it to me.

Those Bureau guys are just used to getting their way.

There was a note from Sea Chunny on my desk. He had forwarded a copy of the snuff tape to Dulles for me, requesting an analysis of the housing, emulsion, production values, camera work, and locale. I crumpled the note and made a high, good toss to the trash can by the window. Then I wandered in to see Wacona.

She was framing something at her desk, and she had a long strip of white tape between her teeth.

"Nice look," I said.

"You can really be a dick sometimes, Max. Have I told you that lately?"

"Call me Tracy."

"How about I call you the Invisible Man?"

"Aw, don't you want a little help with that?" I gestured at the ashwood frame and the neatly cut mat.

"I'm fine. You're in trouble though. I told you not to stay up on that tape case and wander in late."

"I had a funeral," I said. "An old friend died."

"You kidding."

"I don't joke about dead friends."

"Sorry, Max. Now get out of here."

Something in her manner piqued my curiosity. She was always brusque, but she had yet to actually throw me out of her office.

"What have you got there?" I asked, reaching for the brown paper package on her desk. There isn't a postal inspector alive that can resist an unmarked package.

"Private stuff," she slapped my hand aside.

I grabbed it with my second snatch and tore it open. There was an animation cell inside, a Disney scene, 101 Dalmatian puppies looking bright-eyed at their mother.

"Goddamnit, Diamond, I told you to get out of here!" she snapped.

Wacona might have run the domicile, but she was two years my junior and she rarely called me "Diamond."

"It's, uh, very attractive. I hear animation art is really in these days. Did you buy it for the office?"

"I didn't buy it at all! It's from a fraud case I've been running."

"One hundred and one Dalmatians?" I taunted.

"It was a lottery scam, Max. This lowlife bought the subscription list to a couple of fancy magazines for rich people. One on art, another on home furnishings, thick and glossy, six bucks a copy. You get the idea. Then he sent a letter to say a hundred people in different parts of the country telling them that they had been entered in a subscription lottery and that they had won. The letter said that for seventy-nine dollars shipping and handling, they would be sent their prize, a one-thousand-five-hundred-dollar Disney cell." She gestured at the little puppies. "Half the people went for it, sent in the money, and received one of these,"

"Worth about a buck, right?"

"Maybe two," she gave a small smile. "But it's cute."

"So you're hanging it?"

"Only as a reminder that there are scumbags out there."

"Of course."

"By the way, the scam didn't end there," she went on. "The people who bought in got another letter about two months later, offering them a closeout on a three-thousand-dollar piece of art for five hundred dollars."

"Maybe the second piece would have been Goofy," I taunted. "You should have gone for it."

"Out, Max. I'm not kidding."

My grandmother grew up in Austria, in the company of urbane, sophisticated, Jewish academics. Her father was the chairman of the Department of Romance Languages at the University of Vienna, and by the time she was eleven years old she and her twin sister could speak poor Italian, good French, excellent Hebrew, idiomatically rich Yiddish, and, of course, perfect German. On the run from Hitler, she and her family—identical twin sister, mother, father, and a musically gifted brother for whom I was named—moved east. For a time they hid secretly in a summer dacha, and when the Nazis grew near, they were saved by a band of dashing Jewish militiamen.

The leader of the militia, a short but brave fellow named Isaac, provided for the terrified family through the brutal Eastern European winter, smuggling bread and potatoes and the occasional scrap of meat through the snow. When spring came, and the Nazis were still afield, Sara's father—despite an ingrained disdain for Russians—gratefully gave Isaac her hand in marriage. Isaac smuggled my grandmother, and some gold, across the border into Poland. From there they headed to America as refugees, where she gave birth to my father at the age of seventeen. Six months later, Hitler sent Sara's family to Belsen where all of them, including my namesake—a musician who could by all accounts make a wooden violin weep tears—were turned into soap and lamp shades.

Isaac died five years ago, but Sara lives on, anguished by the guilt of the survivor, ending every laugh with a sigh, but still erect, beautiful, educated and charming enough to send Seagrave Chunny, a confirmed bachelor if ever there was one, into a heartsick nosedive. After a lifetime of frustration and brushes with bankruptcy, Isaac had, in his last few years of life, finally learned the commodity futures game. He profited well, and sank the money into the Boca beach house still occupied by Sara. She survives on his legacy—the nest egg retrieved by Chunny—and holds court by the ocean, playing bridge and drinking Manischewitz wine on holidays.

When I walked up her driveway that night, all the lights were on, and I could hear Felix Mendelssohn's violin concerto. I lack my great-uncle's musical ear, but I still love the delicacy of classical music, the way it keeps the outside world at bay and encourages quietude. I rang the doorbell, and Sara opened it at once. Smells of an era past wafted out; perfume and potpourri, garlic, meat, and tomatoes. She was wearing a floral dress that went below the knee and a delicate necklace of garnets. Sea once told me that the way she dressed was what slew him, never in skirts or blouses like other old Florida women, never laden down with jewelry, never with much makeup or with shiny shoes or trendy purses, but always as if she were headed for the symphony in Vienna, to hear her late brother play.

"Did you shoot anybody today?" she asked in her thick Eastern European accent.

"Forty *goyim*, but they deserved it," I replied.

"Did they yell and scream?"

"Actually, they died quietly."

"Did you get paid for it?"

"You know I don't kill for nothing."

"For a minute I forgot," she smiled. "So are you hungry? Would you like to eat something?"

"I'm always hungry after a good shooting."

"Good, because I have cabbage rolls."

I sat down at her table, an old piece of darkly stained wood with carved claws for feet and covered by a white tablecloth and an ivory-colored doily.

"How did you know I was coming?" I asked innocently.

"Certain grandmothers have this rare talent."

Sometimes I wonder if she makes the rolls every day just in case I come over. They're my favorite, garlicky ground beef seasoned with pine nuts, paprika and secret spices, all wrapped up in cabbage leaves boiled in secretly seasoned water. She ladled a heaping portion onto a plate and set it down in front of me, then brought me some water.

"Some rain this morning," she sniffed. "Were you driving?"

"I went to a funeral."

I ladled a dab of sour cream onto the cabbage roll and took a bite.

"Wow!" I rolled my eyes.

"Good?"

"Fantastic."

She gave me a satisfied look.

"The funeral, was it somebody you killed?"

"No. An old friend from college."

She'd given me a boiled potato too, and I split it open, releasing steam.

"*Oy.* Just a child. Was he sick? Was it cancer?"

Isaac, a sun-worshipper, had died of skin cancer. Sara had a mortal fear of the sun. She never went outside unless she was completely covered. Sea often extolled the virtues of her skin.

"An accident with a power tool," I answered, taking a long drink.

"Shows you."

"Shows you what?"

"Power tools are nobody's business. Do you want more food?"

"Couldn't hurt," I said.

This happens when I'm around her. Unavoidably, I adopt her syntax and her cadence.

"You talk with your father?" she asked, bringing me another plate.

"Not lately."

"Your mother?"

"Not in the last couple of weeks."

"Remember, they're still your parents."

"Oh, I remember."

"So much tragedy in their lives. You have to forgive them."

"I do," I said. "I just don't feel obliged to talk to them every day."

She let it go there. Neither of us really wanted to skate on that particular thin ice. I finished the second plate and we retired to the couch, where we played gin rummy and watched the local news; a family killed by a drunk driver, two young boys missing, a serial killer released from prison due to overcrowding.

"Forget the news. Play cards," Sara commanded.

She was immune to news, however bad it might be. Nothing on television could compare to what she had endured in real life. I looked at my cards. A deuce, three sevens, three aces, eight, nine, ten of clubs. I picked up another ace, tossed the deuce, and put the hand face-up on the table.

"Gin."

"Shit," she cursed.

I made an astonished face. This was our private little ritual — she swore and I pretended to be shocked. She shuffled the cards and dealt another hand.

"You hear from Seagrave today?" I asked.

"Oy, is that man a pain in the *tuchis*," she scoffed. "He walks like a bird and says 'understand?' at the end of every sentence."

"He loves you."

"Love," she sighed.

"Why don't you marry him and get it over with?"

"What are you talking about?"

"You alone in your house, Sea alone in his, you enjoy each other so much, what's the point of playing hard to get?"

"Stick to cards, mister," she advised, studying her hand.

The news broadcast concluded without a single positive story. Sara beat me the next five hands in a row.

"Luck," I asserted.

"Skill," she countered.

She brought cinnamon cookies. We had herb tea the Russian way, in glasses, and when we were finished, Sara fell asleep on the couch. Quietly, I opened the fireproof door I had personally installed after her '87 Caddy Brougham burst a fuel hose and nearly vaporized the house, squeezed past the rack of suitcases Isaac had termed "valises" and straddled my 1974 BMW R90S motorcycle.

BMWs have long been known as traveling machines, bikes you can use as transportation, bikes that will take you around the country or around the world. They are simple, elegant, reliable and comfortable, but compared to the Japanese offerings that have dominated the motorcycle industry since the late '60s, they are ponderous and slow.

In 1974, when the European motorcycle industry had been almost annihilated by Japan, BMW managed one last world-beating machine, a 900cc version of its classic "flat" twin-cylinder machine, a factory hot rod with Italian carburetors, racing camshafts, and a sexy fairing, tank, and tail section, all hand-painted in a luscious, custom, burnt orange. The machine won the World Superbike Championship at Daytona Beach, and became an instant classic. Mine came from an old farmer near Ocala who had purchased it while in the clutches of a mid-life crisis. He had fawned over it, changed its oil religiously, waxed it until a gaggle of circling geese couldn't hurt the paint, but never actually put a leg over it.

I rode the three blocks to my house, locked it to a standpipe at the back of my building and gently patted the rear part of the seat, which I hoped might soon support Phayle.

Picard was bumping against the patio door when I got upstairs. It was unusual for him to be active in the dark. The morning's strong rain and the hot sun that followed must have gotten him started. I gave him the last scrap of food I had for him, a head of romaine lettuce, and he devoured it under the porch light. I set up my subliminal learning Spanish tapes—one can't be in law enforcement in South Florida without a command of Spanish—and plugged the player into this relaxation machine I bought years ago when I had a bad coffee habit and couldn't sleep. The machine was the size of a pack of cigarettes, with a jack for goggles and external music. I donned the goggles, went to bed, and listened to Spanish verbs while staring at flashing red lights that were supposed to put my brain in the learning mode.

Compro, compras, compra. Voy, vas, va.

I heard a faint ringing. I sat up and took off the head-phones and picked up the telephone.

"Max? It's Phayle."

"Hi," I said. I was lying on top of the covers, but suddenly I felt the urge to cover up.

"Max, why are you afraid of me?"

"What are you talking about?"

"I'm talking about the fact that we're not together right now."

"We're not together because it's almost midnight."

"That's not the answer I was hoping for."

"I had to work today, Phayle."

"So did I. But we're in the same city now, Max, or at least we're close."

I took a deep breath. "Let's take a little time to catch up, okay? There's no fire."

"Maybe not on your end."

"I've got something going tomorrow after work, but how about the day after? I'll pick you up at seven o'clock and take you over to the Lincoln Road Mall. Place there does fish with an Asian touch, exotic vegetables, great desserts."

"Yum," she said.

"I'm glad you're here, I really am," I said, meaning it.

"Me too," she whispered.

"Good night, Phayle."

"Good night, M.D."

I fell asleep quickly, those little red lights dancing in my eyes.

THREE

Scandals and Secrets was down toward Federal Highway on Clematis street, not far from the U.S.P.I.S. domicile. It stood in a block-long war zone that had yet to come into the Palm Beach of the '90s; a shantytown just the other side of the Intracoastal from the ocean-front mansions of tycoons, princes, and kings. There was a liquor store adjacent to it, the door always open, a brindle pit bull tied outside, stacked cases of Colt 45 and Rolling Rock in the window along with tattered posters of Lowenbräu girls. On the other side was Mr. Happy's tattoo parlor, with two creased and faded barbershop chairs—the kind with separable head- and footrests and a heavy circular base of pitted chrome—visible inside.

I had never visited the place, though I'd noticed it every time I drove east from work. Nobody ever seemed to go in or come out, probably because it was a nighttime business, so I worked late the next day, had a bite and a beer, and headed over about 10:00 P.M. Under cover of darkness, human cockroaches scurried about, keeping their distance from each other amidst the steamy selections on the shelves. Most everyone seemed to wear some kind of raincoat, though it wasn't raining. Spectacles abounded, square ones too small even for John Lennon, as did Greek captains' caps with braided rope above the brim.

The first room was full of paraphernalia; cheap camisoles, crotchless undies, latex rubber outfits for the adventurous and black leather face masks for the dominant. There were dildos and butt plugs and massagers, and there were outrageous, midget-sized, feather-trimmed bras. Trying to avoid looking at anybody, and feeling more self-conscious than Twiggy at a Sumo match, I moseyed up to a glass case and smiled neutrally at the earringed man behind the counter.

"Interest you in a cock ring?" he asked.

"Not tonight."

"How about a pleasure pump? I've got a great new unit from Japan. Really heavy duty, not like the cheap Taiwanese garbage other places carry. Won't crap out on you after one or two sessions."

"Actually, I was looking for some tapes," I said.

He jerked his thumb in the direction of a curtain of rainbow beads. "Back room," he said.

"What I want, you wouldn't have on display," I said trying to sound as nervous as a real customer would. That wasn't hard to do. Undercover work has never been my forte. My palms sweat too much and my voice tends to crack.

"What I got, I put out."

"That's not what I hear."

"You hear wrong."

"Listen," I said, wearing my best conspiratorial face, "help me out here, will you?"

A customer nearby shot me a quick glance. He was examining an inflatable sheep. The box called it an "I Luv Ewe" and said it had pulsing action and a warm water reservoir.

"What's that supposed to mean?" the clerk leaned forward across the counter, narrowing his eyes.

"I like things violent and fresh," I said in a low voice. "And young."

"Man, if you're not a cop, you ought to be," he laughed nastily. "Just for the record, the girls are over eighteen in every tape I carry. Distributors guarantee it. S and M scenes are staged and consensual."

"Me a cop," I huffed. "Pshaw."

I parted the beaded curtain. The back room was slightly smaller than the front, and less crowded. There were walls and aisles of porn videos here, and I started at the left and worked my way clockwise, surveying the titles, skipping the gay sections, focusing on the words "teen," "virgin," and "bondage." I dismissed tapes that showed black women or blondes on the cover, as well as any with ratings or reviews from *Penthouse, Playboy*, or *Screw* magazine. Most of the tapes that met my criteria were sealed, but I opened the ones that weren't, sliding the cassettes out of the box to check the color of the reels—mostly white; the length of the tapes—mostly short; and the numbers or letters printed on or embossed into the plastic.

I was so engrossed in the process that it took me a few seconds to notice that a fleshy circus giant had joined me in the aisle. He had a sagging belly, huge arms, and a military-style haircut that nearly grazed the ceiling. He smelled of sour sweat and onions.

"This ain't no library," he declared.

"Yeah, okay. You ever get anything direct from overseas? India, maybe, or Latin America?"

"We're closed. It's time to leave."

"Really? How come there are customers out there and the sign on the door says you're open 'til two A.M.?"

"Unless you got a warrant, you gotta get out."

"Lighten up, will you?" I spread my hand. "I'm no cop. I'm just looking for that special something."

He closed in. I started thinking I should have come in here with backup, then wondered what good Sea would have done me in the face of this behemoth. Waco might have cut him off at the knees with some smart remark, but there was no way I could have asked her along. Not here. Not at night.

"You should be trying to help me, not hassle me," I told him.

He belched.

"You want kiddie material, you're in the wrong place."

"How about snuff?"

He put two meaty hands on my shoulders. I felt like Atlas, holding up the weight of the world.

"I don't know you," he said.

In one swift movement, I ripped the little Glock out of my fanny pack and stuck the black plastic muzzle under his chin. "A good reason to take your fucking hands off me," I said calmly.

He didn't look scared, but he let me go. I cleared the beads and then the front door. A bum hanging around the liquor store started to hit on me for change, but when he saw the look on my face, he turned and headed unevenly down the street away from me.

"It's a hard, it's a hard, it's a hard raaaaaaaaiin's a gonna fall," he sang the Bob Dylan tune in a voice like a churchyard bell.

The next morning, Regina Diaz came out of a Palm Beach Gardens physical therapy center looking like a Latina movie star with a crack habit. She had high cheekbones and a classy, painted face, but her legs, long enough to win at Hollywood Park, were thin as candy canes. Her worker's compensation fraud case jacket said her back was incapable of supporting her through a day of window duty selling stamps and posting flats, but it seemed to function perfectly well as she strode toward her red Mercury Marquis, hopped in, and headed south on Haverhill Avenue.

I gave her plenty of room. Her right rear quarter panel was missing and her license plate hung loose, so there was no way I was going to lose her to a crowd. She drove as far as Bee Line Highway and made a quick jog over to Blue Heron, then got on the Interstate toward Miami. I stayed a few cars back, dicing it up with a string of green, white, and yellow Mayflower moving vans. She got off at Broward Boulevard, breezed over to the tourist haven of Las Olas, and parked in a private lot behind a row of exclusive stores right on the avenue; purveyors of malachite elephants and ceramic fellating dogs, vendors of purple fainting-couches, chocolatiers, and emporia of espressos and ice cream and thin-crust pizza baked with homemade cheese. I waited in the Porsche until she had entered some back door, then cruised around front and caught sight of her inside a boutique with wedding dresses in the window.

I watched from the car as she turned the sign in the window from "closed" to "open," then I chose a French cafe directly across the street for some breakfast. I ordered Earl Grey tea and a croissant and read the newspaper, keeping an eye on the time, finally switching the Earl for

59

herbal. It was an unseasonably warm morning. Typically, November down here feels great — sky bluer than it ever got in L.A., perfect temperature for driving with your elbow out the window — but instead, I watched clouds dodge and jostle each other like circus clowns; leftovers from the tropical collision that had brought yesterday's rain. It was over eighty degrees and sticky enough to make me slide around in my shoes. I called the office, told Wacona that I would have something on Diaz by the end of the day, and went back to watching the wedding trade.

It was brisk. Women went inside in pairs, and through the lace thicket, I could just glimpse them modeling for each other at the back of the store, a smooth leg here, an excited smile there. Regina brought out whatever they asked for — no sign of having a sore back — and when they left, she read some pulp fiction.

At 11:30 A.M. the manager of the cafe approached me uncomfortably and explained that the window tables were the most desirable ones and asked if perhaps monsieur intended to have lunch. I could have flashed my badge, but instead I ordered an eggplant and aged cheddar sandwich on grilled sourdough bread, garnished with fennel. I read another paper, this one a listing of local business opportunities. There seemed to be a dearth of competent yacht captains, presumably because of the explosion of boats in South Florida waters.

It appears we just can't leave Florida alone. Bad enough we've garrotted the great natural filter of the Everglades — depriving an eclectic worldwide marine fauna of essential nutrients in their Gulf Coast breeding ground — bad enough we've spilled oil and gas into the Atlantic waters offshore, picked the reefs clean, trashed the beaches, and slaughtered the manatees with our propellers. Now, it appears, we need more yacht captains.

The sandwich arrived. It was perfect, light and

crunchy and just chewy enough to be satisfying. When I was finished, I sauntered across the street. A bell tinkled when I opened the door, and I found myself adrift in a sea of gowns packed so tightly that every move I made caused a rustle. Regina appeared as if out of thin air.

"May I help you?" she asked.

I hadn't been this close to her before, and the intimate deception made me feel guilty. I fingered the hem of an ivory dress hanging high and asked for a closer look. Despite receiving twenty-seven hundred dollars a month in disability payments, Regina scaled the ladder like a monkey.

"It's a small," she said, smiling shyly and handing it over.

I made a show of feeling the material, holding up the garment, checking the price tag. I had a fleeting image of Phayle in it, but it was a milky, confused image, a super-imposition of my memory of a college girl and my fantasies of a mature woman. Something about the fantasy brought a frog to my throat.

I turned the dress around, pretended to consider it, then handed it back.

"I'll need to think about it."

She nodded and went up the ladder again to rehang the outfit. This time I took a closer look at her emaciated legs, the way her hip bones showed through the jeans, the minuscule diameter of her forearm as she fussed with the outfit, getting it to stay on the hook. Anorexia, bulimia, or maybe both. I felt a rush of pity for her, felt angry at myself for hassling her. She might be scamming the postal service, but she wasn't on any joy ride. Without medical attention, she'd be dead in six months, no matter what my duty to the postal service might be. I wanted to help her, and instead I had to bust her, on top of which I had a far more pressing case I needed to be pursuing.

Like any job, this one had its occasional tawdry moments.

I followed Regina Diaz home. Her place was in Lake Worth, on C Street, in the predominantly black section of town just west of Dixie Highway. It wasn't the kind of place I expected for a stylish Latina with two incomes. I saw her more as a Tequesta type, or maybe Riviera. I parked a few houses away, unconcerned about keeping a low-profile now that I had what I needed to take her case to the Unites States Attorney's office, left Phayle a message that I'd be late, opened the window, turned off the engine and sat back. I can't say what made me hang out there, just some little tingling sense that there was more to Regina than met the eye.

I was just getting comfortable when the screaming started. Sometimes I think maybe the human scream is the only thing our ears were really designed to receive, and that everything else we hear is just static. The scream receptors seem hot-wired to the brain — able at an instant to override any other mental function save that which directs our diaphragm and bowels. Among the screams I have heard in my life are the scream of a woman in childbirth, of a man watching his brother blown apart by a parcel bomb, and the dying scream — more a high-pitched keening — of a postal worker gunned down in the parking lot by his jealous wife.

The screams coming from Regina's house set me running like a cheetah at prey. I reached the front door in seconds and peered in through the glass. Regina stood in the center of the room, her nose a blossom of blood. A shrieking toddler wearing a Marlins T-shirt clutched her hand, and behind them an infant in a high chair waved a lime green plastic rattle.

A Caribbean black man in knee-length boxer shorts stood with his back to me. He was tall enough to play pro ball. His hands were closed in fists and he was all rangy motion as he closed in for another round.

"No!" I shouted, tapping on the glass.

Ignoring me, the guy took a swing at Regina. She ducked, but he clipped her anyway, lifting her clean off the ground. She fell back on the toddler. Desperately, I yanked at the doorknob, but it was locked. I pounded hard, but the guy didn't even turn around. I set back on my rear leg, shifted my weight, then swung upward and splintered the lock with my heel.

"Hey!" the guy sputtered, as I half-fell into the foyer.

"Get away from them," I commanded.

He chuckled and went back to work. "Maybe this will cure you, you puking bitch!" he spat, and then he slapped her hard on the side of the head.

My left hand found my gun, and my right my badge, but the guy was already rushing me. T'ai chi ch'uan teaches you to regard energy spent against you as a gift. If you use it properly, you don't even need to work up a sweat. As he came in, I stepped aside, grabbed his elbow and twisted my waist, escorting him hard to the floor. His head cracked against the white tile and his eyes rolled up.

"Cristoforo!" cried Regina.

He lay stunned, breathing heavily and staring at my gun. Dried flowers from a tipped-over vase scattered around him like a funeral corsage.

"You're not going to press charges against her, are you?" Phayle asked, horrified at the story.

We were strolling arm-in-arm amidst cafes and restaurants, inhaling frangipani, headed from the Delano to the Lincoln Mall restaurant I had in mind. The humid day had turned into a night so still that tiny gnats—bugs that could be blown for miles by the merest exhalation—circled about us in clouds. Phayle was wearing white, a short skirt, which showed off legs that looked better, thanks to exercise, than they had in college. Her midriff was exposed, flat and tan. The shortened blouse she wore hung over her breasts and down, waving as she walked, blowing her perfume my way. She looked like she might be the editor of a woman's magazine, deliberate in the airs she put on, secure in her sense of herself, and obviously looking to drive me wild.

"She's conning the postal service. It's my job to press charges. Still, she's too sympathetic a character for any judge to convict her; a bulimic, battered, working mother of two, trying to feed her kids and hold her life together in the face of mental illness. I'm betting that the United States Attorney's office will dismiss the case, arrange therapy and foster care, maybe even work her back into the service."

"And the bastard who hit her?"

"She reluctantly agreed to file charges. We'll see. Abuse has its patterns. I'm just glad I came along at that moment. I'm not even sure why I followed her home. I already had what I needed."

"Subconsciously, you were looking for a way to help her."

"Maybe," I shrugged.

A woman in a neoprene suit went by on Rollerblades, pulled by a harlequin Great Dane.

"Nice pants," she called to me.

"I'm glad *she* likes them. What's the bottom line on your baggy phase, M.D.?" Phayle put in.

"I'm a gang-banger wannabe," I replied, guiding her into the restaurant.

Over dinner we talked about the little things; bowling

on the slanted floor in the apartment she rented in Los Angeles when she thought maybe she wanted to be in the movie business, the exciting pace at which Picard had grown since I moved to Florida, a boyfriend whom she had reluctantly accompanied to an Oregon commune then abandoned because of the delight he took in slaughtering farm animals. We talked about the unexpected romance between my grandmother and Seagrave Chunny, and we tasted each other's food—swordfish and scallops—and shared dipping sauces, salads, and finally sorbets of fresh fruit. After dinner we drank sweet dessert wine, then moved to a nearby bar, where, with trepidation born of a fear of hurting each other and beneath framed black-and-white photographs of Miami bowing to hurricanes, we slipped sideways into the delicate subject of our years together at Yale.

"Remember the 'Cruise'?" she asked, referring to a dorm party in which we had ended up half-naked in each other's arms in deep snow. "If I told your boss the things you put in your body back then, you'd be jobless in a heartbeat."

"I'd deny everything," I laughed.

She was on Chardonnay again. I was drinking Lagavulin, a fine single malt Scotch from the Isle of Islay. It didn't mix well with the dessert wine, but it evoked heather and moss and a melancholy kind of beauty that seemed to match my mood.

"You didn't seem too happy to see Clifton and Jeff," she observed.

"It was Twy's funeral, Phayle."

"It looked like there was more going on than that."

"I told you, we drifted apart. College was a long time ago. Look what happened to you and me."

"Did you guys have a falling out over Lyre and Stone?"

Maybe if she hadn't said it so casually, I wouldn't have

been caught so off guard. As it was, I jerked back, spilling the Scotch all over my sport jacket and the plush red upholstery of our snug little booth.

Lyre and Stone is the most secret of the Yale secret societies, an archly clandestine fraternity that exists only amongst the disciples of Eli Yale. Yale men are tapped in their junior year. Membership is built during the senior year and cemented, for most, during the rest of their days. Stone seeks to build lives and careers, to secure power by interlocking the fingers of a select few. Twyman Boatwright had been a member, as had Jeff Grayson and Clifton Hughes. I, Maximillian Diamond, had been the fourteenth Jew admitted in the society's history, being, I was told during an evening of debauched celebration, a unanimous choice.

"I don't know what you're talking about," I said.

"Come on, Max. Lyre and Stone's not the big deal it was years ago. There have been all kinds of news stories about it."

"I wouldn't know."

"You wouldn't know that two U.S. presidents have confessed to being members, or that one out of three of all the Joint Chiefs of Staff since Truman have Lyre and Stone pocket watches? I knew you four were tapped, Max. It wasn't that hard to figure out. Junior year you guys hardly knew each other, senior year you're suddenly best friends."

I stared at her. She wore the easy seriousness of the alcoholic like a broach, and it dawned on me that maybe the mercurial temperament I remembered had been a result of alcoholism and that I had been too young and too smitten to notice.

"You think you're pretty clever, huh?"

"I'm thinking maybe *I'm* the one who should be the detective," she smiled.

"What do you expect me to say?"

"I was just wondering what happened with you and Jeff and Clifton."

"Lyre and Stone was a long time ago. I don't have anything to do with it anymore. On the rare occasion I think about it these days, it just seems like a frat that took itself too seriously."

"Right before I left Santa Barbara, there was a big spread in the *Los Angeles Times* about college secret societies," she said, waving down the waiter and ordering another Chardonnay. "It talked about Lyre and Stone's links to the intelligence community, and about how the wartime OSS and the CIA sang Yale's Whiffenpoof drinking song at parties."

"I didn't get my job through Stone connections, if that's what you're thinking. A postal inspector is a long way from a spy."

The waiter brought Phayle's drink, and she downed half of it before setting it down.

"You've stayed very much in control of yourself, haven't you, Max?" she slurred slightly, as if it were an accusation.

"You say that like it's a bad thing."

"Maybe it is, maybe it isn't. But you being a cop is starting to make sense to me."

"I'll drink to that."

When we finally got back to her hotel, Phayle asked me up to her room for a nightcap. I told her I felt like glue was running in my veins.

"A cop who can't beat back a few boilermakers? What sort of a lightweight are you? What happened to the beer-guzzling college boy I knew?"

"He ran off with my hair. How about a swim instead?"

She liked the idea, so we went out the back door of the lobby and down to the long, shallow, softly lit green pool. We got two big white towels from a pile by the bar and stepped into one of the changing closets that lined the hedges near the pool. The little room was maybe 6' × 4' and inside there was a long futon of puffy cotton laid over a white wicker base. I closed the zebra-striped curtain and pulled Phayle to me.

"Stop digging at the past," I said softly. "Focus on the here and now, okay?"

"I'm sorry," she said, burying her head in my chest. "I guess Twy's death shook me more than I thought it would."

I nodded, thinking that Twyman Boatwright wasn't the first of my friends to die. That would be the guy who had roomed across the hall from me during two of my four years of Yale and died of AIDS a year after graduation. Then of course there was the late inspector Greg Hunter, who had risen above his resentment of Sea's obvious affection — and my easy way with Wacona — to help me learn the job. I thought of the way we had backed each other up, the way men with guns do, at times and in places nobody else would understand. I recalled the sight of his soul following the red geyser of his carotid blood upward and out of his body, suddenly unfettered, momentarily confused.

Phayle lifted her face and brushed my lips with hers. "Will you help me forget everything?" she whispered.

"If you'll promise to stay in Florida for a while."

By way of answer she raised her hands up over her head, inviting me to take off her blouse. I did, and saw the light and dark of her, by the moonlight, through a fine white mesh brassiere. I reached around back for the hooks, and the bra fell to the ground. Suddenly, there were footsteps and a man's face appeared not two feet from us. He was swarthy, with a mustache and a blue shirt with a patch on the sleeve.

Phayle folded her arms across her chest in panic.

"Get lost," I said.

"Hotel security. Curtains must remain open," he replied.

"Show him your badge or something," Phayle hissed.

The security man looked at me inquiringly. I shrugged my shoulders and he moved off, leaving the curtains slightly parted. Phayle slipped her blouse back on.

"Killjoy," she pouted.

"He's just doing his job."

"Not him, you. You could have made him go away."

"I've got a better idea."

I took her hand and led her through the hedge at the end of the pool deck and out onto the dark expanse of sandy beach. We found a small dune, and our clothes were off in moments. She wrapped herself around me. I kissed her breasts, she threw her head back and moaned, and then, suddenly, in the warmth and the quiet and the darkness, I saw the little blue-eyed girl, her high heels tapping on the table, and I pulled away.

"What's wrong?"

"Nothing."

She reached down, and found me limp. "This isn't the old Max."

"No."

"Are you shy all of a sudden?"

"That's not it."

"Maybe we should go up to my room."

"I don't think so, Phayle."

"So what, you're going to leave me like this?"

"I'm tired," I lied.

"So take a rest. I'll wake you up."

Looking into her eyes, I just couldn't bring myself to

say no, even though I was afraid that she wasn't angel enough to beat back my demons, so I smiled and said okay. We pulled ourselves together and we went upstairs.

She did everything a loving, talented, caring woman could possibly do, and I tried mightily, but in the end, it just didn't happen for me.

"What's going on here, Max?" she asked. I could see she was fighting back tears.

"It's not you, Phayle," I said numbly.

"But it *is* me, Max. It's me naked with you in the bed, and I can tell you that right now it doesn't feel very good to *be* me. Maybe I should have gone with that guy on the yacht, you know the guy who was ogling me at lunch the other day when you kissed me?"

"Please," I said.

"Please what? Don't you think I deserve some kind of explanation?"

I took a deep breath and wiped my perspiration off with the sheet. "This hasn't happened before," I began.

"Well thank you very much for that. You sure know how to make a girl feel special."

"Something is going on," I began. "Something that started right before you came back into my life."

"Just my luck. You're not coming out of the closet, are you, M.D.? Turning out to be one of those macho gay guys?"

"Jesus, Phayle."

She stood up. "Is there somebody else then? Is that it? Is this some manifestation of guilt?"

"There's nobody else."

"Am I too old? Is that it? Maybe you keep thinking of me at nineteen and you're disappointed with what you see?"

"Forget that, will you? You were a knockout then and you're a knockout now."

"So you're not gay, there's nobody else, and I'm a knockout. What does that leave? Are you sick? My God, Max. Don't tell me you're sick."

"I'm not sick, okay? At least not the way you mean."

I felt stubborn frustration rising, and attempted to beat it back by thinking first about my father—that always brought anger—and then about the ridiculous man with the shotgun who had threatened to shoot the mail carrier. That last should have made me laugh, but it didn't.

"Then talk to me," Phayle implored. "Is it just that I don't turn you on anymore?"

"You turn me on, Phayle, but there's something I'm involved in at work," I said slowly. "It's an active case, and I can't give you any detail. I *can* tell you that it involves sex crimes."

"Sex crimes," Phayle repeated.

"Terrible things."

"Like what?"

"Murder. Children. I keep replaying scenes in my head."

"Oh!" she shuddered.

"You know, I've seen a man shotgunned in the face, seen fleeing felons tasered until they twitch like dying bugs on the floor, even seen a bomb blow a man to bits, but this thing just eats me up down low."

She put her arms around me and I buried my head on her bare shoulder. I sighed, taking in her aroma as I did so, a cocktail of hormones and nerves, fears and insecurities.

"I'm so sorry, Max," she murmured.

"Me too."

She reached gently and elegantly up for my bald pate, and drew me in tight. We held each other for so long we

71

got too hot to breathe, then finally, gently, let each other go. She put on her underwear and I slipped into my pants. Things got better after that. We raided the minibar and inhaled peanuts, candy bars, potato chips, and orange juice. The tension gone, we channel-surfed the TV. There were infomercials on most stations, two for exercise machines and one for a shampoo that grew hair. I told her I'd tried it. She found a Charles Bronson movie. I switched it off, she switched it back on again.

"What's wrong with Bronson?" she asked.

"It doesn't feel good for you to be ogling the guy right now, that's all."

"Bronson *is* pretty buffed," she mused.

"Not as buffed as I am."

"Doesn't have your sex appeal either."

"Phayle," I said, kissing her, "you're the best."

"You look like shit," Wacona said, with typical tactfulness and warmth.

She was right, of course. I was only just out of Phayle's bed, and had managed no more than a couple of sleeping hours.

"Well, I feel terrific," I said.

"You look fine," added Chunny, who was standing beside her. "At least for a gigolo."

I made like I was going to hit him, and he ducked away grinning.

We were standing behind the firing line at the police qualifying range in Coral Springs; an outdoor facility smack dab in the heart of what used to be the Everglades and used by a variety of different law enforcement agencies. Five Broward County sheriff's deputies were finishing up on the range, and it was our turn next. I hadn't remembered that we had our twice-yearly qualifying drills until I was on my way to the office and Lorraine, our indispensable office clerk, had radioed to remind me.

Wacona was in jeans that fit her like a narrow, tasteful picture frame; not so tight as to be sleazy, not so loose as to look like mine. She wore a T-shirt tucked in, and a vest of distressed leather over her shoulder holster. She was a die-hard revolver shooter, fond of saying that semi-automatics were for soldiers and drug dealers and she was neither. She carried a Smith & Wesson Performance Center Model 66, a .357 magnum in stainless steel with a sweetened trigger, adjustable sights, ported barrel, and custom cut cocobolo grips with heart-shaped ivory insets. It wasn't, strictly speaking, a regulation gun, but nobody I knew was about to chew her out about it. She popped the cylinder out, inspected the ejector rod for gum-up, took a peek down the barrel, and put it away.

"Everything okay?" I asked.

"Perfect as always, Max. It's my gun."

The BSO deputies shut down, and it was our turn. The first drill was to shoot clanging steel plates, and the three of us did fine. The second drill had us running from barrier to barrier, protecting ourselves while we fired at the same targets. Despite his strange birdlike gait, Sea scored better than I did. Wacona, of course, beat us both.

Mercifully, a rain shower came up after that, and we all dashed for the shelter of the target bench. My head was beginning to throb, telling me that my hangover hadn't really yet begun—that by staying up most of the night I had fooled my body enough to delay the inevitable, but not avoid it. I belched up a spot of acid bile and buried my head in my hands.

"Hair of the dog," said Sea, squeezing my neck.

"Hangover or no hangover, you'd shoot better if you gave up that Glock," Wacona declared.

"You just hate short barrels," I said.

"Don't sweat it, Max. I think you're okay despite your anatomical limitations," she quipped.

Sea rolled his eyes.

As soon as the rain stopped, we had to shoot at swiveling poster targets, controlled by the rangemaster, that depicted good guys and bad guys. The public is told that cops are taught to shoot low in a firefight, but in truth we're taught to aim for the chest or belly shot, and if a clean shot is completely assured, the head. When my turn came, I confidently drilled an innocent bystander right between the eyes, barely missed shooting an old lady holding an umbrella, and fatally wounded a lowlife wearing a gorilla mask and holding a knife at a kid's throat. Wacona was wrong about the little Glock. At close quarters, it was more accurate than I was.

I finished the rest of the drill okay, and Wacona followed, making no mistakes. Sea was last, and things didn't go well. He still had a steady hand, and his judgment and his knowledge of the law—not to mention the network of friends and informants he had set up over the years—kept him a living legend in the department, but age was robbing him of his reaction time. Fully half the targets swung back on their posts before he had made a fire decision, and he knew he would have gone home in a body bag for sure if the test had been real life.

Wacona looked thoughtful, and Sea was visibly shaken.

"Just an off day," I said, trying to make light of things. "You don't work external crime much anymore anyway, what do you care? If we need you for backup, Wacona can always get you something in full auto and you can spray the whole damn place."

"It's no joke, Max," he said quietly. "Qualifying is part of the job, understand?"

"We'll get you back out here in a few weeks. You can

practice until then," Wacona said awkwardly.

I felt bad for both of them. Knowing he was nearing retirement and interested in reducing his workload, Sea had voluntarily stepped aside as Palm Beach Team Leader so that he could train whomever the Inspector-in-Charge chose as his replacement. Wacona had been a selection clear out of left field, brought in from Seattle, tops in her division, a woman more than a quarter-century younger than Sea who could shame him on the firing range.

"Sure," he said. "I'll get it back."

The last drill was mock night. At one time the range was open late, but the overtime costs were high, and all the agencies that used the facility opted for daytime training with goggles so ridiculously dark a supernova fifty feet away would have been tough to spot. I watched Wacona walk the range half-blind, drawing quickly and shooting at the spinners. She did well, but not so well, I suspected, as she could have. Perhaps she was trying to ease things up on Sea, and indeed he responded by doing better than I feared he would. When it was my turn, I did okay, but I'd done better.

Couldn't focus, somehow.

FOUR

The next morning, I put a call in to the U.S.P.I.S. Forensic and Technical Services Laboratory in Dulles, Virginia. They told me they had received the videotape, but that they were backlogged and that initial processing might take more time. They seemed unimpressed by the fact that the tape contained a visual record of a woman murdered in front of a nude, dancing child. Frustrated, I dragged the two spare VCRs and monitors into my office, closed the door, and settled back for more screening. If anything, the stack of remaining tapes seemed to have grown overnight, as if the cassettes themselves were coupling, inspired by the scenes they contained. I put three of them in and let them roll.

The TV on my left showed a pool-cleaner scene — woman alone in house, studly boy with a long, thick skimmer comes to take care of the plumbing, the inevitable transpires. The center tube held nothing but 1-900 ads. I called one of them on a lark and asked if they had any little girls I could speak to. Acidly they informed me that all their employees were over twenty-one, then hung up.

The third screen was a bit more interesting. It had begun with a couple of Southern California beach bunnies washing cars, then each other, then stripping, then having outdoor sex, but suddenly the picture wavered, the screen went dark, and the sound track scratched and hissed. A moment later, a view of the tropics appeared; a native village ringed by low, thorny, exotic-looking foliage sprouting from reddish soil. Huts stood in a cluster; primitive mud and timber affairs with brightly colored window frames and doors. The camera panned to a girl, not as young as the table-dancer but still clearly underage. She walked toward a crumbling barn. Inside, she began to gently brush the coat of a black goat with a white stripe down its forehead. She moved the brush from fore to aft in long strokes. A man's voice said something in a language I couldn't understand, she glanced at the camera, and began to touch her breasts in time to the brushstrokes. Then she dropped the brush and climbed under the goat.

I killed the tape and took a break to check my home answering machine. Phayle had left a message. She wanted to make plans for the evening. I returned the call, but she was out. I watched the culmination of the bestiality scene, saw the goat buck wildly and heard the girl shriek, then loaded another three videos, and then another, and then another. After two hours, I found another nightmare.

Like the barn and restaurant scenes, the live, amateurish soundtrack was the first tip-off—the sounds of waves smacking a fiberglass hull and the low rumble of a marine diesel. A deeply tanned man with a thin, scraggly beard and a hooked nose was gutting and cleaning a fish on the stern deck of a power boat—no name on the stern — bobbing in a dark blue ocean dotted with tiny whitecaps. Spray on the lens suggested that the camera was on a different boat, with a telephoto used to good effect. The man's hands were gnarled and strong, and he used the fillet knife easily.

Suddenly a girl-child appeared, perhaps twelve, brown-skinned like the dancer, but with dark eyes, black hair and a certain shyness about the way she came naked up the stairs, her hands straying between her legs. The fisherman greeted her tenderly, putting his hand on her cheek as a parent might wipe away a child's tear. She wouldn't look at him. He bent her gently back over the gunwale. Spray hit the lens again, and a moment later misted the girl's hair. The fisherman fondled what little there was of her breasts. She closed her eyes. The camera zoomed in for a tight shot of his fingers.

His lips were pulled back in a terrible grin, and I was so riveted by his expression that I almost missed it when he picked up the fillet knife and plunged it into the little girl's belly, right below the ribs, angled expertly up at the heart. There was blood, of course, but when the camera shifted to her face, more of the story was there.

The killer heaved her over the side, and I began heaves of my own before her body even hit the water. Waco and Sea must have heard me, because they came running. They tried to soothe me, but no matter how loudly I cursed and spat out the bile, no matter how violently I gasped for air, I knew those precious little ears would never hear me, wrapped tightly as they were in the strong arms of the deep blue sea.

I went home early, took a shower, switched the ringer off my phone, and tried to sleep. My stomach was raw, my mouth tasted like rancid oysters, and my head was ringing from dehydration. The innocent helplessness of the girl and the raw horror of her murder itched me in a place I just could not reach to scratch. I tried to calm myself with Taoist ideas of universal unity and integration and Buddhist notions of karma, but none of these tactics gave me any solace, nor did my relaxation machine, the one with the flashing lights.

When late afternoon rolled around, I got up out of bed more tired than I had gone down. There was a message from Phayle on my machine, just a long, drawn-out sigh with a lip-smack at the end. I called the Delano, but once again, she was out. Picard was hungry, and I had nothing in the house to feed him, so I dashed down to the market in Deerfield Beach.

Two months after I'd moved into the condo, I'd gone late one night and found one of the shelf-stockers, a Nicaraguan kid named Rigoberto, practicing martial arts moves in the back of the parking lot. Everything he was doing was wrong; back not straight, movements too jerky, weight-shifts in the wrong places. Turned out he had never had a teacher, and had been copying moves he'd seen David Carradine perform on late night reruns of *Kung Fu*. I showed him some t'ai chi ch'uan, and we made an agreement then and there—free martial arts lessons in exchange for enough tortoise food to help Picard reach his full eight hundred pounds.

Rigoberto wasn't around, but as always there was a box secreted behind the last in a row of store Dumpsters. I opened it up to find a couple of winter squashes and eight ears of corn. I took them back to my place, and, still feeling dirty, ran a hot bath. I was about to step in when the phone rang.

"Max, it's Jeff Grayson. What are you up to right now?"

"I've got one foot in the tub."

"Well take a shower instead and meet me down in Fort Lauderdale. I've got tickets for the symphony and Gwen's got the flu. Bruno Gelber is in town from Argentina to play Beethoven. He never gets up here. It's an event."

"Who is Gwen, Jeff?"

"My wife," he said impatiently. "Didn't you meet her at the funeral?"

"Actually, I didn't."

"Hmm. Well anyway, say yes. It'll be great music and we can catch up afterwards."

This was Jeff's way. The dozen years of silence between us was nothing. It had never happened. He needed a partner at the symphony and I had answered the phone.

"It's kind of short notice," I hesitated.

"Twy pulled us together again, old buddy, dying the way he did. Go with the flow, Max. I'll leave a ticket for you at will-call."

He hung up before I could say anything more. As in the old days, there was simply no denying him.

There are few things I dislike more than walking late into a packed hall where a performer is making love to his piano. I had taken the BMW bike and illegally split lanes half the way, but Jeff hadn't given me enough time. The old usher, whose tag identified him as a volunteer, looked disdainfully at my leather jacket, and reluctantly showed me to Jeff Grayson's box. Unsurprisingly, it was the best in the house, orchestra right, elevated for a perfect view of orchestra and maestro. I said a quiet hello to Jeff, but he was so absorbed in the cadenza of the Emperor Concerto that he didn't acknowledge me until the performance was over and the crowd was on its feet.

"Max!" he said, as if seeing me for the first time. "Don't you just love the bombast of Beethoven?" I told him I preferred the intellectual intricacy of Bach. He smiled and shook his head.

After the show, he led me to a patron's bash in the symphony's dining hall. Twin buffets served the same mix of soggy sushi, overcooked prime rib, and grainy rotini drenched in creamy faux-lobster sauce.

"Thank God the music was better than the food, eh old buddy?"

I ate sparingly, wagered with myself that the wine and soda offered would not be enough for Jeff. I felt an inspector's satisfaction when he grabbed a waitress by the arm and slipped her a ten to go find him some name-brand bourbon.

"You still active in Stone?" I asked, watching him chow down. Clearly, piano music made him hungry.

"No small talk for you, huh?" he chewed.

"I just figured that's what kept you and Cliff and Twy connected," I shrugged.

"So you're a postal inspector," he announced, avoiding my question.

I remembered that this was the way with Lyre and Stone. It was as if membership in the society bestowed permission upon each member to use a crowbar upon the heart of the others. In a certain sense, membership in that fraternity was not that different from the badge I carried. Both entitled a certain brutal frankness, but whereas an officer of the law did what he did for the good of the many, Stonemen did what they did for the good of the few. I suspected that exclusivity and power turned college boys into vicious men.

"It's reassuring to know there are files on me," I said. "That way, posterity will remember me for the prince I really am."

"We always liked you, Max. If you change your mind, it's not too late to come to a meeting. It really is the way the thing was billed to us at Yale, a network, nothing more. People helping people."

"Thanks, but no thanks."

"Right. Well the offer stands. 'Once a Stoneman,' like they say. Lots of guys we know have risen to the top during the last few years. Senators, congressmen, heads of Fortune five hundred companies, some particular names that would surprise you."

"Like who?"

"People close to you. People you work with."

In the U.S.P.I.S.? I doubted it. "I'm happy with my life, Jeff."

"Good to hear," he grinned. "So how's your father?"

This was just like him, and one of the reasons why I had instinctively been wary of his motives when we first met at school. He wore a calculated face, a persona he could change at will so that nobody would ever know exactly what was going on inside him. It made off-balancing shifts of conversation easy for him.

"I bet you know the answer to that, Jeff. I feel pretty shitty about him, if that's what you're trying to dig out. How about *your* old man? Did he ever retire to that farm near Moultrie? He fit in well in southern Georgia as I remember, surrounded by hillbillies and pickup trucks, representing pig farmers in suits over land titles and runaway sows."

Twy and Cliff and Jeff and I had spent one spring vacation on the Grayson farm near Moultrie, daydreaming aloud of willing teenage southern belles. I had enjoyed the airgun plinking, if not the rattlesnake hunting, but found it hard to relax among the locals.

"He sold the place and retired to Martha's Vineyard," Jeff said tightly.

"Leaving you his law practice."

"But no pig farm," he brightened. "We each have our

own thing. Twy handled corporate work—he did some jobs for Disney and recently contracts for the proposed Orlando-Miami rail. Cliff focuses on divorce and family law, estates and so on. Personally, I like real estate law, especially development."

I winced.

"Don't tell me you're a save-the-Everglades type, M.D.?"

"We don't know what we're doing, with our building and our canals. Changes to the 'glades affect animals that come from half a world away to nest in the Ten Thousand Islands."

"I shoulda known," he smiled, shaking his head.

The waitress showed up with his bourbon. He downed half of it immediately—no ice, no water, no hesitation.

"More people are moving down here every day—the old, the sick, the weak, the failures, filling in the state from both sides. That's the inevitable truth, old buddy. Nobody can stop it, and nobody can change it. What we can do is make sure the place doesn't turn into a trash heap. We can supervise and organize the growth, keep the get-rich-quick sleazeballs out, the people of integrity in. Lend order to the chaos, Max. You should be able to understand that."

"I understand it fine, Jeff. Now how about telling me how Twy died?"

His face darkened. "Horribly," he said. "Did you know he was into woodworking?"

"Phayle mentioned it."

"You seen her since the funeral?"

"Uh-huh."

"Wonderful. What did you two talk about?"

"Old times, her work. Let's get back to Twy."

He wet his lips with what was left of his drink, suddenly looking as if he wanted to savor it. "Twy had a hell of a shop out behind his place," he said, the booze rising to his eyes. "Edgers and cutters and grinders and saws."

"Furniture, right?" I kept on it.

"Stuff you never even dreamed of. Beautiful pieces. Christ, I swear his rocking chairs belonged in a museum."

"Maybe now they'll get there. He always had good taste."

"You got that right. You should have seen Nora when they met. Not like she looked at the funeral, but full of Twy's own brand of ruddy-faced happiness. Her smile would have stopped your heart in mid-beat."

"So what happened, exactly?"

"He was using a table saw. Cutting some piece of African hardwood. Dense stuff, dark and heavy. Somehow the fence—that's the adjustable piece that sticks up from the table and holds the wood in place against the saw—was set slightly crooked. Twy kept pushing the wood against the saw, hard, you know, to make the cut, and because that fence wasn't straight the wood kicked back on him."

"You know a lot about power tools, don't you Jeff?"

"I learned a thing or two from Twy. He was always in that shop. Anyway, the wood went through his throat like a missile. I didn't tell Phayle, but it basically took his head clean off. Nora found him."

"Oh no."

Jeff nodded, took a giant stab of pasta and wound it around his fork. I wondered how he could keep his appetite and talk like he did. He saw my expression and put his fork down.

"I made my peace with Twy the night it happened," he said, his voice suddenly thick. "Wherever he's gone, I'll see him again."

FIVE

The plainclothes sheriff's deputy at Palm Beach International Airport hardly seemed to remember the case.

"Porn tapes," he said thoughtfully, chewing on an unlit cigar.

He was one of the new breed of smokers, I could tell that much, men who went for cigars the same way they went for Harley Davidson motorcycles — a marque of no interest to the intelligent rider — because both Hogs and stogies were cultural icons, symbols of masculine power. The cigar he was smoking had a Cohiba ring, but I could tell by the quality of the wrapper that it was a knock-off, not a Cuban; a two-dollar, maybe a three-dollar cigar. His suit looked like Adolfo, though. Nice. He would blend well with a crew of business travelers, and that was the idea.

"Come on. You turned the courier on the case. He's a confidential informant for you now."

His eyes narrowed as he put it together. "What do you want with him?"

"I've just got questions. Follow-up on something I've got going."

"We tend to tuck our informants well under our wings."

I pulled a Te Amo Meditation from the inside pocket of my leather jacket.

"Ever had one of these?"

He took the cigar, inspected it.

"Don't like the dark ones."

"They're called Maduros," I told him. "What you've got in your mouth, that's bitter."

He pulled the cigar out of his mouth and looked at it.

"Are you kidding? This is a Cuban."

"Cuban name, maybe," I shook my head, "but the cigar looks Nicaraguan to me. Cost you what, a couple of bucks?"

He nodded. I clucked.

I had learned about cigars from my Grandpa Isaac. In the early years after his escape from Russia, Isaac had sold produce off a pushcart on the Lower East Side of Manhattan. Garment workers—they considered themselves bigshots then because they got deals on clothing and sometimes a suit here and there as a bonus—would pass their good fortune on to my grandfather in the form of an occasional stogie. In return, the customers would expect a price break on some sweet corn or access to the secret, coal-warmed knish drawer in the bottom of the cart, out of sight because it required an additional license.

Good cigars in those days were always Cubans, and Isaac soon acquired a taste for them. Too, he had a spectacular nose, as sensitive as it was imposing, and he was able at six inches to distinguish a dry cigar from one left too long in a vest pocket during hot or rainy weather, or, more easily, a good Cuban from a bad. He learned about wrapper leaf—Connecticut Shade was considered first-cabin—and about filler leaf, the tightness of draw, even the art on the ring and the box. For my bar mitzvah, he gave me his collection of cigar rings and box art. I don't know if they are worth anything, but to this day I keep them stored carefully under my bed.

"A real Cuban would have cost you thirty dollars," I told the deputy. "But don't feel bad. Cubans aren't what they used to be. The soil has gone bad under Castro. No agricultural management, no more nutrients for good tobacco, the use of artificial chemicals in the filler. All the talented cigar makers have moved to the Dominican Republic, Jamaica, Honduras or Mexico."

The detective stared at me. I pulled the Te Amo out of the cellophane and handed it to him. "Guys who know cigars go for these."

"Mexico," he frowned, reading the ring. "I'd a figured you'd be smoking some confiscated Cubans yourself."

"That's Customs. Postal inspectors don't get them much. Anyway, what's in your hand is tobacco from the San Andres Valley. Inside word is that it's some of the sweetest, best leaf around."

"Well, we can't smoke it in here," he said.

In response, I took him by the elbow—he was a burly guy, but soft—and led him out through the security doors to the airport police parking lot.

"My first postal inspector," he shook his head and disengaged his arm.

"I'm not taking you to bed, man. I'm just giving you a cigar."

That made him laugh. I snipped the end off the Te Amo for him using Grandpa Isaac's old gold cutter out of my pocket and gave him a light with my own classic Dunhill.

"Ha," he said, drawing and puffing.

"Sweet, right?"

He took another puff, dropped his old cigar on the ground, mashed it with his foot. "The C.I. you're looking for? We can't prove it, but it's pretty obvious he tipped the bad guys when he tipped us. We've used him for some other stuff in the meantime. He tends to hang out around the airport—he's friendly with some of the bag handlers. Say, you ride a motorcycle up here?"

I nodded. He pointed at the far end of the lot. A Harley Fat Boy sat all by itself, gray with yellow pinstripes, chrome everywhere, solid wheels, leather saddlebags with shiny rivets and a fringe. I smiled to myself for having called it.

"That's mine," he said proudly.

I made jealous noises and handed him another smoke.

"For later," I said. "After your ride home."

He scribbled something on a card and handed it to me. "The guy you want is in Lake Worth lockup," he said.

"Why?"

"I'm trying to find that out. He called me screaming of course. His one phone call. Look, don't tell him I sent you."

"No problem."

"And hey, where can I get more of these Mexicans, you know, just in case I decide I like 'em?"

"Your supplier is but a phone call away," I grinned.

He grinned back.

Sometimes it's that easy.

"What a beautiful motorcycle!" Phayle exclaimed, as I pulled into the lot behind my building and shut the R90S down.

"How did you find me?" I asked. My address and number were unlisted.

"A woman named Lorraine at your office told me where to come. How about pretending you're glad to see me?"

She was right, of course, but I felt like my privacy had been invaded. "Sorry. It's just that in my line of work a guy has to be careful. I'm glad you like the bike. I told you I'd have one someday."

"And I've waited fifteen years for a ride, so I can wait a little longer and take you upstairs for a hot bath and backrub."

"If I didn't know better, I would think you were trying to seduce me."

"Busted!" she cried.

My cell phone sounded off. I picked it up and found Wacona on the other end yelling something about a bomb. I wrote down the address in a hurry. It was a Riviera house, one of the yuppie eruptions behind Boca Raton's crown jewel, Mizener Park. Depending on whether there was water access or not, the place might run up as high as seven-hundred-and-fifty-thousand dollars! I told her I'd get right on it.

"What about our tub?" Phayle pouted.

"Duty calls," I spread my hands. "Bomb scare."

"Oh, Max, I have to go!"

"Don't be silly."

"I mean it! I want you to take me. I want to see you in action."

I thought about it for a minute. Waco wouldn't be there, that was why she was sending me, and I could park at a safe distance. "All right," I agreed.

She whooped, and I dashed upstairs for an extra helmet and we took off. The R90S may be slow compared to the current crop of Japanese repli-racers, but it still beats most sports cars on the planet to sixty mph.

"I love this!" Phayle cried, wrapping her arms tight around me as I powered out onto the coast road.

I headed west at Palmetto Park Road, crossed the Intracoastal Waterway and turned north. I found the house by following the flashing red lights. Boca P.D. cruisers clustered around the house like geese around a frog pond. A news van with a dish antenna on top rolled in.

I told Phayle to stay with the bike and went through the front door. In the living room, a man in a white terrycloth bathrobe was whining to a Boca P.D. sergeant. I held up my shield and followed the sound of voices to the kitchen, where I found a bomb squad guy in a moonsuit, drinking a can of soda.

"S'up?" he asked me.

"You tell me. My team leader just sent me over here."

"Your team leader. Oh. You're a Fed. Here, take this."

He handed me a package the size and shape of a shoebox, wrapped in brown paper, one end torn open.

"Give it a shake," he suggested.

"Oh sure."

"No, really. Go ahead."

I shook it. It started buzzing. You don't need bomb training to know buzzing is a bad sign. I put it down and took an involuntary step back.

"The highly trained federal investigator," he said sarcastically.

"Maximillian Diamond, United States Postal Inspector," I said, prying the box open with my fingers.

The sergeant from the living room walked in. "The wife's in the bathroom and she won't come out," he announced. "Says she didn't order the thing."

I pulled a long white marital aid out of the package.

"Duck!" screamed the cop. He and the sergeant

howled. I took out the battery and the buzzing stopped.

"You've got the touch, Inspector," said the bomb boy.

I gave him the finger and slid the evidence into my jacket. Outside, Phayle asked what had happened. I unsnapped her jeans, turned on the dildo and pressed it against her.

"False alarm," I said.

In nearly four years working the West Palm Beach domicile, I had never been to the Lake Worth station. A small, older community suffering the blight of crack cocaine, Lake Worth boasts a few nice neighborhoods like College Park and a lot of dicey ones. Geographically dead center of town is Dixie Highway, the main thoroughfare down to Miami and the Keys before the Interstate came in during the late '60s. Now the road is overrun with motels good mostly for an hour with a hooker, and though I've heard talk of gentrifying the waterfront area by Bryant Park and the old Gulfstream Hotel, in the face of drug dealers and Haitian migrant workers any such work would be like building a sand castle during a hurricane.

I pulled into the Police Department's lot just off of I-95 and parked in a reserved spot. A converted forty-year-old school, the building was ramshackle and sprawling. I prowled the walkways looking for a way in, and came across a uniformed officer holding up a child's doll for one of his chums. He yanked at the dress, stripping the doll to its tiny diaper.

"Daddy, daddy, why don't you send the support money?" he falsettoed.

I cleared my throat. The cop dropped the doll. Holding up my shield, I asked for directions. Embarrassed, the cop led me personally through a maze of white rooms and straight to his lieutenant, a 315-pound bodybuilder named Pete DeNoso.

"If that's your car, maybe I should go local," I told DeNoso, shaking his hand and pointing to a poster of a Lamborghini Countach on the wall.

"I wouldn't even fit in the driver's seat," he smiled.

"A man's got to dream."

"You got that right."

"Looks to me like somebody dreamed up this station," I told him.

"Thanks. We're proud of it. My men cleaned, spackled, rebuilt, set the place up. We've got computers, a Tac room for S.W.A.T training, the whole nine yards."

"This used to be the principal's office?"

"Nope. The chief has that one. You know how chiefs are. This place was the little boys room."

We had a good laugh over that, but he didn't look so happy when I asked to see the confidential informant.

"We're holding him and the Palm Beach Sheriff's Office wants him sprung. Talk about a clusterfuck."

The C.I. was whining about how shitty the food was, and I recognized his voice before we were even through the sallyport. The confidential informant on the tape case was the son of a bitch who'd beat up Regina Diaz.

"What do *you* want, motherfucker?" he said when he saw me.

"Mostly I'd like you to stop beating up women and children."

"You didn't tell me you were the one who busted him," DeNoso broke in angrily.

"I'm working two cases. I didn't know this was the guy. Give me a couple of minutes with him, would you?"

I entered into the bright pink holding cell. The place wasn't intended for long-term incarceration, so there was only a metal shelf, no mattress, and a video camera in the corner pointed right at the shiny steel john. On the wall behind him a message was stenciled high up, in black letters:

IF YOU HAVE INFORMATION OF A CRIMINAL
NATURE, WE MAY BE ABLE TO ASSIST YOU.
CONTACT AN OFFICER OR DETECTIVE.

"Why don't you leave me alone?"

"I came to talk to you."

"Go fuck yourself."

"Cristoforo Cruz," I said, reading his file. "Be nice and I'll order you a pizza. Now I happen to know that you carried a package of tapes out of Palm Beach International.

"Man, that's ancient history," he groaned.

"Sheriff busted you, you gave up your contact, then you tipped him off."

"Whatever you say."

"I want that contact's name."

"After what, six months?" he crossed his arms. "There's slow, and then there's you, postal man. Is this why I'm still sleeping here in this shithole, no sheets, no privacy? So you can come and get in my shit? I know my rights. You can't hold me here without a lawyer."

"I'm not holding you at all," I said mildly, looking back at his sheet. "Let's see. Receiving Prohibited Material, International Smuggling, Purveyance of Prohibited Substances."

"They planted that dope on me," Cristoforo whined.

"They didn't plant attempted homicide, bro. I saw you try to kill Regina Diaz, and I'll testify to that in a court of law."

"She won't press," he said, defiant again.

"She will after she and I have a little talk. And when she does, it will be you, a convicted smuggler and drug pusher, against that delicate girlfriend of yours, her two little kids, and the federal officer who saw you whack her. How do you think the jury will vote?"

He blew up big, like a puffer fish, locked eyes with me and balled his fists. I thought we were going to have a little rumble, right there in the pink tank, but I stayed calm, still, and relaxed and after a while he shrank down.

"I ain't no smuggler," he said.

I smiled.

"You need to get me outta here."

"And you need to tell me about the men that sent you for that package. Was it the first time you did the run?"

"First and only."

"You sure?"

"Course I'm sure."

I raised my hand in a signal to the control room, and the door clicked open. "Be seein' ya'," I waved.

I went outside into the hallway and stood quietly listening to Cruz mutter and curse and pace in his cage.

"Hey, postal man!" his cry came finally, full of desperation. "Come back!"

I painted the Regina Diaz case unprosecutable, and Wacona and the U.S. Attorney's office agreed that a social worker for the kids and medical care for Regina was the cheapest and best solution to her illegal second job. Getting Regina to file a restraining order was easy, because Cristoforo Cruz's blow had rendered her permanently deaf in one ear. Talking Lake Worth P.D. into enforcing the order with regular drive-bys was a little harder, but when I pointed out that I could make their tiff with the Palm Beach sheriff over Cruz disappear, they bit.

What Cruz got from me was freedom, along with the promise that if he fed me a line or showed up at Regina Diaz's place just one more time, I'd take him down so hard he'd be staring at the ceiling of a federal cell for the rest of his life. What I got from him was more than he had given anybody, namely a description of the guy he said had hired him to pick up the package at PBIA — an older, light-skinned Cuban who wore an antique rose gold wristwatch with a small second hand in the center. He'd noticed that watch, he said, because it was the kind rich Miami Beach Jews wear, and he'd wanted really badly to steal it.

He consented to work with a police artist, provided I took him out of the cell, and so DeNoso got somebody to do sketches of the perp and the watch. She was an older lady, but her legs were good and Cruz looked at them more than he did the paper. It took better than forty minutes for him to be satisfied with the sketches. If the artist had been a man, it might have taken half that. Before we sprang Cruz, I made copies of both sketches, rolled them up and shoved them into my pocket.

Once set free, Cruz became his previous, cocky self, giving me the finger twice on the way to the front door of the station. The lock-down sergeant looked on disapprovingly. "You're patient. I would have brained him," he said as soon as Cruz was gone.

"Can't do that."

"I wouldn't have told on you."

"I know, and believe me, I wanted to do it, but you can't give into impulses like that. You gotta keep some self-control, or you end up a woman-beating, child-kicking, drug-pushing piece of shit like him."

"You only say that 'cause you're young," the sergeant shook his head. He was an old guy with a thick gray mustache and the kind of belly that requires a car with a tilt steering wheel. "No matter how many times you brained him, you wouldn't be like him."

"Even so, it's my code."

He chewed on that for a minute. "Your code, huh?"

"That's right. No beating up scumbags like Cruz."

The sergeant appeared to be thinking hard about something. "You wanna know my code?"

"Sure."

"Personally, I don't arrest johns."

"You don't?"

"Nah. Say you go into a Seven-Eleven and stick the place up. Then you get caught. You're a young kid, maybe you're a hurting junky, but you got no priors. Any good lawyer gets you three years probation, and you walk. If you've got a job, you probably won't lose it, your friends don't shun you, your family doesn't even have to know. You made a mistake, that's all. Now say you pull your car over next to a sweet-lookin' hooker, 'cause you got the devil in your pants. The two of you talk. You agree on a price. Twenty dollars for a BJ. You give her the twenty, she pulls a badge and arrests you. A policewoman. We've got reverse-stings like that running. Next morning your picture is in the paper. Your wife splits, your kids have no use for you, your boss fires you, you spend thirty days in the klink. I won't do that to a guy 'cause he got a hard-on—won't take a guy down for a victimless crime. He wants to die of AIDS, he wants to cheat on his wife, that's his business, not mine. It's a victimless crime."

"You have your code and I have mine," I shrugged, and headed out to my bike.

A misty kind of rain had begun to fall and it was nearly dark. The bottom of my helmet was damp on my neck. Steam rose from the opposed cylinders as I eased off the choke and ran the engine up, let it fall back, then ran it up again until it warmed into a steady, organic idle. When

I got home to Boca, there were two messages on my machine. The first began with a buzzing not unlike the dildo-bomb, followed by a giggle from Phayle. The second was a high-pitched, nearly hysterical message from Clifton Hughes telling me that Jeff Grayson was dead.

SIX

Although Hitler's genocidal war had never touched him directly, my father wore all possible connections with the Holocaust like a thorny crown.

"There is one thing that is true of every Jew," he told me when discussing the importance of a bar mitzvah when I was thirteen years old, "and that is that no matter how high he climbs, no matter how much he owns, no matter what treasures he has buried, deep down he is afraid that late one night, with no warning at all, somebody is going to break down his door in the middle of the night and take it all away."

"Who would do that?" I remember asking.

"Them," he said simply.

"But the Nazis are gone."

"They're still around. They're just hiding. They'll probably come back, and even if they don't, sooner or later there will be a revolution among the Have-Nots, probably

101

the blacks, and the result will be a frenzied feeding on the Haves."

"But they wouldn't single out the Jews," I protested. "They would just go after rich people."

At that time I didn't realize how close my father was to being rich, nor did I have even a meager grasp of the finely nuanced relationship between African Americans and Jews.

"The Jews will be the first attacked," he said. "They always are. Then, perhaps, what remains of the Gypsies and the Poles."

"I don't know any Gypsies and I don't know any Poles."

He nodded knowingly. "Just mark my words, we're only guests here in America. The invitation can be revoked at any time. The key to survival is to become indispensable or, even better, invisible."

My father seemed to forget his own admonitions as he grew in wealth and power. During high school, when I had little of his attention, I roamed New York City alone, taking advantage of the way his name opened doors to softly lit paths all over town, many of which seemed to have pots of gold at their end. It was during these prowlings that I first became aware of feeling like an imposter, aware that when people looked at me they weren't seeing me at all, but were seeing dear old dad, the crook-to-be.

Even now, there are minutes, hours, sometimes even whole days when I go around feeling as if I'm wearing somebody else's gun and badge. I felt that way as I pushed past my own dread and stepped lightly across the yellow tape barring the door to Jeff Grayson's bathroom. The police presence there was small, a single young officer outside—more and more cops are looking like kids to me these days—and a medical examiner just finishing up.

I looked down upon the grisly sight of Jeff's naked, fit,

tanned body. My former classmate still managed to radiate a certain presence, as if he might be able to suddenly gather his horribly contorted limbs underneath him, spring up with his hands held wide and that charming grin on his face, do a little naked jig across the bathroom tile and convince you somehow that his death was a ruse. But there would be no jig, and deception had fled for drier climes. There was an empty Emerson, Lake and Palmer CD jewel case under the sink—it appeared to have been flung there during Jeff's death throes—and a portable stereo lay half in the water, half on his chest, the black power cord snaking out over the tub's white porcelain like an asp. Grayson's crisped and blackened fingers were wrapped around the outside edges of the unit, palms over the speakers.

"Haven't seen you around here," the M.E. said casually.

"I'm federal," I said, staring at Grayson's hands.

"Yeah? This a mob case?"

"Guy's a friend of mine."

"Ah. My condolences."

"Thanks. What happened?"

"Near as we can figure it, he was reaching to adjust something and the boom box slipped and fell into the water."

"They dust for prints?"

He looked at me suspiciously. "Why would they do that? Guys die in the tub every day. His wife and kid were in the other room when it happened."

"Wasn't there a GFI protector in place? I thought all outlets around pools and in bathrooms had them."

"Only in new construction. This house was built back in the sixties. Rebar concrete, hurricane-proof construction, quality through and through," the medico winked sarcastically.

The LCD on the front of the boom box showed track number 6. Careful not to touch Jeff's hands, I pushed the button and released the cover over the CD player and checked the title of the song.

" 'Lucky Man,' " I muttered.

"Not from where I'm standing."

"The name of the song he was listening to."

"Oh yeah. I remember that one. It was on the radio all the time. Real popular. *Oh, what a lucky man he was . . .*" the doctor sang.

I put the disc into an evidence bag. "Look, I'm going to talk to the family, keep them occupied while you get him out of here. I don't want them to have to see him like this, okay?"

The M.E. cocked himself up in a sick and stupid imitation of Jeff's corpse, grinned, and nodded.

Gwen Grayson's makeup was perfect and her shining hair put up so that nary a strand escape. I'd seen such careful couture before and recognized it as a sign of denial. I hoped someone was going to be around with soft mats to cushion her and a hose for the fires of grief when she finally crashed and burned.

"Max," she blinked.

She was wearing black already, but it was tight, designer stuff, a matching skirt and blouse, not the robes of mourning.

"I wish we'd met earlier," I said, "before this. Is there anything special I can do?"

"The thing is, there isn't," she said distantly. "He left everything in such splendid order—our bills paid, insurance up-to-date, a trust fund for our daughter."

I was surprised Jeff had only one child. He always seemed to me the kind who wanted an army around him, field soldiers to direct, campaigns to launch, a support network that would never let him fry in a bathtub.

"I'm sure he loved you very much," I said, taking her hand.

She nodded. "Jeff had funny ways of showing love. Everything was order, structure, military precision. The way you knew he cared was that he had you on his team. You were on his team once, weren't you Max? Seems like he said you were."

"That was a long time ago," I said. "I've never been much of a team player."

She leaned forward as if she were about to tell me a secret. "I'm not either," she whispered.

I gazed around the huge living room—cathedral ceilings, a view to a manicured backyard. Jeff had obviously given her free reign decorating, as everything was floral and overstuffed and comfy, accented with early American antiques. The glow from shaded lamps made small suns on the hardwood floor, and I could just make out the faint musk of old books.

"Do you need help with the arrangements?"

Gwen almost laughed. "Do you know what he did? He made the arrangements himself."

"Recently?"

"No. Apparently he had a long-standing contract with a funeral home in Coconut Grove. Cliff informed them about what happened and they called me this morning. They were very nice. There isn't going to be a burial because there isn't going to be a body."

"I see."

"His will said he wanted his ashes sprinkled offshore. He wanted us to have a party. I'm not going to do it."

"Maybe you'll feel differently after some time has passed."

We watched elephant ear philodendrons wave against the window in a sudden wind.

105

"When did you last see him?" asked Gwen.

"At the symphony," I answered, omitting the horror of the bathtub. "Seemed like he loved that kind of music."

"And he died listening. That's funny, don't you think? I mean, you figure dying doing what you love might happen to a race-car driver or a skydiver, but you'd never guess it would happen to a music lover."

"I gather from his interest in the symphony that he was a classical music man."

"Of course," Gwen managed a wan smile.

"Ever hear him listen to rock-and-roll?"

"Not in a long time. When we were first married he used to have a convertible. He would put down the top and tune into the pop stations sometimes. He liked the song "Radar Love." It was kind of our thing. He said we were linked like that, a wave from above. He always knew when I wanted him to call me from work."

A little girl came in. Slim and dark, with extraordinary white hands, she might have been Gwen's tiny clone.

"This is your Uncle Max," said her mother. "And this is Brooke. Brooke was seven last week."

"If you're my uncle, how come I've never met you before?" she asked, staring at me with huge brown eyes floating over dark semicircles of pain. She was trembling, trying desperately to emulate her mother's self-control.

"Your daddy and I were friends in school," I said, shaking her hand solemnly. "I've been away for a while."

"She has her daddy's preoccupation with detail," Gwen put in.

"My daddy's dead," Brooke said simply. Gwen inhaled sharply and dropped into a chair.

"How would you like to show me where your daddy kept his CDs?" I asked.

She shrugged.

106

"I would sure like it if you would," I said.

"Max?" Gwen said, puzzled. I made a sign with my hands as if it were something I could to to bond with Brooke, to make her feel better, and Gwen nodded.

Brooke led me to a family room dominated by a projection TV and a hugely expensive sound system. There were shelves of discs everywhere, divided into sections for opera, baroque, symphonies, piano pieces, choral works, and Brazilian jazz. Finally, at the very bottom, tucked away in one corner, I found a few vintage rock-and-roll titles; Fleetwood Mac, the Grateful Dead, the Eagles, the Rolling Stones.

"Daddy loved music," she said philosophically.

"I know, honey. And what music did he listen to the most?"

"Violins," she said immediately.

Gwen was still slumped in her chair when we got back to her. I could tell she was starting to lose it, and I felt that since I didn't know her well enough to be there when she did, my presence could only embarrass her. I handed over my card.

"If you think of anything you think the police should know, give me a call first," I said.

"Are you here professionally?" she glanced at the card.

"I didn't intend to be."

"But something changed your mind?"

"I'm not sure," I said carefully.

"But it's possible?"

"Yes, it's possible."

"Are you going to take care of us now that Daddy's gone?" Brooke interrupted.

I felt my eyes filling up and I didn't want the little girl to see them, so I backed out with my best gentle smile.

———

In the early part of the seventeenth century, invaders were everywhere, and the social, economic and political fabric of China was unraveling. Chung Cheng, the last Ming emperor, urged his intellectuals to learn the art of war, take up arms, and defend home and country. Chen Wangting, an officer in charge of the Shandong Province garrison, gained fame for repelling a thousand invaders with an impossibly tiny force that he'd trained in his Taoist version of the martial arts of the day. The resulting complex of movements, t'ai chi ch'uan, was a triumph of intellect and elegance amidst turbulence and war.

As I stood meditating by the edge of the Intracoastal Waterway behind my apartment that evening, I thought about Chen denying the inevitability of the odds. What internal discipline that must have taken! What cleaving to conviction, what strength of mind! Inspired, I pushed my tongue against the inside of my upper teeth, imagining that a cord was coming down from Heaven and attaching to my head at the Hundred Meetings point of my crown. I felt a small fire at what the Chinese called the "Bubbling Spring" behind the ball of my foot, where the earth's energy entered my body and filled me. I sought to move through the Chen family form with intent in my hands, and with my heels gripping the ground, but I couldn't stop thinking about Jeff's body crisped and twisted in the tub, and about Twy's corpse under the ground, his head only slightly attached to his torso.

I couldn't get past the certainty that both men had been murdered. It seemed odd and somehow important that Jeff Grayson had chosen to listen to rock-and-roll in the bathtub, and I wondered if and how this small fact related to Twy Boatwright's beheading. I raised my hands in the first, salutary movement of the form, and lowered them again, pretending I was standing chest-deep in a stream and that my hands were on an algae-coated log which I needed to press straight down past my waist without letting it slip away. I continued through the first part of the sequence, the postures known as Buddha's Warrior Pounds the Mortar, Lazily Tying Coat, White Crane Spreads its Wings. It was hard to keep from thinking about my embarrassment with Phayle, about how I felt diminished, how the snuff tapes had gone far beyond the realm of work, insinuating themselves into the most private possible part of my life.

There were boaters on the Intracoastal, but they were speeding and seemed not to notice me in the setting sun. I have found that despite t'ai chi ch'uan's exotic look, there is a certain contraction of energy that attends its performance, resulting in a delightful invisibility. I began the second section of the form, and was halfway through the set of side and heel kicks, when the background rumble of boat engines on the Intracoastal grew into the churn of water at the dock just over the retaining wall. I tried to keep Chen Wangting in my mind, to open and close my hip joints with precision, and to keep the flow going through the movements, but the boat engine below me shut down and FBI Special Agent Ron Dryden came bounding up the steps to my practice pad. I had to fight to maintain my one-legged stance.

"You dress like a beatnik and you stand like a bird," the FBI man shook his head.

"What the hell are you doing at my place, Dryden?" I demanded, my hands staying in the traditional position. "I'm off duty. Go home and call me at the office tomorrow."

"Sure. No problem. DeNoso's people made a match on Cristoforo Cruz's contact, but you can wait until morning to find out who he is," he said casually.

I dropped down out of my posture. A loud speedboat zipped by. "You're in my space and you're on my case," I said.

"You're on *my* case, actually," he observed. He didn't step back but he didn't step forward, either.

"And what case is that?"

"International smuggling of prohibited materials, child pornography, and murder," he said smugly.

"You meddling fuck."

"Hey, I got it all from your supervisor, Inspector Wacona Smith." I knew Waco wouldn't have talked to him without bringing me in, and then only if she absolutely had to. This was the Bureau flexing its muscle, pure and simple, and it pissed me off.

"Who did Cruz finger?" I asked tightly.

"You might want to sit down for this."

"I'm not asking you upstairs, if that's what you're suggesting."

"You should play nicer."

"Why? I can get the name from DeNoso right now."

"Cuco O'Burke," he revealed, watching my face.

I made Dryden wait by the dock—a petty slight, but it felt good—while I donned a square-cut navy blue suit, a white shirt with a mandarin collar, a pair of thin Ralph Lauren dress socks, and black, Swiss, Bally weaves. FBI informants had tipped Dryden that Cuco O'Burke, Latino crime lord extraordinaire and himself reputed employer of more federal agents than a typical field office, was holding court in his club downtown. We made a full-power, cool-spray-on-the-face dash down the Intracoastal in the agency's confiscated Cigarette. The boat got us close, but it took a Bureau Crown Victoria waiting by the dock to get us the rest of the way.

"I still can't believe Cruz knew O'Burke's face but not his name," I shook my head as we drove into Little Havana. "Bastard played me good. Probably still laughing about it."

"A scumbag like Cruz isn't that smart," Dryden scoffed. "He probably didn't know. O'Burke is ruthless and anonymous and runs his operation as if he were admiral of the termites, all holed up where nobody can see him while the troops chew up the town. Who knows what Cruz knew and what he didn't?"

Dryden's point was a reasonable one. Although O'Burke was a famous hood, he kept a low profile. A variety of investigative journalists in South Florida had linked him to a notorious Mexican drug king, but had never published a good clear photo. As recently as two weeks ago, the *Miami Herald* ran a story about a Soviet nuclear powered submarine brought to South Florida by members of the Russian mafia—themselves former KGB agents—and seized in a foiled DEA sting before the deal could go down. The article speculated that the sophisticated warship would make a worthy addition to O'Burke's drug-running fleet, but again ran no image of the Don. O'Burke could have hired a drone like Cruz by just flashing some cash.

"He didn't have any termites between him and Cruz, though," I mused. "The Don himself sent that worm to the airport."

"I know, and that worries me."

"Like it's part of a bigger picture?" I asked.

"Exactly."

We pulled up in front of the New Havana Club, right behind a red Ferrari with more louvres and wings than the space shuttle.

"Ever been in here, Diamond?" Dryden inquired.

I shook my head.

"You're in for a treat," he smiled smugly.

Now and then, the lords of chaos who rule our world belch out a wee bit of nonsense that doesn't belong in the space-time continuum. Cuco O'Burke's New Havana Club was one of these cosmic eructations. The building's facade was brick, and there was a line of palm trees leading to the front door, illuminated from the base by spotlights. The setting—on Miami's Calle Ocho, next to a discount store and across from an old guard restaurant serving *moros* and *empanadas* drenched in lard—couldn't have been more incongruous. The valet parkers stared at Dryden's Crown Vic like it was a pile of stinking fish bones.

"Private club," a musclebound bouncer declared as we got out. A good-looking blond couple in his-and-hers Armani duds slipped past. Dryden's pockmarked face screwed up, and he took out one of his unfiltered Camels and lit it in a motion so fluid I never saw the match. He drew in the smoke, squinted his eyes, and slowly, calmly, put the cigarette out into the bouncer's collar. The man's eyes grew wide, but Dryden's Sig Sauer automatic was discreetly jammed hard into his belly before he could make his move.

"Federal agents," he said. "We have an invitation from the boss."

"Mr. O'Burke is not in the club," the man gasped, pronouncing the name oh-BOOR-kay.

"We'll just have a drink anyway," Dryden said, leading me through the double doors and into another world.

The walls were murals of Havana's glory days, recreating the harbor, famous edifices, gardens, and trees. We followed a walkway lined with miniature palms on a course that led between dance floors toward a raised dais in the back of the club. People were smoking cigars everywhere, but the air smelled only of roses. I remembered reading somewhere that the club's air handlers recharged the environment every ninety seconds.

I wanted O'Burke, but I also wanted to go slow, to take in the place, the beautiful people, the samba music, the popping champagne corks. Dryden, however, was a heat-seeking missile. His suit, the same one I had seen at the warehouse by the airport, had looked rich that day, but in here it looked shabby, and his pockmarked face and greasy hair didn't help. People avoided his glance as he walked by, and I made sure to stay a few steps back.

"O'Burke is Cuban-Irish," I heard him mutter. "What a street dog combination."

It was early and there were only a few people in the club. A man in a gray suit toasted a beautiful redhead whose white dress did a poor job of containing her artificially enhanced breasts. A trio of beautiful young boys in tuxedos held hands atop their table. An old couple danced, the man using tentative, Arthur Murray moves, the woman a whirlwind in a twirling skirt that showed surprisingly fine legs. A long narrow table of businessmen passed documents back and forth, signing papers with Montblanc pens and flashing gold cuff links.

"Maybe," I answered, mostly to myself, "but the mongrel has taste."

Dryden made his way briskly to the dais, jostling waiters out of the way, peering rudely into every nook and cranny. I took him by the arm.

"You don't have a warrant, do you?" I asked quietly.

"For what, a conversation?" he snorted.

"Exactly. You're not here to arrest the guy, you're here to talk to him, maybe get him to cooperate and give up the film gang. You want to avoid charges his rich lawyers can beat, right? Keep big-footing around in here and you'll blow my case."

"I'm not going to blow anything," he huffed. "We'll just work him a bit, maybe press him into making a mistake. That okay with you, *Inspector?*"

Before I could answer, he had steamrolled through a door at the end of the room. Reluctantly, I followed.

I had learned something about body language during my years of martial arts training, so the two thugs casually aiming machine pistols in my direction barely increased my heart rate. I took in the snarling pair of Italian greyhounds—one brindle, one white—with equal equanimity, and the small round table laden with oysters, wine bottles, ice cream and red grapes with some interest. I saw Dryden flash his shield and saw Cuco O'Burke—dressed in a white linen suit and wearing a shock of silver hair like a crown—lose his smile. But what was of far, far greater interest to me than any of that was the woman sitting by the gangster's side.

Drizzling emeralds, she was a portrait of Castilian elegance—translucent white skin, high cheekbones, erect posture, shining jet black hair, pouting lips, a high-collared sea-green dress to match her enormous eyes, just enough chin, and the body to start a revolution. Her eyes met mine for an instant, then dropped as O'Burke waved his bodyguards aside and spoke.

"Would you like some port wine, Special Agent Dryden?" he inquired in a slight Cuban accent. He spoke as if we had been sitting at his table all evening, in a tone so flat and calm and dangerous, I did a cartwheel inside my own skin. Dryden, no doubt feeling the menace, overcompensated with braggadocio.

"I wouldn't drink with you if this was the last oasis on a desert planet," he spat.

O'Burke's eyes narrowed. In another setting, I imag-

114

ined that such a change of mien might be construed by his gunmen as an execution order. Then he smiled, and the moment passed, and he was the genial host once more. "Your loss, I'm afraid. It's a ninety-year-old Portuguese *colheita*, quite spectacular, really. How about you, my bald friend?"

Reluctantly, I turned my attention from the woman in green, nodded and approached the table.

"Hey!" Dryden barked.

"Mister O'Burke," I said, careful to use the correct pronunciation, "my name is Maximillian Diamond, and I am a United States Postal Inspector. We are here because the federal government is in possession of evidence connecting you to certain contraband videotapes."

"Goodness. What a thing to say," O'Burke remarked mildly, handing me the snifter of port. I accepted the drink. At close range, I could see that the skin on the crime boss's face had been pulled tight by repeated operations, leaving him with a mask that could be molded, with difficulty, into one of a few stock expressions. He could have been anywhere between forty-five and sixty.

"Goddamnit, Diamond," Dryden chafed.

I knew he was thinking regulations, but I was neither fraternizing with the enemy nor getting sloshed on duty. I was just performing a minor social nicety that would make my job a lot easier. "Don't be such a boor, Ron," I swirled the snifter. "A drink isn't going to kill you."

The beautiful woman smiled at me, and O'Burke noticed. "Forgive me. Inspector Diamond, this is my daughter, Guiomary. Guiomary, Inspector Max Diamond."

His daughter. Just my luck. She dazzled me with a smile, and I felt a squeeze deep inside. "A pleasure," I said. "Now about those tapes . . ."

"Of course I don't know what you are talking about. I am a legitimate businessman, a restaurant owner. If you really had the evidence you say you have, you would be here with a warrant, no? And there would be handcuffs?"

I caught a glimpse of his gleaming Patek Phillippe wristwatch with the subsidiary second hand, a classic executed in red gold. "We have the evidence, sir," I said carefully, conscious that I was in a chess game with O'Burke, and just as on the board, the opening moves would determine the final outcome. "We're just trying to make this easy on all concerned."

Dryden shifted impatiently, setting off a storm of snarls from the elegant little greyhounds. O'Burke took off his hat and patted his white pant leg. "Come here, my darlings," he cooed in a falsetto, putting his legs together as a ramp. The dogs ran up to his lap, onto his jacket and nuzzled under his neck, gurgling and licking, leaving brittle hairs on his suit.

"You work out of West Palm Beach, am I correct, Inspector?" he asked fondly, kissing each dog on the snout.

"Papá," said Guiomary in a voice as creamy and deep as banana ice cream, "Maximillian seems like a friend. I think he has come to you because he respects you and he wants your help."

Maximillian. I never used that name, but, strangely, I just had. I wondered why. I thought I knew. It sounded big, exotic, important. I wanted to impress this woman. If the conditions were right, I was capable of stunning idiocy.

O'Burke regarded me with new interest. "Is that right, Inspector? Do you want my help?"

"You don't help us on the tapes, you're going down deep and slow," Dryden interrupted. "Think about it."

He spun on his heel and went out, leaving me time for only a quick taste of the port. It was as spectacular as billed — a four hundred dollar bottle, I reckoned.

O'Burke saw that I enjoyed it.

SEVEN

Wacona was in my office the next morning, even before I'd poured my first cup of Red Zinger tea. She was wearing a classy purple suit, amethyst earrings, and the faintest hint of Angel. When she perched on the edge of my desk she showed a good run of firm thigh, and seemed not to care. She knew she slew me.

"Your pal Cristoforo Cruz violated his restraining order," she said.

"Now there's a surprise."

"Lake Worth P.D. has him locked up again, and they're filing charges."

"I warned him."

"I'm sure you did."

"He welshed on our deal. I want to testify against him."

"I had the impression you were going to back off those tapes until Dulles could prove they were real."

"I don't need Dulles to tell me what I already know. And by the way, thanks for sending Special Agent Pockmark to my house."

"How did you expect me to avoid it? He called me at home. Quoted the rule book."

"I gather you told him all about the tapes?"

"I had to. What are you doing poking around Cuco O'Burke?"

"He's involved somehow. I'm trying to piece it together."

"Yeah, well Dryden isn't the only one calling. I got a message from a Metro-Dade homicide dick named Todd Steiner. He wants you to call him about somebody named Grayson. Wanna tell me about it?"

"It's a personal thing."

"A personal homicide?"

"Friend of mine was killed."

"This the one you buried?"

"No."

"I'm sorry to hear that, Max, but when too many of your friends start dying it's usually the universe knocking hard on your trap door. You hear what I'm saying?"

"I hear."

"Now call this guy, will you?" she handed me a slip of paper with Steiner's number on it. "And tiptoe around O'Burke like you're on land mines hidden in egg-shells."

"You got it."

"One more thing," she said, getting up off my desk. "Greg's replacement will be here at the end of the week."

That was a shocker. I hadn't even seen any interview-ees floating around.

"Who is he?"

"Name's Mozart Potrero," she said, heading out. "The I.N.C. selected him for us." John Clark, the Inspector-in-Charge in Miami, had picked Wacona, too, so I wasn't about to make any smart remarks about the new guy's name.

"Great," I said.

She stopped in the doorway just long enough to glance over her shoulder and see me checking out her ass. I braced for the worst, but she just smiled and kept walking.

"Heard you were poking around Jeff Grayson's place," Steiner's gravelly voice came over the line. Another chain-smoking policeman.

"He was a friend of mine."

"No professional interest?"

"It's hard to ignore a fried corpse in a bathtub."

"Don't see what it has to do with the mail."

"I'm not sure I do either," I agreed, staring at the remaining stack of videotapes in the corner and daydreaming of Guiomary O'Burke's incredible skin.

"What *I've* got is a titillating coincidence. There's this guy Boatwright, worked with Grayson. Last week he gets his head chopped off by a table saw."

"That titillates you, Steiner, you're in the right line of work."

"It's been said. This Boatwright a friend of yours too?"

"Old college buddy."

"You didn't kill them both, did you?"

"Whoops, you caught me. If you come to my house, you'll find their livers in the fridge."

"You're a weirdo, Diamond. I couldn't joke about dead friends like that."

"There's you, and then there's me," I replied.

"Yeah, so we got a man poking around the law firm, trying to figure out what might be going on there, but he can't seem to get anybody to talk."

"Rich clients pay dearly for tight lips."

"Your two buddies paid dearly too."

"Maybe. Any leads at all?"

"The firm did divorce work, among other things. Right now, I'm thinking maybe a pissed-off ex-husband. What's *your* theory?"

"Don't have one yet. You dust that tape player for prints?"

"Sure. Found the victim's on the dry parts. Did Boatwright's garage, too, just for kicks, but it's a wash. The wife was through everything, farming it out to the needy. Wanted to take the place down to the bare walls so she didn't have to be reminded of the accident."

"Keep me up to date, will you?" I asked.

"If you do the same for me."

Sea Chunny wandered in just then, and Steiner and I signed off.

"You get wind of the new boy?" Sea asked.

"Just his name."

"My bet is he doesn't play a note."

"My bet is you're right."

"I heard about your college buddy, Grayson. Terrible."

"Yalies are dying all over town," I sighed.

"Just make sure you're not one of them, understand? Waco says you had a talk with Cuco O'Burke. You don't want to go there, understand? Leave him for the Bureau or the DEA. Nothing you're into can connect to him."

"I'm thinking maybe it can."

"The tapes?"

I nodded.

"Then forget 'em. I don't want to be driving your grandmother to your funeral."

"Not going to happen. And speaking of my grandmother, when are you two getting hitched?"

"She won't talk serious with me," he sighed. "All she does is beat me at cards."

"She beats everybody at cards, Sea. It's her job."

"You think she'll ever have me?"

"She doesn't trust your motives. Thinks you're too young for her," I grinned.

"Damn if I'm not doing my best to look older every day."

"Just keep loving her, Sea. She'll come around."

I spent the rest of the day going through the remaining box of videos. The end was in sight and it galvanized me to keep going long past the point where my eyesight went fuzzy and my lower back began to ache. I saw girls coupling on trains, men and women pleasuring each other amidst spring wildflowers, transsexuals in rapture behind mosquito netting, and one particularly sad, black-and-white amateur rendition of a middle-aged man making love to his wife, taken through an open window by a video voyeur.

When there was just one stack left, I literally couldn't focus my eyes anymore, so I turned off the screens, donned my leather jacket and headed for home on the R90S. There was a dense fog outside, but I elected to take State Road A1A along the beach anyway. Inhaling the ocean air, I wiped my visor with a damp leather glove and kept my eyes peeled for brake lights. At irregular intervals, I tooted my horn and flashed my high beams to announce my presence in the gloom.

The nearby crash of the surf reminded me of the long lost July when my father had rented a Long Island beach house. It was right after my sister Rachel left us, and I guess he thought we all needed a change. Most days, while he was at work in Manhattan, my mother hunted seashells in the morning and tended herb plants in the afternoon. One particular morning, the sound of my father starting his car woke me, and I crept outside naked. The fog, thick as the cloud cover of Venus, hid me while I snuck down to the garage and did what I had wanted to do for months — start up the red Vespa scooter that belonged to the owner of the rented house.

Intoxicated by my own daring and the sound of power and the smell of two-stroke exhaust I rode the scooter down the beachfront lane, aware that I could be struck by a car at any time, ignoring the chill, and reading the messages sent by the tarmac through the handlebar and tires. I stayed afield until the sun began to break through the fog, and then blasted home. I returned the machine to the garage and ran back up to bed before anyone was the wiser, a crust of salt on my eyelashes, grime on my shins, my heart beating like a bird's.

The ride home from the office wasn't as thrilling, but it was just as dangerous. At one point a pickup truck blasting country music nearly ran me down, its lights appearing suddenly in my rearview mirror. There was a loud squeal of brakes and strange shadows as the pickup skidded on the damp road to avoid me. I pulled far to the right and as he drove by, the driver lowered the window and flipped me off. I returned the gesture with a friendly wave, knowing that nothing I could have done would have annoyed him more.

I stayed on A1A the length of Palm Beach, and crossed a piece of Lake Worth before entering Manalapan and Ocean Ridge. Just before Gulfstream, I came across an old Eldorado convertible. The top was down, and the rich leather was getting wet. As I motored carefully past, I saw a grinning teenager with thick, black, horn-rimmed glasses at the wheel. He was listening to a Beethoven sonata, and I thought how Jeff Grayson might have been like this kid, with his rich father and his taste for classical music. I half-expected the boy to give me and my bike the thumbs-up, as teenagers often do, but he was lost in a world of violins and never even saw me. I rode down through Delray Beach without incident and into Boca Raton.

When I got home, I wiped away the leaves and flowers the damp air had deposited on my jacket and pants, washed the salt off the bike with a hose, and went upstairs. Low temperatures generally make reptiles torpid, but I found Picard strangely alert, as if he were expecting something and was fighting the slowdown in his metabolism by sheer force of will. I gave him some sweet corn and turned on the infrared heater I provided him on cool nights. He ate quietly, watching me while I listened to Phayle's messages on my answering machine.

She talked a little bit about antiquated inventory management at the department store that had hired her, and about the trouble she was having interfacing her software with their system, but underneath the chatter was the sullen implication I was avoiding her, and she knew it. I let her go on and on about the fact that I shouldn't be embarrassed about what happened between us at the Delano, that it was okay, that this kind of thing happened to everyone now and then and that she didn't take it personally and only wanted to help. In all that, she never mentioned Jeff Grayson's name, which made me wonder how she could not have heard the news.

I made myself a Mediterranean platter—Greek olives, grape leaves, hummus, tahini, babaganough, and falafel balls—deep-frying the last in a skillet of canola oil and garnishing them with habañero peppers so hot that I had to spear them with a fork to avoid burning the skin on my fingers. I turned on the local news, and as I ate, I watched a young woman report Jeff's electrocution. There was a brief mention of the fact that my old friend was the partner of the late Twyman Boatwright, pillar of the Miami legal community, followed by the assertion that police were investigating his death but as yet had no reason to suspect foul play. There was a picture of Jeff outside the Florida Philharmonic, and another of him smiling at Gwen and holding Brooke in his arms. The report ended with a shot of the outside of Jeff's mansion and an aside by the commentator that the death of a man with so much to live for was a tragic thing.

I switched off the set and watched Picard polish off the last of the corn cobs. My brain was on a wild rally course, rounding the curves that were Phayle, powering toward Dryden, slowing down at Wacona's plum suit, climbing Guiomary's mountains in low gear, flashing my brake lights at O'Burke's evil eyes, and coming to a screeching stop in front of the dying, knifed girl.

The balanced, Taoist tempo of life I craved was all shot to hell. I wondered if my grandmother would ever say yes to Sea Chunny and what kind of a fellow the new man Mozart Potrero would turn out to be. I thought of trudging through a New England blizzard with Jeff and Twy and Clifton in our senior year, munched-out from drinking beer and smoking pot, fixated at 3 A.M. on a falafel meal much like the one I had just finished.

I put my head back against the couch and I guess I must have drifted off, because the next thing I knew I was awakened to the sound of my heart pounding in time with someone's fist on my front door.

"M.D!" came the cry as I fumbled for the knob.

"Who is it?"

"Open up! They're going to kill me!"

I yanked the door open and a terrified, shaking Clifton Hughes fell onto me. I put my hands on his shoulders and pushed him away. He was a wild-eyed, unshaven mess — his tie hanging loosely around his neck, his collar gray with dirty sweat. His navy, worsted wool suit jacket hung unbuttoned and open, and there were two vertical sweat stains on his shirt.

"Get a hold of yourself, Cliff! Jeff's dead!" he panted.

"I know. How did you find out where I live, Clifton?"

"From Stone, okay? Listen, they're coming after me next, I know they are!"

I steered him to the couch and sat him down. "Who's coming after you?" I asked, smoldering at the news that my home address was available to a Yale secret society to which I no longer belonged.

"You have a gun, right?"

"Yes, Cliff. I have a gun."

He pointed at Picard. "What the hell is that?"

"My pet tortoise. Now what makes you think someone is after you?"

"Twy and Jeff both dead within a week? Do I need to spell it out for you?" He was still breathing wildly and I noticed that his fingernails were bitten to the quick.

"There's no hard evidence of foul play, Cliff."

He rose and started flapping his arms like a swan. "No evidence! Are you nuts? A table saw launching wood through the air? Electrocution in the bath? Twy worked in his garage every single night of his life, ditto for Jeff listening to music in the tub. Those were their habits, the way they lived. Don't you think it's just a little too much of a coincidence that there should be two fatal accidents, one right after the other, and that the victims should be partners and old friends?"

"As a matter of fact I do," I admitted. That stopped him, and he dropped back down onto the couch.

I opened a Hurricane Reef for him. He took a long

pull, then pressed the cold bottle against his forehead. "Pet tortoise. You always were pretty fucking eccentric."

"I'm allergic to animals with hair, but thank you for the compliment. I treasure my eccentricity."

"You could get a parrot," he offered. "Teach it to talk."

"The one thing I don't want in the house is a lot of talk, Cliff, and I'm allergic to feathers. Can't even sleep on a down pillow. You getting enough rest?"

"You're joking, right?"

"Get some pills from a doctor," I suggested. He shook his head.

"Funny, huh? The four of us reuniting with Twy in the ground, and now this."

"The five of us," I said quietly. "There's Phayle."

"Phayle. Right. You seeing her much?"

"Couple of times."

"She talk about the old days?"

"Not much. So Cliff, here we are. Jeff and Twy are dead and you're scared shitless. You wanna tell me what you think is going on? Does this have to do with the practice? A disgruntled client or employee? A skeleton in the closet?"

"We deal with so many people," he sighed miserably.

"You overcharge someone? Sue someone you shouldn't have? Unfairly accuse a husband of wife-beating? Saddle some guy for life with an alimony burden he doesn't deserve?"

"All of the above," he smiled a sickening smile.

"But you haven't pulled a Johnnie Cochran, right?" I pursued, hoping my disgust showed.

"What?"

"Gotten a killer off the hook?"

He waved his hands around. "Who knows who's really guilty? Anyway, we don't do criminal cases."

"Well, something you did may have gotten Jeff and Twy killed and may be threatening you too. I suggest you make a list of the guys you've screwed over. Check all your family cases, Jeff's real estate and corporate deals, whatever else you're into. When you've got the list, we'll get together again and I'll share it with Metro-Dade."

"To tell you the truth, M.D., it's going to be a long list."

"Tell me something I don't know."

He picked up the television remote and started clicking through the channels like he was sitting in his own home. "Nice quiet waterfront you got here," he said at last.

"Cliff, do you think the murders have anything to do with Lyre and Stone?"

He looked up in surprise.

"What a strange question."

"Just trying to cover the bases."

"We didn't have much to do with Stone anymore, Max. At least I didn't. A few meetings here and there."

"Maybe a favor or two? A private address, maybe?"

He looked genuinely wounded. "Hey, you're not sore I came over here, are you?"

"No, Cliff. Of course I'm not. I want to do everything I can to help."

He nodded, and found *I Love Lucy* on the tube. I sat beside him through the entire episode, wondering what had become of my innocence and my youth.

The next morning was Saturday, and I awoke to a message from Phayle. Bright and cheery, she asked if I would take her to Monkey Jungle down in South Miami. Someone at Burdine's had told her that monkeys ran free there while the humans were in cages, and she said she had always loved monkeys and just *had* to see the place. I grabbed a bagel and tea and ate it in the front seat of the Porsche while heading down the Interstate. It was a blustery day, not warm, not cold, and the sun ducked in and out from behind the clouds. I scanned the radio news for any follow-up on Jeff, but the headlines were dominated by political strife in the Balkans, a gang war in Homestead, and the capture of a twenty-foot Great White shark off Key West. Still, Phayle's silence about Jeff troubled me. I figured she had to have word of his death by now.

When I arrived at the hotel, she was standing out front in a pair of tight white jeans, blue flats, and a braless purple tank-top, causing an absolute riot among the help.

"Pretty hot number you're almost wearing," I said, gesturing at her top while I opened the door for her.

"The bellboys seem to think so," she said, getting into the car.

I headed across to the causeway, unable to help myself from staring at her legs. "I'm not trying to pressure you sexually, I hope you know that," she said.

"Just hoping to get the old juices flowing?"

"Something like that."

I made it across the MacArthur Causeway, then took the Dolphin Expressway to the Florida Turnpike. The jazz station I like was playing a new George Benson tune, and Phayle tapped her foot to it while looking out the window. In stark contrast to my own strange, growing anxiety, she seemed happy and relaxed. I took the 216th Street exit just south of Cutler Ridge, and drove through a rough section; bombed-out buildings, graffiti-covered trestles, police substations in the middle of battered shopping malls. I stopped at a light and Phayle happened to glance over and see a black kid shooting up in an alley behind an apartment complex. He saw her too, and turned away in shame.

"Is he doing what I think he's doing?" she whispered, putting her hand on my arm.

"Probably heroin," I said, trying to sound matter-of-fact.

"What terrible karma," she said.

"I beg your pardon?"

"What he must have done in a past life to deserve this one, it makes me shudder just to think about it."

"You don't really believe that, do you?"

"Of course I do. It's the only way I can make sense of the world."

We came to a red light. "Do you think that junkie has the same options as we do?" I asked, looking at her.

"No. Like I said, I think he has his own karma to deal with."

"Does that karma include being born with AIDS because his mother has it, or taking a bullet in a drive-by shooting?"

"Max," Phayle said, gentling me with a hand.

I shook her off, my anger surprising me. It was the little girl in the pinafore I was thinking of, more than anyone else, but I was also thinking of the poor stabbed child on the fishing boat, and of course of the girl blown apart at the restaurant. I was thinking of them as victims of raw circumstance, not karma.

"Religion is so damn convenient," I said. "It's always been what the Haves use to keep the Have-Nots in line. Let's talk about responsibility. Let's talk about the Fourth World, a rising underclass so big soon nobody will be able to contain it."

"If you could only see the larger forces at work," Phayle began.

"Poor me. I've never been good at the big picture. I see someone shooting up, I get upset. I see a little girl

129

murdered, I get upset. I see people starving, I lose sight of larger forces right away."

"You don't have to be sarcastic," Phayle countered. "The fact is the tragedy is less than you think because each of those people has many other lives to live."

"You don't know that."

"Yes I do."

"I envy you then," I said, gunning the car as the light changed. "Personally, I have to be content with believing only what I can see with my own two eyes."

We drove for a few miles without saying anything. A leaf got trapped in the windshield wiper. The vent window brought a dragonfly in, and it caught in Phayle's hair. She didn't notice, and I didn't mention it. I'd been getting ready to tell her about Jeff Grayson, but the right moment kept eluding me.

"Have you considered the possibility that this might not be the best job for you?" she said finally.

"I've considered carefully that it's the *only* job for me," I said, "because the only thing worse than not facing bad things is doing nothing about them."

Monkey Jungle is a private enterprise, grown up around a troupe of crab-eating macaques that some importer had let loose to study many, many years ago. Every hundred feet or so along the screened-in walkway, a tin cup is attached to a chain hung below a hole in the screening. Phayle bought some peanuts and put them in the first cup and suddenly, as if by magic, a monkey appeared—a bearded, well-hung male who used his dark, human-like fingers to pull the cup up by the chain and eat the nuts. Phayle laughed with delight over this, buying more peanuts, and sunflower seeds and raisins, until she had fed monkeys at half a dozen cup stations. Exhausted with pleasure, she leaned against the rail and looked out into the tropical park. There were smaller macaques hovering in the distance, young ones and females waiting for permission to come forward for their share of the loot.

"Phayle, I've got some bad news," I began.

She winced. I remembered that wince, reminder of a past where everything between us had to be happy and airy and light, where there was no room for serious conversation, no room for talk of long-term commitments, no digging at issues that hurt. The wince was emblematic of the part of her that had finally broken us up. "I wish you didn't," she sighed.

"So do I, but Jeff Grayson's dead."

She cocked her head at an unnatural angle, as if she were a puppet or a marionette, or something bad had happened to her neck. "I beg your pardon?"

"Jeff's dead. He died two days ago, at his home."

The shock came down like a curtain over her countenance, starting at her brow, dropping to her questing eyes, her full lips and finally settling on her lovely chin. She flew into my arms. "What happened?" she whispered, her lips muffled by my jacket.

"He was in his bathtub listening to music on a portable stereo. It was perched on a stool, stupidly close to the water. He reached up to change something, the volume maybe, or the track he was listening to, and somehow the whole unit fell in and electrocuted him."

"Oh my God. Did he suffer?"

"Not it all," I lied, thinking of his contorted features and his fried, scaly hands. "It was over in an instant. He didn't feel a thing." I waited for her to make some remark about karma. I wasn't sure what I would do if she did that.

"Life is like a bad dream since I came down here," she

said instead. "Not seeing you, of course, but all the rest of it. What about his wife? Is she okay? What about his little girl?"

"Too soon to tell about either of them. The wife seems worse on the surface, ready to fall apart, I think, but Brooke is holding everything in, maybe letting her hurt turn to anger. That could lead to bad places."

"I don't really know them, but I should go visit anyway," Phayle murmured.

A monkey hooted a distant warning, and the sound echoed through the trees. We started walking again, then stopped for Phayle to give Sunmaid raisins to a white gibbon; a mother who in turn fed them languorously to a tiny baby with pink fingers.

"Do you want children of your own, Max?"

"If I had them, I'd need to be able to protect them all the time. They'd make me feel so vulnerable, tearing down all my illusions of being on top of things, of keeping things under control."

"The only thing you can control is yourself," she said. "That's a lesson I learned long ago."

I almost said something unkind about her drinking, but I didn't. The path divided, one way to the orangutans, one way to the gorilla and siamangs.

"Does what happened to Jeff have anything to do with what happened to Twy?" she asked abruptly.

"I think they both were murdered," I said simply. "I can't prove it just yet, and I don't know who did it or why, but I doubt either of them died by accident."

"But the power tool. . . ."

"Maybe somebody sabotaged that saw. We may never know. Nora gave everything away immediately."

"And Jeff?"

"Not much evidence, but Metro-Dade says they're working on it."

"You think someone came into the bathroom and pushed the stereo into the bath?"

"The Grayson mansion is palatial," I replied. "There must be twenty ways to get in. Jeff's bathroom was on the ground floor. There were no signs of forced entry, but that doesn't mean much. A garden or patio door could have been left open. Someone could have cased the joint, known Jeff's habit of listening in the tub, planned the whole thing, then pulled it off without his wife or kid ever knowing anybody was there."

" 'Cased the joint' " Phayle repeated as if she were tasting the words with her tongue.

"I'm trying to help Metro-Dade figure out a motive. Something to do with their law practice, probably, or something else they had in common."

"There's Lyre and Stone," she offered.

"What makes you think of that?"

"Just something they had in common."

"You didn't see much of those guys, did you, Phayle?"

"I live in California," she replied evenly. "I already told you I'm here on business. If I hadn't seen Twy's obituary in the Miami paper, I wouldn't have even known they were down here."

"But you didn't see anything about Jeff on the news?"

"The last couple of days have been so busy, I haven't even had time for the paper. What is this, anyway? The Spanish Inquisition?"

I squeezed her hand. "I'm just looking anywhere I can for clues to help me understand what happened. There might be something that you remember, something one of them said or did that would lead to a new line of inquiry."

"I doubt it," she shook her head.

We walked past the orangutans, who looked sad despite their lavish moated enclosure, and on to the gorilla, king of the apes, who was entertaining a group of old women by masturbating behind the glass. Another time, I would have found it funny.

"We could be enjoying the monkeys, and instead I feel like we're fighting over the memory of dead friends," Phayle said suddenly.

I kissed her gently, and bought her more peanuts. She seemed to brighten with the strengthening sunlight, and I started to feel much better about everything too.

Then, without any warning, she began whistling "Lucky Man."

I've said it before, and I'll say it again; I would never make it undercover. In order not to reveal that my heart was in jeopardy, I pretended that my beeper was vibrating in my pocket and dashed off to the nearest pay phone. I made a fake call. I spoke theories in hushed tones to no listener. Perhaps Phayle simply loves Emerson Lake and Palmer, and this is all a coincidence, I said to myself. Hearing her whistle the song stirred some vague memory, but it was so overlaid with thoughts of Jeff's corpse that I couldn't place it. Perhaps they both heard someone singing it ironically at Twy's funeral. Yes. That had to be it. Building mental sandbags against the flood of my fears, I bid the receiver adieu and rejoined her at the chimps.

"Gotta go," I announced.

"Now? On a Saturday?" she asked, plainly crushed.

"Crime never sleeps."

"Can't someone else handle it?"

"I'm not exactly top of the totem pole, Phayle."

"What's happened?"

"A possible break in a case I'm working on."

"What kind of a break? Can I go along?"

"It's an ongoing investigation," I shook my head. "I can't even tell you about it."

"Is it the case with the children?"

"No. Something different."

I led the way to the car. Phayle followed at a distance, like a reluctant child being taken from a party. "I know it sounds selfish, but I was looking forward to spending more time with you," she pouted as I pulled out of the parking lot.

"Me too. I'm sorry." I found that I could cover my anxiety by pretending to be concerned about the spurious call. I frowned, I let my hands get tense on the wheel, and I erected an emotional barricade the size of the Middle Kingdom in the small space between us in the car. Phayle sensed it of course, and pressed against the door in response, leaning as far as possible from me.

I needed to poke around some, to check with the hotel regarding her whereabouts, perhaps even have a chat with her contact at Burdine's. Most of all, I needed to be in my own space, to think through how to handle this, how to find out what I needed to know without tipping my hand. I drove quickly, with the bubble on the dash for effect. Under other circumstances, Phayle might have enjoyed that, but the thick air between us kept her quiet. I pulled up in front of the Delano, and she got out.

"Call me, okay?" she asked.

I nodded.

I did my best to smile. I'd be calling her all right.

I don't remember anything of the drive. I'm not even sure if I took I-95 or the Turnpike, but somehow I ended up in the office parking lot. The sky had turned drizzly, and dark enough to match my mood. Instinctively, I must have known that in order to look at the situation objectively — to try and ignore my feelings for Phayle — I needed to surround myself with the familiar trappings of law enforcement.

I let myself in the back door only to find all the lights on and the copy machine humming. This was strange, as I often stopped in over the weekend and had never caught Lorraine slacking on her shut-off duties. Even though Wacona never worked Saturday or Sunday—what she did during her spare time was perhaps the greatest mystery at the West Palm domicile—I ducked into her office to see if she was around. The room was empty, dark, and neat as a pin. I checked out Sea Chunny's digs and found them empty as well. After glancing into my own quarters, I began to get uneasy, and that was when I noticed light coming from under the door of Greg Hunter's old office. My mouth dry, I unzipped my fanny pack and put my hand on my Glock and knocked once, harshly.

"Come in," said an unfamiliar voice.

We postal inspectors keep a low profile, and federal facilities like U.S.P.I.S. domiciles are pretty secure places. This didn't add up.

"How about you come out?" I commanded. I heard a chair push back, a couple of footsteps, and the door slowly opened to reveal a tiny black man. His cologne smelled like a forest fire, his eyes glimmered brightly above his delicate, almost pretty features, and his head bobbed like a bird's.

"Who the hell are you?" I demanded.

He reached into his jacket pocket.

"Easy," I said, my mind racing with the possibility that some perp had gotten in and was digging through his own file to destroy the evidence.

Slowly, looking slightly amused, he pulled out a shield. "Inspector Mozart Potrero."

I let go of my fanny pack and sagged against the wall, feeling like an idiot. "Shit, I'm sorry, Potrero. It's a bad day for surprises, and nobody told me you were coming."

"I talked to Chunny on the phone. He's got a heartbeat like a whale's. You're too jumpy to be him. I guess you gotta be Diamond."

"Max," I said, offering my hand.

He shook it, then plunked himself back behind his desk. I sat down across from him. The office was mostly bare — Greg's stuff was long gone — but the file cabinet was open and I could see that Mozart was busy sorting a stack of papers.

"So I guess you guys don't work weekends too often," he ventured.

"I'm usually the only one here."

"Wacona Smith?"

"Never. She's too organized. Gets everything done in half-days."

"Yeah, well not me. That's why I'm in here now. My condolences about Hunter, by the way. Were you guys close?"

"We were friends."

"I heard he was a good man. Say, what the hell kind of shoes are those?"

"Birkenstock clogs."

"Ha! Hippie shoes. You were never in the service, were you?"

"Never."

"I knew it. Nobody who's been in the service could ever wear Birkenstocks. Me, I was in the Marine Corps. Had a chiropractor put me on one of those pivoting tables that hang you upside-down so I could make the height requirement. Stayed on the thing for thirty-six hours. I was three-quarters of an inch taller for almost a week after that."

"Do the same thing to get this job?" I asked. We had our requirements too.

"Didn't need to once they found out I'd been in the Corps," he grinned.

"You see action?"

"One tour in the Nam."

I figured the guy had to be a radar tech or a medic, and apparently he could see the wheels turning in my head.

"Tunnel rat," he said. They sent me in with a gun and a miner's lamp and I crawled around NVA territory and knifed guys point-blank in the dark. I was a natural."

The new guy on the block was, among other things, a natural tunnel rat. I nodded. It was good to know.

He pointed at a calendar on the wall, the sole remaining link to Greg. There was a crude skull and crossbones drawn in black magic marker over a date in the middle of the page. "So, was that the day Greg Hunter died?"

"I believe it was."

"His handwriting?"

"Maybe."

"Think he had a premonition?"

"Looks like it."

"You believe in shit like that?"

I picked a pencil off the desk and held it up. "If I told you sixty years ago that this little pencil was made up of particles so small that trillions of them could fit on the head of a pin, you would have thought I was nuts. If I told you that smashing one of those infinitesimally tiny particles would release enough energy to blow up West Palm, you would have had me committed. There are forces at work in the world, Mozart. Who's to say Greg didn't feel something coming?"

"I heard you were strange," he said.

"So that question was a test?"

"Let's just say I'm curious about the people I work with."

"Me too. Tell me more about yourself."

He leaned back in his chair and put his hands behind his head. "I'm from the Dominican Republic. My mother was an accountant and my father was a cop who loved music. He picked my name. I don't play any instruments, I don't care for sex with women, and I'm five-foot-four without shoes. I'm forty-five, I've been an inspector for eleven years, and I've busted more scumbags than anybody who works in this building, including Chunny. Any other questions?"

"No," I answered meekly. It took effort. I don't do meek well.

"Good," he said. "Now how about them Dolphins?"

"The Miami Dolphins haven't won a game since dinosaurs roamed the Earth," I replied without enthusiasm.

"That's okay. I don't really care about them. I just asked because I thought maybe you did."

"You thought wrong. Tell me, what *do* you care about, Mozart?"

"You know," he winked.

"Besides that."

"I like busting somebody who thinks they're smarter than me, or somebody who never saw me coming. I like Ping-Pong, too," he said, leaning way back in his chair, which meant sliding down so his head was almost invisible and putting his tiny feet up. "I was state champion two years running." He snapped his fingers. "Hey! You're into kung fu, aren't you? One of the guys in Miami told me that. What style?"

"Chen t'ai chi ch'uan."

"You teach me that shit sometime?"

"It's sort of a lifestyle thing," I responded. "You can't really learn it in a lesson here and there."

"Maybe if we work together for a while, I'll have a chance to learn it in a meaningful way," he said.

There was something surprisingly earnest, almost na-
ive, about the way he said that, and I found, to my enormous surprise, that it didn't sound like a bad deal.
"Maybe," I answered at last.

"You'll see," he grinned. "I may be a natural rat, but I
can be very charming."

EIGHT

The night manager of the Delano Hotel was an elegantly dressed Indian man who frowned at the sight of my badge.

"Will there be violence?" he inquired in a sing-song voice.

"No violence."

"No shooting, no breaking of furniture, no loud noise?"

"None."

"Because I am only here for emergencies. If there is to be unpleasantness, you will have to wait until my supervisor comes in at ten A.M."

"I'm only here on surveillance," I reassured him. "Now I'd appreciate it if you would find me a waiter's uniform."

"The problems of the lady in room nine-sixteen are not really the problems of the hotel," he said hesitantly.

"Help me, or they will be."

With a great sigh of resignation, he led me to the staff changing room in a dingy basement smelling strongly of rodents. We searched through rusty lockers until we found a uniform that fit. He waited outside while I changed and hid my street clothes on the bottom shelf of a serving cart. The pants were too tight, but anything without an elastic waist feels tight to me. He led me to the kitchen, where he equipped me with a tray covered with dishes and a full pitcher of ice water.

"Champagne would be good," I said.

"Forget champagne. It's four A.M. on Sunday morning."

I rode the elevator to the ninth floor, where I used the house phone to call Phayle's room and make sure she was in. I hung up when she answered groggily and then positioned myself where I could watch her door.

At seven o'clock, a red-headed call girl slipped out of room 910 and made her way to the emergency stairs, a pair of hose sticking out of her purse. At eight-thirty, a tall man with runner's legs, brand-new Nikes, a perforated tank top, and spandex tights, emerged from room 912, brushed his cowlick aside, nodded at me, and rang for the elevator. At eight forty-five, an overweight middle-aged couple in matching Bermudas emerged from room 904. They were arguing about breakfast. Finally, at 10:10 A.M., while I pretended to fuss with a Sterno burner, Phayle Tollard came out of her room wearing a bikini that would have gotten a gasp from God. I took the service car downstairs, and found a position just inside the mezzanine where I could watch her on the pool deck without being seen.

She seemed agitated, unable to adjust her deck chair to a comfortable angle, oblivious to both the admiration and the resentment her skimpy swimsuit elicited from the other guests. Looking at her, I wanted ugly suspicions to go away, I wanted to be a boy again, to nestle against her, to know nothing of little dark girls dying and of bathtub electrocutions and the kickback of table saws. She raised a long leg to slather it with oil that I knew, even from this distance, smelled of papayas and mangoes and coconuts and cream. A moth fluttered in my chest, and I was over-come by sadness at what my life had become — skulking around after a woman I had once loved. A heavy hand on my shoulder interrupted my reverie.

"Don't you have work to do?" It was the security guard who had hassled us in the cabaña the week before.

"Just on break," I told him.

Suspicion turned to recognition. "I know you," he said, lifting the cover off one of the empty plates on my cart.

"I doubt it."

"Yes I do! You were with that woman last week, out by the pool."

Reluctantly, I flashed my I.D., explaining that Phayle was under surveillance.

"What you two did on the beach that night, that was surveillance too?"

"Part of the job," I said, trying to hide my embarrass-ment.

He looked at me a long moment. "This makes me feel stupid," he said. "I'm in charge of security here. I should have been told."

"I'm sorry."

Phayle got up and started walking to the elevator, her towel wrapped around her midriff, just below her navel. I made as if to follow.

"Boy, am I in the wrong line of work," the guard shook his head.

She left the hotel an hour later. Her cab crossed the MacArthur Causeway, turned south on Brick-ell, proceeded along the eastern edge of Miami and turned

143

east onto Rickenbacker Causeway. I paid the toll and followed her across the long, low bridge that separated Key Biscayne, the most northerly of the Florida Keys, from downtown. We drove past Miami Seaquarium and the University of Miami, and onto Crandon Boulevard, past the park and golf courses and down into Key Biscayne's small, exclusive, residential area.

The cab stopped at a red light. A stunning black woman on an enormous pink Harley Davidson pulled up beside me, posing like Cleopatra straddling the sphinx. I cranked up the volume and scanned radio stations, stopping when I heard the Rolling Stones play "Ruby Tuesday." The light changed, and the cab turned right. Three minutes later, the driver stopped in front of the expected address on Harbor Drive—a conservative gray Cape Cod with white trim. My last, faint hopes dashed, I hid the Porsche behind a Ford minivan. The cab roared away and Phayle made for the front door. I could have stopped her right there, maybe I should have, but something held me back. She reached into her purse. I pulled my Glock. She came up with a compact, checked her lipstick, then rang the doorbell. When nobody answered, she walked around to the side of the house, and let herself in through the wooden gate. I ran lightly across the street and followed her in.

Clifton Hughes was lying by his pool reading the front page of the Sunday paper, a cordless telephone resting on his stomach. He didn't see his guest until she was almost upon him, and neither of them saw me peering around the side of the house, my weapon at the ready.

"Phayle!" he exclaimed, leaping to his feet. A gust of wind blew the sports section into the pool.

"I thought we should talk," she said.

"Of course." I could see that he was tense. My finger crept close to the trigger, waiting for Phayle's move.

"I'm very sorry about Jeff," she said, swinging her purse.

"What?" he rocked back slightly.

"I just heard from Max."

"I know you don't want to hear it," he said, dropping back down into his chaise longue. "But I'm sure that if Jeff and Twy were still alive . . ."

"You're right," Phayle held up her hand. "I don't want to hear it."

He nodded miserably. "Look, about our other business . . ."

"I still want to go through with it," she said slowly.

Cliff took a deep breath. "This isn't the best time," he said.

"Make it the best time," she snapped.

Somewhere behind them, a door slid open and an enormous brunette appeared. Devoid of makeup, she was draped in a flowered sarong that couldn't hide her enormous heft, her triple chin, her wide flat feet, and her thick ankles. A little dog followed her out, running in glad circles around her, overcome with love. I held my breath and hoped the wind wouldn't blow my scent his way.

"I didn't know we had company, Clifton," she said, looking resentfully at Phayle's curves. "You know how I like to be told when you're expecting somebody. The house is a mess and so am I." The dog went up to Phayle, sniffed her, ran back to his mistress.

"You look wonderful, darling, and so does the patio," Cliff said warmly. "Phayle, this is my wife, Memphis. Memphis, this is Phayle Tollard, an old friend from school in town for a few days."

"I don't believe I saw you at Twy's funeral, Memphis," said Phayle.

"It wasn't a good day for me to go out," Clifton's big wife replied curtly.

A seagull wheeled in the midday sun, then headed out over Biscayne Bay. A freighter, riding high in the water and showing rust-stained anchor holes, emitted a puff of smoke and sounded its foghorn.

"Memphis," said Cliff. "Why don't you offer Phayle a drink?"

"I'm not much of a drinker," Phayle lied, shading her eyes and looking at the ship. "I just came by to say hello."

"Just in the neighborhood?" Memphis challenged.

"That's right."

"Well, we're certainly glad you did," Memphis nodded.

There was another moment of awkward silence.

"Cute dog," said Phayle. I had to give her credit for trying.

"His name is Daniel," said Memphis. "A bichon frise champion. The only stud for miles."

Cliff winced and so did I.

"Where are you staying, Phayle?" he asked.

"A hotel in South Beach."

"Got a car?"

She shook her head.

"I'll drive you back, then," he declared.

"I think Clifton is forgetting that the Petersons are bringing their bitch in heat to meet Daniel at one o'clock," Memphis said in a condescending tone.

"Maybe you could handle that without me," Cliff suggested.

"I really don't think so. You know how wild males can be at the sight of a pretty girl."

"I'll just phone for a cab," said Phayle.

"Please. Allow me," Cliff picked up the cordless phone.

I slithered away, feeling like a snake, having more questions and no answers at all.

The next morning I walked into the wood-paneled Palm Beach County courtroom where Cristoforo Diaz was to be arraigned for violating his restraining order and for assaulting Regina Diaz, and found it nearly empty. I learned later that the usual gawkers were next door for the trial of a Seminole Indian who had raped a seventy-year-old Palm Beach woman. Wacona was there, though, in a middle row, sitting beside Dave Beard, the assistant U.S. attorney assigned to the Diaz comp fraud case. I slid in beside them.

"You're late," Wacona hissed. "Cruz will be here any minute, and Diaz should have shown up already."

I could have explained to her that I was late because I'd been following my college girlfriend around Miami. Instead, I just muttered something about traffic on the Interstate.

Beard leaned across Wacona. "Heard you talked to Cruz in his cell."

"So?"

"If opposing counsel can show prejudice, it's going to hurt our efforts to dismiss those worker's comp fraud charges."

"What are you talking about?"

"They'll make it look like you had a hard-on for Diaz and a grudge against Cruz."

"Come on."

"These people use what they can."

"But I never set eyes on either of them before the day Cruz beat her," I protested.

"I hope you can prove that," Beard sighed.

The doors to the hallway opened, and Regina Diaz came in. She was accompanied by a dapper man with a briefcase and white streaks in his dark, oiled hair. She looked as if she had been mainlining fettueine Alfredo for a week. Her features were fuller, softer, and more round, and she filled out her conservative blue suit with impressive curves and bulges. I caught Beard staring.

"You call that a pathetic figure?" he hissed.

"She didn't look that good the other day," I said weakly.

"Oink," grunted Wacona.

Cruz came in a moment later, looking like a refugee from the Cotton Club in saddle shoes and a three-piece brown tweed suit.

"Nice to see you again, Inspector," he taunted, showing brilliant teeth.

I might have popped him right there had his attorney — a big-boned woman — not stopped to say hello to Beard. They chatted as colleagues do, about some ruling they had both read about in a law journal, about the food at the courthouse cafeteria, about how the coffee could be used to strip furniture. The moment passed.

"All rise for the Honorable Manny Saperstein!" bellowed the bailiff.

The judge came in. He was bent horizontal by scoliosis, and hillocks of hair exploded out of his ears like Everglades sawgrass. Before he could even tap his gavel, the two attorneys approached the bench for a conference. What they had to say didn't take very long, and it made a tropical storm of the judge's face.

"The charges have been dropped. The case is dismissed," he clapped his gavel down.

It was over that fast. I felt shock, dismay, confusion. The courtroom buzzed. Cruz took Regina Diaz in his arms and smiled at me. Unable to help myself, I stood and headed their way.

"I can't protect you now," I told Diaz. She looked away.

"If you don't leave us alone, I'll have to get a restraining order on *you*," Cruz snapped, forcibly turning Regina Diaz around and pushing her toward the door.

Wacona appeared at my elbow. "Let them go, Max. There's nothing you can do."

"You *know* he threatened her," I said.

"It's always more complicated than that," Wacona said, resignedly. "Co-dependent. Weird. Inexplicable. I found that out when I volunteered at a shelter in Seattle. Some women get help, work it out, turn their lives around. Others wind up dead."

"Believe me, that prick's bad business."

"I do believe you. It's just not your fight. It's hers."

We walked slowly down the hall. Ten feet ahead of us, the lovebirds reached the end of the long hallway and pushed through the glass doors that led to the street.

That was when the shooting started.

At first, between the screams, I wasn't sure where the bullets were coming from. I hit the deck and waited for the noise to stop. When I finally looked up, Cruz was dead, a gaping hole in his chest, a look of complete surprise on his face. Regina was down beside him, her legs out in front of her, a piece of her skull dangling like an earring. For a moment, everything was so quiet I could hear the plop-plop of her blood dripping down the concrete steps. Then Beard came running up behind us, accompanied by a few cops, their weapons drawn. I heard a squeal of tires and a black Infiniti peeled out down the street, its license plate deliberately obscured by mud. I started running for the R90S.

"Max, don't!" Wacona cried.

"Diamond!" echoed Beard. "Not on a motorcycle!"

ARTHUR ROSENFELD

Ignoring them, I jumped aboard turned the key, twisted the throttle, pushed the start button and took off on full choke. A cloud of gray smoke came out of the twin pipes as I roared away. Ahead of me, the high-output sedan sped toward Dixie Highway.

Before I-95 was built, Dixie Highway, laid down along the rail line, was the main route to Miami for vacationers from the Northeast. After the completion of the Interstate, the road was abandoned by travelers and streetfront real estate plummeted. Businesses closed up, and the strip became the roughest part of most coastal towns, literally and figuratively. The macadam near the tracks was a washboard, and the flying Infiniti fishtailed over a railroad crossing just as the red lights began flashing and the train bells sounded. I almost made it through, but had to grab a handful of brake as a locomotive burst into view. The Infiniti got across and turned north.

My front wheel skittered sideways. I fought the bars mightily, but I lost. The bike went down, pinning my right leg. I lost the feeling in my toes and smelled the gasoline spilling onto my shoes. The train thundered by. My heart raced, my adrenals squeezing their elixir into my bloodstream. Feeling like I could use a planet for a bowling ball, I lifted the bike. The twin cylinders were still firing, so I pointed the front wheel off the pavement and twisted the throttle. I hit the tennis-ball-sized rocks of the trackbed, but could manage no more than 20 mph, about half the speed as the freight train.

Box car after box car after box car went by, and the deafening clatter of steel wheels disoriented me to the point of nausea. Each second I stayed upright was a miracle. I craned for a look beneath the train but saw only an impossible blur. I wrestled with the bouncing bars and wondered how far to go and how fast. I figured that the killers might have stopped and doubled back, might have lost themselves in the subdivision on the other side of the tracks before heading to the freeway, might even have taken refuge in someone's garage. I slowed down. Flatbeds went by, as did refrigerated containers marked with the imprint of Midwest meatpackers. When the caboose finally passed, I made it to the other side. The Infiniti was nowhere in sight. Aware that squad cars, choppers, and radios could do more than I could, I turned around and headed for the office. I was hoping to get in and out of there before Wacona tried to stop me from doing what I knew I had to do.

I came through the front door so fast and hard that Lorraine dropped her coffee cup when she saw me.

"Inspector Potrero started today," she said, trying to make conversation as I rushed past. "My God, Max, your leg is bleeding."

I looked down. My right ankle was soaked in blood where the motorcycle had fallen on me. "Doesn't hurt," I said brusquely.

I headed for the supply room, where I grabbed an MP-5 machine gun, two clips, a radio and a couple of other supplies. Mozart Potrero stuck his head in the door while I was shoving the gear in a duffel bag.

"Oh, you look good," he said.

"Go away."

"I thought you were going to be in court with Inspector Smith."

"We were in court. Now we're out."

"Better have someone look at that leg."

"I'll get to it."

"MP-5?" he motioned at the duffel.

"That's right."

He put his coffee cup down on a shelf and rubbed his hands together as if his fingers were cold. "Little mission?"

"Something like that."

"Going alone?"

"You bet."

"Inspector Smith know?"

"Why don't you call her Wacona?"

"I will when she asks me to. Does she know?"

My ankle was starting to throb. I didn't want to look at it. "She's probably guessed."

"Want backup?"

"No thanks."

"My bite is worse than my bark."

"The answer is still no."

"Want to tell me what case you're working on?"

I pushed past him in the doorway, but he wouldn't take the hint.

"Well?" he pressed, following me.

I turned to look at him. His face was about even with my breastbone, and he was shaking with excitement and purpose.

"Trust me, Potrero, you don't want to go where I'm going. You just got here. Give Wacona time to get to like you before you piss her off."

He hesitated. "What you're doing, is it going to upset Inspector Smith?"

"That's probably a fair statement."

"Will you break the law or discredit the service?"

"You never can tell about me these days."

He searched me for a second with his eyes, and then he followed me out the door.

We took his Chevy Suburban—a vehicle he told me had been seized in a Miami drug bust. He had to slump down so low to reach the pedals that the top of the steering wheel was almost even with his forehead.

"You should have gotten a smaller car," I said.

"Nah. This is perfect."

He put his foot in it, and zoomed out of the lot. I pointed him to I-95 southbound and dialed FBI headquarters in Miami. I asked for Ron Dryden. There was a delay, a couple of beeps, and he came on the line.

"Where can I find O'Burke?" I demanded.

"I heard about the unpleasantness at the local courthouse."

"It was unpleasant. Where's O'Burke?"

"Probably at home."

"What's the address?"

"Gee, I don't know, Diamond. You sound pretty strung out. What do you want with the Don?"

"Cruz ratted him out."

"So you think O'Burke did him on the courthouse steps just to send us a message?"

"To send *me* a message. You weren't around."

"The woman's dead too, from what I hear."

"Mother of two and she's missing half her head. Now gimme the address before I show up at *your* house."

"That a threat?"

"It's a promise."

He gave me the address, telling me it was my funeral.

"You wouldn't be talking about *Cuco* O'Burke?" Mozart asked casually, putting the blue bubble on the dashboard.

"I warned you not to come along."

We drove a little farther. The radio came to life. Wacona was yelling something. Mozart reached down and turned her off. "Not what they used to be, these radios," he said. "I couldn't understand a word of that. Some kind of weather report, wasn't it?"

"Thanks," I said.

"For what? Listen, your foot is bleeding all over my truck. Why don't we stop someplace and take care of that?"

I looked down. The blood had completely soaked through my pants and was making a puddle in my shoe on one side, dribbling down to the floor mat on the other. I rolled up my cuff. There was a half-moon shaped gouge above my ankle, deep enough to show white connective tissue and red meat. I pressed the raw and angry artery with my thumb. "Later," I said.

We raced down the Interstate, passing through Fort Lauderdale too fast for me to read the billboards. Mozart gave two seconds of siren to an Oldsmobile trundling along in the left lane.

"How about filling me in before we get to the Don?" he said conversationally.

I gave him a quick and dirty version of Cuco O'Burke's connection to the snuff tapes. Then I told him about Cruz and Regina Diaz.

"You think Diaz was intentional?" Mozart asked.

"Maybe."

"And Cruz was your only link to those tapes?"

"Right. And even though he walked, I would have caught up with him again, worked him over the first time he pissed in an alley," I shook my head.

"Now all you've got is O'Burke."

"Right. And I can't stop thinking about Regina's two kids."

"The courthouse steps," Mozart shook his head. "What was that *Cubano* thinking? If it *was* him, the Bureau is going to shut him right down."

"Oh it was him all right, and he's not going to have to wait for the Bureau."

"Because you're running around for revenge with your leg cut up?"

"With my leg cut up and an MP-5 in my bag," I said, tapping the duffel with my toe.

"You sure you don't have any Latin blood?"

"I'm sure."

"You're not planning on murdering O'Burke, are you?"

"I went to the club, I sent the S.O.B. the message that I was personally interested in this case," I said.

"And he disrespects you by killing Cruz and Diaz."

"More like he gives me the finger."

"So you *are* planning to kill him."

"No."

"So why show up at his house with guns?" Mozart persisted.

"Stir the pot, things float to the surface," I replied, staring out at the road.

Southeast of Coral Gables and north of Matheson Hammock Park, the Coral Gables Waterway wends its way east to Biscayne Bay. The houses that surround the exclusive canal are protected by guard gates and patrolled by private security forces. What makes the artificial oasis possible, however, is not these heavy-handed trappings, but the same police presence that protects Coconut Grove and South Miami Beach from being overrun by penniless hordes. I considered the irony of one of Miami's most notorious gangsters having chosen this elite part of town for his home as Mozart pulled the Suburban to a stop at the guard gate.

"You sure you want to do this?" he asked. "We could still back out."

"I'm sure," I said grimly.

The guard emerged from his booth. He was clean and young and blond, with knife-sharp creases on his pants, a gold badge with a blue enamel eagle in the middle pinned to his shirt, and a .45 Kimber automatic on his hip.

"Some piece," muttered Mozart. "Where does a rent-a-cop kid get off wearing a gun like that?"

"May I help you?" the guard asked with a frozen smile, looking through the window at Mozart's tiny body.

Mozart pulled his shield smoothly. "Federal agents. Open the gate."

The kid looked at Mozart's badge. *"Postal Inspector?"* he said doubtfully.

Mozart let out a sigh. He'd heard it before, and so had I. "Open the gate right now, before I cuff you for obstruction," he said.

The kid opened the gate. Mozart powered through.

"You're a patient guy. I would have shot him," I chafed.

"O'Burke's man, no doubt," Mozart shrugged. "I doubt this subdivision's seen so much as a broken beer bottle since the Don moved in."

We drove through archways of tall palms, past Mediterranean-style villas and Tudor-style mansions. There were Jaguars and Hummers and Beemers in most driveways, Benzes too.

"Tough business, being rich," I observed sarcastically.

"You said it. Terrible thing to be at the mercy of gardeners, house painters, fence men and tree doctors."

"Mechanics," I added.

"Postal inspectors," he said. We actually laughed at that.

I pointed to a huge house whose lines were punctuated by towers.

"Figure that for Casa O'Burke?" said Mozart.

"I do."

"We're probably under surveillance right now."

"No probably about it. And don't forget the missile launchers, poison gas, grenades, and the army of mean guys. I get hungry just thinking about it all."

"I don't really know you at all, do I?" Mozart smiled.

The house was styled after a French country villa, with dark green shutters and white plaster showing through ivy walls. The circular driveway was littered with the leaves of a magnificent oak whose gnarled roots had broken through the pavement in places, imparting a mixture of opulence and decay.

"Not what you expected, huh?" I asked Mozart.

"To tell you the truth, I was looking for a house built like a Lamborghini. Something flashy, something fast, something that makes your heart speed up when you see it."

"O'Burke's been building his empire for years. He's the slow and steady type — big on foundation, tradition, not a man for modern edges, skylights or picture windows. You can be sure there's ten, twelve million in this place."

"And they say crime doesn't pay."

"Of course it pays. That's why people do it."

Mozart pulled the Suburban in behind a cream-colored Bentley Mulsanne convertible and turned off the key. The silence was broken only by the faint ticking of the cooling engine. "So here we are," Mozart said after a minute or two

"O'Burke murdered my witness."

"And now?"

By way of answer, I climbed out of the truck.

"You sure you want to go in with that machine pistol in your hand?" Mozart asked.

Nodding, I walked straight to the front door, found it open, and stepped inside. The foyer was like a Monet still-life. A large, dark, antique table sat in the center of the room, grapefruits in a glass bowl atop it, surrounded by flowers. Beyond it was a vast patio, and beyond that, a beautiful swimming pool fed by water coming out of a trio of statues of young boys riding dolphins. In the distance, a sailboat mast, just visible above the trees, moved along the bay.

"Born to suffer," said Mozart from somewhere off my left elbow. He'd been so quiet, I hadn't even known he was there.

Suddenly there was a thundering sound. A jet plane came out of nowhere, not more than a thousand feet above us. Glass rattled. I ducked. Somewhere, a parrot squawked. "Hope the Don got a deal on this place," Mozart added. "We're right on the approach to MIA."

"I get a deal on everything," Cuco O'Burke's voice floated eerily to us. He was watching us from the shade of an awning by the pool, a thin line of smoke drifting up from the cigar in his hand. He wore sandals, bathing trunks and a shirt unbuttoned to show a lean, gray-haired chest. His sunglasses were so dark I couldn't tell where he was looking.

"Cuco," I said.

"Inspector Diamond and friend. To what do I owe the pleasure?"

"You orphaned two children on the steps of the Palm Beach County Courthouse today," I answered.

"I don't know what you're talking about."

I limped forward. My ankle had begun to swell below the wound. The Don's two tiny greyhounds emerged from beneath his chair and snarled as their master put down his cigar with great deliberation, raised his sunglasses, and gazed at me. Mozart took an involuntary step backwards. "Fourteen sniper rifles are trained on you," O'Burke said calmly. "Please put your gun down."

I hesitated.

"Max," said Mozart.

I lowered the MP-5.

"Thank you. May I get you either of you some lunch?"

"No, thank you," Mozart smiled.

"A drink, then? Iced tea, or perhaps something stronger?"

"Where's the black Infiniti?" I interrupted.

"I don't own a black Infiniti," the Don replied smoothly.

"You probably figure that I don't care about a piece of human garbage like Cristoforo Cruz," I said quietly, "and under normal circumstances you'd be right. But I needed him, and you knew that so you took him away."

"I wish I knew what you were talking about," O'Burke moved his glasses back down over his eyes.

"And then there are the Diaz kids," I added. "You didn't have to shoot the woman."

"If not a drink, how about a cigar? A Cohiba perhaps?"

"Cubans aren't what they used to be, Cuco. And I don't just mean cigars."

"Really? That sounds like something a self-important *yanqui* might say. Are you self-important, Inspector Diamond? Do you fancy yourself more significant than you really are?"

I wanted to answer, but suddenly I felt dizzy. My ankle grew hot. Something roared in my ears, but when I looked up I saw no airplane.

Then everything went black.

I woke up in O'Burke's lounge chair. The Don and his little dogs were gone. Mozart Potrero sat in a chair beside me, my Heckler and Koch MP-5 ostentatiously slung around his neck.

"How long?" I asked.

"About ten minutes."

"Some mission this turned into. Where's Cuco?"

"I don't know. Gone."

"What happened?"

"You fainted from loss of blood," said a familiar, creamy voice.

I rose up on my elbows. Guiomary O'Burke knelt on the ground by my leg, a medical kit beside her. She was wearing blue jeans and a bright yellow blouse, unbuttoned just enough to reveal the white tops of her breasts. She was breathtaking.

"Maximillian," she smiled.

"Guiomary."

"I'm afraid I'm going to have to stitch this up."

"I was hoping you would," I said. "In fact, that's why I fell down."

"She's a doctor," Mozart informed me. "She went to Harvard Medical School and she practices Internal Medicine at Mercy Hospital."

"I see you two have been talking."

"Don't worry, I'll anesthetize the area first," she promised.

"I'm not worried. I'd let you stitch me if you were a bus driver with Parkinson's."

"A sense of humor," Guiomary smiled. "No wonder my father likes you."

"I don't want your father to like me," I said. "I'm going to put him in jail."

"This is just his clumsy way of being charming," put in Mozart.

"Actually," she said, as she raised a small vial, shook it, plunged a hypodermic in and drew back a small amount of fluid, "I think my father likes you because he is a fan of Cervantes."

"What is that supposed to mean?"

"He wrote Don Quixote," Mozart put in.

"I know what he wrote. I still don't get it."

"He likes your sense of honor," said Guiomary.

"And appears not to care that you're nuts," Mozart groused.

"I think he does care," Guiomary argued, wiping me down with an iodine-soaked gauze pad. "That's why you two are still alive."

She tapped the syringe and put the needle expertly in near the wound. When the leg was numb, she broke a second needle out of its sterile envelope, threaded it, and began to repair my torn flesh. I lay back down with a groan.

"You would never have made it in the Marines," Mozart gibed.

"You're just jealous 'cause I'm getting all the attention."

Guiomary laughed at that. It was a deep laugh, more the rumble of distant thunder than the tinkle of a bell. "I'm doing the muscle first," she told me. "Next I'll do the skin. Your friend won't be jealous when the anesthesia wears off."

"You look beautiful in yellow," I said.

"I hear that from all my patients."

"I bet you look good in that Bentley, too."

"Obnoxious, I know, but very heavy and safe," she smiled.

"I appreciate the patch job, but I really did come here on business. Your father had two people killed this morning."

Guiomary paused in her work long enough to look up at me.

"Don't talk about my father when he's not here to defend himself," she said.

"So you pretend not to know that he runs the biggest crime syndicate in South Florida?"

"Max," Mozart warned.

"There you go again, tilting at windmills," Guiomary smiled, making a final knot in the stitch and cutting it carefully with small stainless steel scissors. She handed me a bottle of pills. "The wound was dirty. I cleaned it, but there is still the risk of infection. Take two of these a day for one week, after eating. And stay away from alcohol."

I looked down at her handiwork. The stitches were neat, the skin drawn tight. "Thank you," I sighed.

"You're welcome. Now go quietly, like I promised my father you would." With that, she took one of my arms and Mozart took the other, and they lifted me out of the chair. Together, we hobbled past the pool, through the French doors and the foyer and out to the front, where the Suburban sat in the shade of the giant oak. Mozart got in his side and I got in mine. Guiomary stood watching.

"Adios, Dulcinea," I said, leaning out the window.

"Good-bye, Maximillian," she smiled as Mozart started the truck.

"Today, I discovered that you are an idiot," he announced.

By the time we pulled into the office parking lot, my leg was burning so hotly it was a wonder it didn't set my trousers ablaze. "You better get some rest," said Mozart.

I pointed at Wacona's chocolate-colored Porsche.

"You don't know her like I do," I said. "The longer I put it off, the worse it's going to be."

"You were upset about the killings," Mozart said smoothly. "I suggested a little range time with an MP-5 might be just the thing. Grudgingly, you agreed, and when we got back you went home to take care of your leg."

I stared at him.

"What?" he continued. "You think O'Burke's going to call and complain?"

"I owe you one."

"Of course you do," he smiled wryly. "Now go drink some soup or something. And don't forget your pills."

I mounted the R90S gingerly and drove off feeling like a naughty schoolboy. Five P.M. traffic had reached a full pitch by the time I reached the Interstate, and there was a cold front moving in, a long, dark ridge to the west. For a time, the front remained stationary, but then, as if suddenly making up its mind to attack, it moved east, drenching the highway and driving a cold rain straight through my leather jacket and into my bones. By the time I got home, my nose was running and there was a bloody seepage from the cold, blue flesh around my stitches.

I took a long, hot bath and thought of Guiomary O'Burke's touch, and of the way she called me "Maximillian." The adrenaline that had driven me to Cuco's had worn off, leaving with it a profound conviction that there was nothing I could have accomplished there, particularly with a machine gun, and that Mozart was right about me being an idiot. When I had thoroughly thawed, I got out of the tub and rummaged through my drawers until I found my old octagonal Lyre and Stone pocket watch. I took it to the couch, wound it, and sat there listening to it tick until I fell asleep.

At 3 A.M., I awakened shivering on the couch. The bath towel in which I'd been wrapped lay on the floor. Picard was bumping up against the slider, as if trying to get in. Shit. I'd forgotten to bring him in as I do every night, except in summer, and there had been a big drop in temperature. Giant tortoise immune systems don't function in the cold. His breath was coming in wheezing gasps, his eyes were running, and his nose was bubbling—a sure sign of pneumonia.

163

Naked and hobbling on one foot, I dragged him into the bathroom, leaving a streak of dirt on the carpet. I put a heat lamp on him, pried his beak open with a soup spoon, and forced a couple of Guiomary's antibiotic tablets down his throat. Then, to warm him up as fast as possible, I curled around him on the bathroom floor. Instantly I dropped into a dream wherein I was being battered against cold rocks by a fast-moving river, getting nowhere in a hurting hurry.

NINE

The seafood palate of South Florida Jews tends to favor either gravlax — raw, marinated, and salted fish — or the pink, buttery flesh of the smoked salmon of Nova Scotia. Personally, I like the flaky, white, smoked salmon from Scotland, more expensive and harder to find, but always worth the time and money. At two-thirty the next afternoon, after a fitful sleep, I ran out for a couple of fresh bagels, one sesame and one poppy, brought them back, toasted them and covered them with the special fish, topping off the sandwich with capers, fresh lemon juice, and fresh ground pepper. I brewed some Ethiopian Mocha Harrar coffee to go with the feast and ate out on the balcony, watching the boats go by. Then I drove my Porsche sedately in to work, pretending that I was not worried by the fact that I hadn't heard word one from Wacona or Mozart or Sea. Lorraine greeted me with a worried look and told me that John Clark, the Inspector-in-Charge of the

165

Miami Division, had made one of his rare appearances, and that he and Waco were behind closed doors.

John Clark was a born manager with a penchant for efficiency. He had risen through the ranks in Seattle, where he had come to know Wacona Smith, and then moved to the service's headquarters in Washington, D.C., before being assigned to Miami. He was said to wear a gun only at the range, and he looked so much like Jimmy Stewart that it was hard not to expect him to break into a soliloquy about a run on the bank.

"Think I should interrupt?" I asked Lorraine.

"Actually, Max, I would have trouble thinking of a worse idea. How's the leg?"

"Better, thank you. I had it looked at."

I wandered down the hall and found Sea Chunny working on his computer. Frowning, he waved me into his office.

"Heard you played Lone Ranger outside the courthouse yesterday."

"Just figured I might be able to catch up with the bad guys on my bike. Figured wrong and cut my leg for my trouble."

"Mind if I have a look?"

I rolled up my pant leg and showed him Guiomary's handiwork.

"Hurt much?"

"As a matter of fact it does."

"But not too much to go off with Potrero for a little MP-5 range time."

"Yeah, well."

"How's he shoot?"

"Not as good as you."

"Then he'd better be fucking Sherlock Holmes," Sea sighed.

"He's pretty solid."

"You guys buddies now?"

"Sure. I went to O'Burke's place. Potrero backed me up."

"I figured. What were you hoping to accomplish?"

"Maybe shake the bastard up a bit, I don't know."

"Did you do that?"

"No."

"Do you feel better for going?"

I sat down opposite Sea's desk. "Actually," I said. "Things just got more complicated."

"I'm sure you realize that carrying a machine pistol over to the home of Miami's most notorious crime boss in the company of the new guy in the office labels you a complete dunce."

"So I keep hearing."

"Clark's in with Waco right now."

"Am I going to get fired?"

"I don't know. Waco's pretty pissed about you ignoring a direct order, and about Regina Diaz getting clipped, understand? She's not happy about you spending so much time on those tapes either. You know Clark, he just wants things cool and orderly again."

"I gather there's nothing on the Infiniti sedan?"

"West Palm P.D.'s been through the neighborhood probably a hundred times. Could be in someone's garage under a tarp, could be at the bottom of some drainage canal, could be chopped to parts and sailing to Mexico."

"Where's Potrero?"

"Waco sent him to spend some time in the West Palm L.O.G. No suspects, just routine."

"Great," I sighed. "His reward for helping me out."

The Look Out Gallery at the West Palm Beach Station is an enclosed, elevated catwalk that runs the length and breadth of the work floor. Most large urban post offices have these structures, useful for spying on postal workers and keeping them honest. The advent of video surveillance cameras has made them far less useful, and being sent to spend the day in one, particularly when there wasn't anybody in particular to watch, meant Mozart was spending a day alone in the dark—a clear sign of Wacona's displeasure.

"He is a small but noble soul," Seagrave smiled. "He should get along well with the other noble souls around here."

"So you think I'm noble now? Does this mean you admit that the snuff tapes are real?"

"What makes you think I was talking about you?"

I threw up my hands and retired to my office. Sitting there waiting for Clark to chew me a new orifice didn't appeal to me, but it didn't seem wise to flee. I wasn't in the right humor for paperwork, so, reluctantly, I took the last handful of videos from the sole remaining stack, set up a couple of screens, and sat back to watch.

I had avoided finishing the tapes, not only out of fear of finding another horror show, but out of concern that even the tasteful erotica wouldn't arouse me at all. Since my experience in Phayle's hotel room, I had begun a pattern of subconscious sexual avoidance, and only Guiomary—with whom the idea of any kind of romance was abstact and probably as idiotic as Mozart had declared it—lit even a flicker of interest.

There were only four tapes left, and I was relieved to find that the first one showed nothing so tasteless, cruel, and degrading as what I had seen before. The action chronicled the adventures of a bevy of shipwrecked lovelies—as might an X-rated, lesbian episode of *Gilligan's Island*—and contained almost enough character development and snappy dialog to keep my mind off the meeting happening down the hall.

The next tape followed the exploits of four private detectives who happened to be young, attractive, scantily clad women. They made it their business to use whatever means necessary to extract the information they were after, and they were far more effective than anybody in the United States Postal Inspection Service. There was a certain puerile humor in their antics which elicited a reluctant smile from me.

The third tape was a jerky, grainy documentary of a bachelor party at which absolutely nobody appeared to be having a good time. The girl who popped out of the cake looked to be disgusted by the icing adhering to her privates, the groom glanced at the door to the hotel room at least every fifteen seconds as if expecting his fiancée's father to walk in with a shotgun, and the rest of the men amused themselves by drinking directly from a keg of beer and then slobbering foam all over the stripper's ample chest. I wondered whether I might find another job as a porn critic should John Clark dismiss me. Certainly recent events had left me as dispassionate as an imperial eunuch, and my critical faculties, having seen hundreds of porn videos, were in full flower. Feeling grim, I inserted the fourth and last tape.

The horror show began without preamble. The setting was an industrial interior, a vast cavern with huge, sloping concrete walls. Gigantic machines soaring several stories high filled the interior, and their output made a low rumble. The camera zoomed in on an enormous control panel replete with dials and levers and buttons and knobs. Next to the control panel was an empty wall, and before the wall stood an array of naked, brown-skinned, dark-eyed children looking to be between the ages of eight and fourteen years old. They were likely drugged, as there was little shifting or fidgeting. As the lensman panned the line like a butcher showing off meat, I counted thirty kids.

The view shifted to another location within the same industrial area; a corner where two of the massive concrete slabs came together. Shiny metal eyelets had been screwed into the concrete, two high and two low, and handcuffs dangled from each of them. The lighting was harsh and the shadows were long. I pushed the pause button and rubbed my eyes, blurring the video image and focusing on my bald, pale reflection on the surface of the screen. There were new crow's feet at the edges of my hazel eyes—the irises were more yellow than usual—and the kind of dark circles I usually only get when I've had too much to drink. The stubble on my chin looked gray.

"My God, this has to stop," I said out loud.

I continued watching the tape. A man in denim overalls and a white T-shirt appeared, his face hidden by a black executioner's hood. He had a young girl by the hand, and as he pulled her to the wall and clicked the handcuffs closed around her little wrists and her little ankles, I recognized her from the restaurant snuff. In that tape, the girl had seemed downright disinterested, and she looked the same way here. She didn't object to being fastened to the wall and she didn't object when the man began to systematically cut away her shorts and her blouse with a pair of garden shears. She didn't object when he strummed her nipples with his thumbs, and she didn't object when he lit a small blowtorch with a cap lighter and tuned the flame to a brilliant white. When he knelt before her and began to bring the flame close to her thighs, the camera drew in on her threatened flesh and I thought I could hear the breathing of the cameraman, a faint, rough rasping that grew stronger and clearer the closer the child came to burning.

For an instant, perhaps at the shock of actually smelling seared flesh, the cameraman jerked his instrument skyward, revealing details I hadn't seen before. There were rust stains on the top of the slanting concrete walls, and, indistinctly because the camera was focused for close-up work, I could make out a latticework of girders, or perhaps a catwalk. Then the lens was back to the business at hand, and the torch was drawing a line of fire down the inside of the little girl's thigh.

Her skin bubbled under the torch, and disinterested no more, she began to writhe and scream. The camera moved up to her face—here devoid of the inappropriate makeup she had worn during her table dance—to show eyes wide with terror and a mouth open in agony. Tears were coming, and so was saliva, and the tendons in her neck stuck out like knives. She twisted her head from side to side, yanking at her restraints.

My fist crashed down hard on the VCR and the screen went solid blue. A spot of blood on my desktop caught my eye. I had bitten through my lower lip, and although I didn't feel pain, the flow was copious. My office was silent but for the whirring of the VCR. Someone cleared his throat. I looked up. John Clark was standing in the doorway to my office, looking at me as if I were Charles Manson. Wacona stood behind him, quiet and pale.

"Inspector," said Clark.

"Sir," I said, rising.

"This case you're working on. It's become more than any of us had expected."

"Yes, sir," I wiped my lip.

"The pursuit of the killers at the courthouse, the unauthorized visits to Mr. O'Burke's home and place of business, the hours spent viewing these tapes when you could be working on other cases . . ."

"Excuse me," I interrupted, holding up my hand and smelling my own nervous sweat.

"Max, keep your mouth shut," Wacona warned.

"I'm happy to listen to whatever complaints you've got against me," I continued stubbornly. "In fact, I'm willing to give over my shield and my weapon if that's what you want. But before you make any decision—before you say one more word, I need you to give me exactly ninety seconds of your day. Would you do that, sir?"

Clark caught my eye and held it. I could see the indecision there.

"Max," Wacona interjected. "The I.N.C. doesn't have time . . ."

"Ninety seconds," I repeated.

I saw the specter of budget and efficiency rise to the surface of Clark's soul, and it drove me past desperation and into the arms of a wild gamble, a real stab in the dark, something that had been lurking in the back of my head since my night at the opera with Jeff Grayson and his allusion to my secret society and the inspection service.

"Lyre and Stone," I said.

"I beg your pardon?" Clark's cheeks turned instantly red.

"I'm asking you as one Stoneman to another. Will you do this?"

His carotid throbbed wildly in his neck. "Wacona, would you give us a moment alone?" he asked.

"No," I said flatly. "I work with her. I trust her. She stays."

Wacona glanced back and forth between us. Clark gave a small nod. I offered him my chair, and he took it, careful to avoid the blood on the desk.

I started the tape, and didn't stop it until Wacona opened her eyes and Clark had stopped nervously cracking his knuckles.

"I'm hoping I'm wrong, Max," Phayle's voice issued from my answering machine, "but I have the impression you're avoiding me. If it's something I said, I'm sure you misunderstood, and if it's something else, if there's some*body* else, I think the least you could do is give it to me straight. Anyway, it's not clear that my arrangement with Burdine's is going to fly, but I'm still trying for a software fit, so I'll be in town a while longer. I'm leaving the Delano, though. It's expensive, and the other day I had the spookiest sensation that someone was watching me. Probably some creepy guest with a crush. Can't blame him, knockout that I am, right? I've rented an apartment in Coral Gables. Here's the address and number. Call me, okay?"

Mechanically, I wrote down the information as she read it off. I would call her, and I would go back to poking around the murder of my old classmates, but I couldn't do it right then. I had to get my balance back first. I went to check on Picard. I'd made a therapeutic hothouse out of the john with the infrared heater, and the bubbling at his nose had lessened. I wasn't sure whether to offer him water or withhold it for fear he might drink too much and clog his windpipe with pathogenic mucus. Galapagos tortoises are adapted to such a brutally dry environment that when they have the opportunity to drink they behave like Nero Wolfe at a catered orgy. In the end I gave him a small bowl and watched with satisfaction as he submerged his plated head in the bowl and drank it all down. Afterwards, I forced one more of Guiomary O'Burke's pills down his throat, then took one myself for good measure.

In many ways the last tape had been the most horrible of the bunch. Although it showed no murder, the degradation and torture was nearly as bad, and the line of naked children held the promise of more and worse to come. Still, John Clark's reaction had transformed my private hell into a case I knew the inspection service would now commit to solve, and somehow this lessened my burden. No longer was this my private crusade, I thought with grim satisfaction, and no longer was there any reasonable doubt that the events had been staged. The knot that had been inside me loosened just a fraction, and suddenly I found myself hungry as hell.

I headed for Sara's, hoping for cabbage rolls.

Regrettably, there was no food around and my grandmother was in a foul mood, snapping and cursing at everything in sight.

"Take that Nazi motorcycle away," she snapped. "I don't want to look at it anymore."

"Let me take you out for Chinese food," I suggested.

"Gives me gas," she said irritably.

"Cabbage doesn't give you gas, but Chinese food does?"

"You're a gastroenterologist now? They use oil, it gives me gas. Just wait until you're my age. You won't be able to eat it either."

"Cuban then?"

"Lard," she sniffed.

"Vietnamese?"

"What is it with you and the Orientals? You have some reason you can't eat normal food?"

"Vietnamese food is normal for Vietnamese people," I defended weakly.

"Don't talk like a fool."

"Tell me what's bothering you, Grandma."

"Nothing's bothering me."

"You know better than to lie to me."

"Because I don't want you should permanently leave

that Nazi machine in my garage, this makes me seem up-set?"

I took her hand and led her to the living room couch.

"What happened?" I asked. "Did you have a fight with Sea?"

"Fight is maybe not the word," she sniffed.

"When was he here?"

"Last night."

"And?"

"And nothing. He gave me a ring."

"What kind of ring?"

"Never mind, she said, looking away."

"What kind of ring?" I repeated.

"A diamond," she sniffed.

"May I see it?"

"What is it your business?"

"It's my business because you're my grandmother and he's my friend."

"Some friend. Ha! He walks like a bird."

"Sara," I said threateningly.

She stood up from the couch, looking less vital than I had ever seen her—smaller too, as if Sea Chunny's mar-riage proposal had taken something off her frame and she was no longer able to stand quite as strong and stiff.

"Oy, Max, I don't know what to do."

I rose and took her in my arms. She smelled faintly of lilac water, which was surprising, as she very rarely used the stuff. Last night must have been something.

"You're worried about what Grandpa Isaac would think, aren't you?"

"You think I don't know what he would think? Me tak-ing another man to my bed?"

"You didn't choose Grandpa Isaac. You are free to choose Sea."

"Never say that!" she pushed me back.

"But it's true! You've told me so yourself. It was a different world, a different life, the war, the militia, your father. You did what you had to do and you grew to love him, I know you did. He was a good man. But still, life changes. This is a new chapter now, a new chance. Wherever he is, Grandpa has learned enough to know that. He would want you to be happy. Don't sell him short."

"Who made you the rabbi all of a sudden?" she demanded, puttering around with pots and pans. She dropped a plate, and it shattered on the tile floor. I picked the pieces up.

"You think that because of what happened in the war, the terrible way it all ended for the people you loved, that you don't deserve to be happy," I said. "I think you're wrong."

"You don't know what you're talking about," she snapped.

"If you're saying I don't know what it means to lose my family to Hitler, you're right, although I could argue that your loss was my loss too. But I do know that you doubt you deserve good things, and I'm telling you Sea Chunny is a good thing. He adores you."

Her face brightened a little bit, then fell again. "A boyhood fancy," she said.

"He's not a boy and you know it. And it's one hell of a fancy. He hasn't talked about anything but you in the four years I've known him."

"He's a talker, that's for sure."

"So did you accept the ring or not?"

"I did," she whispered, her eyes filling with tears.

"So that means you said yes?"

"Just shut up, will you, Max?"

"Lemme see it."

"I put it away."

"Well, take it out!"

"All right. Just wait here," she said conspiratorially.

I complied, pretending that I didn't know about the wall safe in the bedroom. As we get older, our habits become tougher to break and our secrets become more important to us. Obviously, Sara did not recall that I was the one who had installed the safe, hiding the door behind a tattered, sepia-toned picture of my grandfather's family, clustered together in front of a temple in a small town in Russia, snow falling all around, the trees bare and black with winter.

She emerged a few moments later with a little jewelry box in hand.

"Four-point-two carats," she said. "A perfect stone."

I held the magnificent gem to the light, where it shimmered and glowed in its platinum setting as if Sea's love were a physical source of light within it.

"It's registered with the FBI," she told me.

I didn't doubt it. Even with Sea's contacts, I knew the diamond must have cost him thirty grand. With it, my friend had unwittingly uncovered a corner of Sara's survivor complex, for even after I talked her into going for Chinese dinner, and even after she gave obvious signs of relief at having shared the secret of the ring with me, she refused to wear it out of the house for fear it would be stolen.

I chose a restaurant on Hillsboro Boulevard, about four miles from Sara's house. We started our meal with a large order of hot-and-sour soup. I added hot sesame oil to mine while Sara clucked disapprovingly about ulcers. Next came Buddha's Delight vegetables, which Sara found too chewy, and chow mein which I found too greasy. We both drank plenty of green tea, which Sara said was a powerful antioxidant guaranteed to make us live longer.

Later, we enjoyed a game of making up stories about the people around us in the restaurant. As always, Sara surprised me with her wit and imagination, concocting a richly textured fantasy about the couple next to us—he a closet ballooner who wished more than anything else to float around the world at high altitude, listening only to the wind and sharing good times with passing gulls, she a seamstress who really wanted to get a good shawl business going.

"Shawl business? Nobody wears shawls anymore!"

"Well she certainly should. Those pudgy, bare shoulders are crying out for coverage," Sara declared.

At her insistence, I came up with my own tale. The family in the booth across the way was in a crisis born of the fact that the child was adopted from China, where female infants are summarily drowned after birth because families prefer male children. The kid was just old enough to begin recognizing that she didn't look like her parents, and they had come to the restaurant tonight as part of a slow process of familiarization with Chinese culture.

"But those people are blond!" my grandmother hissed. "Even the little girl is blond. Who ever heard of a blond Chinese?"

"They are doing very sophisticated things with hair color these days," I said seriously.

"Oy, are you crazy. And what is this business about killing children? You shouldn't even *think* of such a story!"

"I have a wild imagination."

At last, our fortune cookies arrived. The two of them contained the same message; the insight that my grandmother and I would both always war with our past.

"I want insults, I'll call my bridge partners," Sara fumed. "What a load of bullshit."

The Victoria Court section of Fort Lauder-dale—a yuppie, gay community of mostly two-income homes, is not far from Las Olas Boulevard, where the late Regina Diaz had sold wedding dresses. Mozart Potrero lived in an elegant two-story townhouse; new construction with a black electric iron gate across the driveway, sealing in the inspection service's Suburban. There were two bay windows, a one-car garage and a small fenced yard in back.

"It's Max," I said. "I'm here to thank you for covering my ass."

"Fuck you. I just came in from eight hours of L.O.G. duty."

"I heard. I'm sorry. I just had dinner with my grand-mother, but would you let me buy you a beer?"

"How'd you find me?"

"I called Lorraine at home."

"You're just disturbing everybody tonight, huh?"

"That's about right."

There was a click, the gate slid open, and Mozart met me at the door. He was wearing a silk housecoat, and he looked smaller and more slender than he did in a sport jacket and tie. I wasn't sure, but I thought I could faintly make out eyeliner and blush.

"If you have plans, we could make it another time," I offered.

"Routine surveillance! First time in six years I've spent more than an hour in one of those fucking catwalks, and on top of that, it was a total waste! There are video cameras everywhere these days. They should tear the damn look-outs down," he groused, gesturing impatiently for me to come inside.

The place was decorated in the wild colors of a Phuket beach house. A giant pink papier-mâché fish hung from the ceiling above the sweeping staircase, and other, equally jubilant, pieces of folk art—an Indonesian dragon

179

chair in vibrant green, a pink, large-breasted Balinese flying sorceress, a bright blue Mexican iguana — were carefully placed for maximum impact. Between these there was
a tangle of rusting iron furniture; tables, a couple of
uncomfortable-looking high-backed chairs, a quintet of
enormous standing flower vases, each holding a different
selection; fresh cut daisies, roses, birds-of-paradise, cro-
cuses. There were other plants too, veritable trees of a spe-
cies I didn't recognize, with generous fronds that added
to the tropical feel. In the center of the room, on a raised
dais not far from the fireplace, sat a purple fainting couch,
and an overstuffed sofa and love seat combination, both
striped in white and tan. All in all, the place had an artis-
tic, feminine look.

"Beautiful," I murmured.

"Not what you expected, eh?" he smiled. "Inspector
Smith called the range, you know. They told her we hadn't
been there. She even looked at all the MP-5s to see if any
had been fired."

"Terrific," I shook my head. "Look, I appreciate what
you did."

"I know. It's not like I didn't try and stop you. Anyway,
I picked up some bananas on the way home. Would you
like a daiquiri? I warn you ahead of time, I use 151 rum."

"Blend away."

The kitchen was small and opened to the living room.
While he clattered about, I busied myself with a lucite box
of tiny drawers, each holding a diminutive stone animal
carving. I pulled out an onyx eagle and a turquoise bear
with a red arrow to its heart.

"Those are Zuni fetishes," he called from the kitchen.
"I've been collecting them for years."

"There's food in the box here," I said, brushing off a
few grains of rice and a dried pinto bean.

"You have to nourish them in order for them to have

180

power. From time to time I give them some of my dinner."

"Yeah? What kind of power do they have, Mozart?" I asked sarcastically.

"Protection, mostly," he said, looking up from peeling a banana. "I carry one on me all the time as a good luck charm. I've only been shot once in all my time on the job, and obviously it wasn't fatal."

"You attribute your survival to carrying a stone carving?"

"Works for me," he shrugged, dumping a big handful of ice into the blender.

I picked up a sandstone frog with violet jasper eyes and pressed it first to my cheek and then to my lips, hoping I would feel something. There was something about the energy of Mozart's place that encouraged such behavior. "Which ones do you carry?" I asked.

"Snakes, turtles, lizards, or frogs. The way the Zunis see things, primitive animals that ignore the impulses of the mind in favor of the laws of survival are strongest, as they are closest to their true nature. More advanced animals are weaker because they are confused by conflicting thoughts and lack connection with the laws of the universe. I have a few mammal fetishes, but mostly I favor the amphibians and reptiles."

I turned a pipestone turtle in my hand. It was the color of terra-cotta tile, and had white lines etched into the carapace, well-defined feet, a short tail, and eyes of quartz. Mozart ran the blender for a long moment, then brought me a daiquiri glass filled to the very top. The drink was salmon-colored, and garnished with a juicy blackberry.

"I've a pet turtle," I said.

"Yeah?"

"Lives on my porch. Listen, what you said about animals, you think it's true of children too?"

"You mean that they're closer to their true nature because they haven't yet been polluted by the mad world of adults?"

"Something like that."

"Sure, I think that's true."

"Then why are they so helpless?"

"There are different ways to be powerful. Kids manipulate us through our heartstrings. Their weakness is their strength."

"They're strong all right," I agreed.

"So is Cuco O'Burke," he said. "You better stay away from his daughter."

"Probably right. But here's to her stitching my leg, and here's to you for taking the rap for me with Wacona." He smiled and we clinked glasses. The cold daiquiri made my sinuses ache, but it was delicious.

"How do you afford such a nice spread?" I asked.

Mozart tucked his silk robe in tight around his bare legs and shook his head. "You're tactful like a steamroller, especially since I hear you've got money of your own put away. The place belonged to a rich friend, okay? We were together for eight years. When we split up, I kept the house. Any other questions?"

"You seeing anybody now?"

"Just playing the field."

"Safely, I hope."

"Listen to you. Probably learned to talk like that from your granny."

"It's just that Palm Beach can't afford to lose another good inspector," I said, feeling sentimental.

"Don't worry, I'm like a balloon vendor in a rose garden. How about you? Anybody in your life?"

"Sometimes," I smiled. "Recently an old flame showed up."

"Yeah? Personally, I never play the same instrument

twice. Way I look at it, there's a whole orchestra out there."

"It's complicated," I said.

"It's always complicated."

"Mozart, let me ask you something, and don't be offended, okay? But when you look at a guy, do you, you know, turn on the x-ray vision like I do with a girl?"

"You turn on x-ray vision?"

"Sometimes, yeah."

"You mean strip them down in your mind, see what their hips look like, their belly looks like, their chest, everything?"

"Well, not always in such anatomic detail, but yes."

"You're asking me whether I use my eyes to strip search every cute guy I see?"

"I guess I am."

"I guess I do." He refilled our glasses from the blender. "This'll be better than the first round. The flavors have had more time to interact."

He was right. The second drink was tropical heaven. "151-proof yum," I stretched. "Nothing quite like it. Nothing quite like Guiomary O'Burke, either. You gotta admit she's a class act."

"I don't gotta, but I will. Look, Max, can I ask you a favor?"

"Go."

"I'd like to see a little t'ai chi ch'uan."

"I'm not big on demonstrations."

"Maybe not, but you owe me."

"I don't practice when I'm tight."

"I won't run a camera."

I looked around. They say you can practice t'ai chi ch'uan in four square feet, but Mozart's place was so cluttered, Minnie and Mickey would have had trouble with a mouse minuet. "There's not much room."

"We could go out to the deck," he persisted.

When I didn't say anything, he flung the doors open wide. The setting wasn't bad. It had been a warm day, and the city lights made the clouds glow like ghosts.

"Okay," I held up my hands. After all, I did owe him.

The orange and grapefruit trees were blooming, filling the yard with their sweet scents. Mozart lit the CD player—I didn't have the heart to tell him that music ruined my concentration—and the strains of Strauss's Acceleration Waltz came wafting out of the house. He pulled a metal chair out of the dining area and sat across it backwards, his robe falling open on a ropy little chest with a thin line of dark, central hair. He looked wispy and vulnerable and not at all like a cop. Maybe there was something to those Zuni fetishes after all.

I started the form, working my way through the press and the push, the traps and the blocks, the spins and the kicks. I increased my tempo in time to the music, finishing with a speedy but precise flourish as the Strauss crescendo peaked.

"Fantastic!" Mozart cried admiringly.

"Just a matter of practice," I responded, flushed and breathing hard.

"The way I've seen old people do it in the park, I figured it was just a dance. Your movements look stronger, but weirder too.

"That's the way the real thing looks," I nodded. "It's all about marrow and muscle and tendon and bone, breathing and alignment. The internal landscape. It's not really *supposed* to look pretty."

"Do you imagine an opponent?"

"Usually not. The overarching principle of it is just to keep your own equilibrium. Basically, I'm ignoring my adversary and concentrating on myself. That's why they call it an internal art."

"So it's purely defensive."

"In a way, yes. But it's also totally devastating. The cruellest, nastiest thing there is."

"You think so?"

"Try to work a come-along on me, like I'm a bad guy and you're going to take me in."

Suddenly, he was trying to put my arm behind my back as he would a perp's, straining the shoulder, getting ready for a takedown or at least a cuffing. I relaxed, going with it, spiralling into him, returning the trap and lightly following through. He went into the air like a child's top and careened across the garden. He gained more altitude than I had expected he would, partly because his stiffness locked his body, stopping him from absorbing any of my energy. His arms and legs wheeled crazily in mid-air and his robe flew open, revealing silk boxers decorated with giant, turn-of-the-century pedal bikes. "Wow," he managed, coming to rest on the grass.

"You all right?"

He brought his hands to his chest and felt himself timidly. "I think so. What the hell happened there?"

"You attempted to rob me of my alignment, and I wouldn't let you."

"What does that mean?"

"It's all based on Chinese medicine," I explained. "Meridian theory, the idea of energy, *qi*, flowing through the body along pathways and nourishing the organs."

"I've heard of *qi*. They use the same term in aikido," said Mozart.

"All Oriental martial arts and medical systems have the concept. Even yoga has it. Calls it *prana*. Different words for life force. It flows through my body like water through a network of garden hoses. Attack me—kink or compress one of the garden hoses—and I have to straighten those

185

hoses out. What happens to you is incidental, as far as I'm concerned."

"Thanks," he said dryly, rubbing his back.

"But you see the philosophy behind it. Keep your own equilibrium."

"Even if it causes someone else heavy trouble."

"The heavy trouble comes as result of what *they* do, not what I do. If you didn't try and grab me, everything would have been fine. The energy you put in came right back to you."

"You put in more than I did," he stood, rubbing his back.

"It always feels that way, but actually I didn't."

"So anyone that touches you goes spinning off into the wild blue yonder? Shit, if I'd known about this I wouldn't have tried to talk you out of rousting O'Burke."

"It doesn't work against bullets," I said.

"There is that."

"There is. You don't have to go spinning away, though. If I return your force with less spin and more penetration, I can disrupt internal organs."

"Like the death touch in kung fu movies? Delayed damage that shows up later, so you can't be blamed?"

"Or right away."

"Still not as effective as an M16," he said.

"Not as effective as our MP-5 machine pistols either, but you don't always have those with you. My skill, though, is always in my body."

"Incipient violence. The human bomb. It fascinates you, huh, Max?"

Suddenly the booze came back and I felt a wave of fatigue bordering on nausea. "The elegance of the system is something I adore," I said. "And the lessons it teaches me about personal balance, well, they're everything to me. But the violence . . . Frankly Mozart, it repels me more than you can imagine."

TEN

The Virginia air bore the crisp crack of young winter as I left my rented car, the blowtorch video tucked under my arm, and strode across the parking lot. The concrete building before me was squat and compact, the windows trimmed in red metal, the walls lightened by blue stripes. Second in size only to the FBI's facility, the National Forensic Laboratory in Dulles handled everything but serology, and was the largest of several U.S.P.I.S. labs across the country.

I gave my name to the receptionist, and a few moments later, a fresh-faced young inspector, fit and blonde and WASPy, appeared at the thick bullet-proof glass doors to the inner sanctum. He buzzed me in and introduced himself as Ron Woodward.

"John Clark asked that we extend you every courtesy," he said, taking my hand in a hard shake. "I hear this case of yours is a runaway train."

"It sure keeps getting worse."

"We've been working on the other tapes all morning," he told me, leading me down the hall.

"Anything?"

"I'll let the tech fill you in. You been up here before?"

"No. Only to the Memphis lab."

"I'm just learning the ropes myself. They're miracle workers, you know. Last week, we handled a case where this guy mailed a bomb to a rich couple for revenge and blew them both to atoms. The field boys couldn't nail him because he cleaned his shop out so well you could have performed open-heart surgery in there. On a lark, the inspector on the case had a look under his kitchen sink, found a red plastic toolbox with Stanley screwdrivers, a cheap socket set, gaskets for the garbage disposal, and a pair of fifty-buck wire cutters; fancy Solingen steel, curved handles."

"The kind of thing a guy would hate to throw away," I ventured.

"Exactly. So the inspector brings the snippers in here, and we do a microscopic match between the marks on the blade and the nicks on the wire. We're talking a wire as thin as a human hair, but the match held up in court and the guy went down for life, no parole."

I stopped for a moment outside a room that looked like something out of my old high school Science room.

"Chemistry," Woodward said off-handedly.

"Poison by mail?"

"Sure. Drugs, too. We can I.D. a particular kind of crack or snow by how strong it is, what's used to cut it. If we can tie manufacturing and production to pushing or using, the sentencing guidelines change. Also, sometimes we can make a case by proving the stuff comes from a particular batch."

We turned the corner, and I noticed photocopies of enlarged fingerprints tacked to the wall. One of the hanging prints showed whorls that made a happy face. Another seemed to clearly read "666."

"Our fingerprint techs do serious work with photos, laser, cyanoacrylate, and ninhydrin, but they have a sense of humor. This Satanic print belongs to one of the secretaries. A sweet old lady who makes shortbread cookies for the whole lab every Friday."

"Feed one of those cookies to a lab rat before you eat it."

"You're not the first to suggest it," he laughed. We headed down a staircase covered by hard-rubber matting and into the bowels of the lab. "This is where we make the AT-three and the AT-four" he said, pointing to an electronics lab on the right and referring to the tiny, high-tech tracking transmitters used in controlled deliveries.

"Any new toys I should know about?" I asked.

"I doubt it. Mostly those guys are just looking for new ways to hide surveillance cameras. We've got false transformers on the tops of power poles, we've got cameras in traffic lights and mailboxes."

"Sounds like Big Brother to me."

"Keeps those postal workers honest, and keeps guys like you from having to live on stakeout."

"God bless electronics," I said, thinking of Mozart in the L.O.G.

The tour ended at the video lab, where Woodward left me in the company of a technician named Rudy Schlimmer. He looked about eighty. He peered at me through thick lenses and stuck out his hand impatiently for the tape I had brought.

"I've been waiting for over a week for word on the first three tapes we sent. Now you're in a hurry?" I said acidly.

Schlimmer gave me a hard look and pointed at the wall

of evidence—audio tapes, video tapes, still negatives, prints.

"Inspectors all over the country are waiting for word too. You just got clout all of a sudden, that's all."

If he was trying to make me feel guilty, he failed. I didn't care about cases all over the country, I cared about this one. "Just tell me what you've got so far," I snapped.

"There was no visible serial number on the Gold Cup Colt, and the menus were blanks. The vegetation on the goat film looks South American, but that's about all I can say."

"What about the language the guy was speaking?" I interrupted.

"Nobody here was able to identify it. We have consultants who may be able to do better."

"And the murder at sea?"

"Without any coastline or I.D. on the boat, it doesn't offer much."

"How about the soundtracks?"

"Every amateur tape has background sounds. Wasn't much there, though."

"You think the snuff was real?"

Schlimmer lowered his thick glasses onto the bridge of his nose. "You're kidding, right?"

"Sure as hell seemed real to me, but my team leader thought the guy fired a blank."

"A blank doesn't spatter a woman's gray matter across the table."

"Sea Chunny said the brains might have been Hollywood."

"Seagrave Chunny said that? He ought to know better."

"What about the casings?"

"Whoever made the tapes was clever enough to use a generic Taiwanese cassette, sandwiching the bad stuff right in the middle of run-of-the-mill porn, not even splicing so we could analyze the emulsion, but recording right over legal scenes. We've already checked with the distributors of the tape. They claim to know nothing and we believe them. A handful of tapes out of the tens of thousands they wholesale is an insignificant number, and of course we have no retailers to grill."

He popped the new tape into a player, and the next instant the sad line of nude children popped into view. Schlimmer swayed suddenly, like he was about to fall down, and his hands flew to his face. I caught a glimpse of faded blue digits on his left wrist.

"Hey, Schlimmer, I'm sorry," I said.

"At Dachau, we were thinner," he replied distantly. Suddenly I could smell his breakfast on his breath—cream cheese and chives, a hint of sesame seeds.

"I didn't know. I would have given this to someone else."

"I was about that age when they took me from my parents. I never saw them again. I have images in my brain, snapshots that don't fade. It's what led me to photography. I thought I could work them out on film, exorcise them. When I first got to this country, I worked weddings, trying to replace what was in my head with happy scenes. Then I went into forensics, to stop the denial."

"Did it work?"

"I'm still here, right? Lots of people I know overdosed on sleeping pills."

"Maybe now you understand why I used clout to get your help."

"Maybe," he murmured, advancing the film frame by frame with digital controls.

"It's in my head too," I said. "I know it's not the same."

"No," he said curtly, "it isn't."

For a moment I wanted to try and tell him what had happened in my life since I'd seen the first tape, but I didn't know where to start. I let it go. "You think you can pull something out of this one?" I asked instead.

"This is video image enhancement software specially developed for law enforcement. I can do most anything with the images."

Indeed, the resolution was far superior to the player in my office. I could see tiny hairs on the arms of some of the children. "Check out that control panel," I pointed at the screen. "What do you make of it?"

"Some kind of factory," he said, tugging on his white beard. He used a computer mouse to draw a square on the screen, enveloping a panel beneath one of the dials, a panel on which tiny letters were written. He punched a couple of keyboard keys, and the outlined area was magnified. The lettering was blurred, but still easy to read.

MW/H

"Megawatts per hour?" I asked.

"A generator," Schlimmer nodded. He used his mouse again and identified another, larger readout, this one digital.

M^3/S

"Cubic meters per second?" I speculated.

"Flow," Schlimmer said thoughtfully.

"A generator with a flow meter?"

"A hydroelectric plant," he said suddenly. He let the tape roll on, then stopped on a flash of international orange, and cleaned up the image. It was a triangle with an exclamation mark in the middle—a warning sign. He enlarged and enhanced it so that we could read the writing on the bottom, above the rusting metal edge.

"*Itaipú Binacional,*" I read slowly. "What the hell is that?"

Schlimmer settled back into a chair and stared at me through his thick glasses. "Iguaçu Falls ring a bell?"

I shook my head.

"It's where they dammed the Paraná River—on the border of Paraguay and Brazil—to make the largest hydro-electric facility in the world."

"Paraguay," I repeated.

"It's a wonder of the modern world."

He ran the film back a few seconds to the soaring interior, the cantilevered catwalk. "I bet this is inside the dam!" I breathed.

Schlimmer ran the rest of the tape on high-speed-forward. I turned away, unwilling to watch the burning for a third time. Schlimmer's armpits grew dark, and the smell of his nervous sweat wafted my way. The odor brought back a memory.

Sara's husband, my grandfather Isaac, was driving me across the Brooklyn Bridge on the way into Manhattan one winter night when I was still a teenager. The lights of the city were twinkling before us, and the air was frigid and spitting snow flurries. Suddenly we heard a crash ahead. My grandfather slammed on the brakes in his ratty old Chevy Nova, but we hit one of the slippery steel plates on the roadway and went sideways. Something had flown through the air and thumped loud and hard beneath our wheels. When the car stopped, Isaac was frozen at the wheel, *davining* the way Jews do in synagogue. I'd jumped out and found the crushed and twisted body of a young woman lying beneath the car. Her extruded tongue was blue, and blood was streaming from her nose. Isaac came slowly out of the car, in some kind of shock, and we both stood there staring at the corpse. The smell of my grandfather's nerves flew right through the night like a missile

193

to my nose. It took nearly an hour for the police to conclude that she'd been dead before we hit her, a homicide victim dumped on the roadway. Isaac sobbed like a baby at the news, and even though I barely knew how to drive, I took the wheel and somehow got him home.

Schlimmer stopped the tape on a frame filled mostly with the white flame of the blowtorch. The fingers that held the torch were shown in amazing detail.

"Take a close look at that hand," he said, pointing at a little half-moon shaped scar in the webbing between the right thumb and forefinger, "and try to keep the image in your head."

He ran the fisherman tape forward, stopping at the moment of the killing, and zoomed in on the grip and the knife. "Same scar!" I exclaimed.

Schlimmer nodded matter-of-factly. "But what's really interesting is the thumb; how clear it is. Very unusual for video. Let's see what we can do with it."

The technique that followed was a tour-de-force of computer imaging. Schlimmer took a computer "snapshot" of the thumb in the burning sequence and in the knifing scene. He printed the images on a high-resolution printer, and then scanned them into his computer. Once he had both thumb images in memory, he carefully superimposed one on the other until he had a complete thumb. It wasn't until he had zeroed in on the finger pad that I realized what he was doing.

"You're going for a *fingerprint*?" I asked incredulously.

He nodded vigorously, his spectacles bobbing on his head. I watched as he continued to juggle the image until the edges of the thumb lined up smoothly and perfectly. "Getting it clear enough to actually do the print is going to take time. I have to clean up the lines, separate scratches or marks on the emulsion, erase any artifacts of the joining process."

"How long?"

Schlimmer shrugged. "It's painstaking work. There are no shortcuts. But know you're at the top of my list."

ELEVEN

I figured that with John Clark on my side, I could afford to stretch things a little bit with Wacona. I called in and let her know I had ceased official business and was taking a little personal time. I promised I'd work out the difference between ticket prices when I got back to West Palm, then hopped a commuter flight to White Plains, New York. I rented a Subaru because it looked like it might snow, and drove the Merritt Parkway to Westport, Connecticut.

In the days before World War II, nobody commuted to Manhattan from Westport. The hustle and bustle of the city seemed a thousand miles away, and potters and water-color painters enjoyed true peace and quiet. There wasn't much more to the town than the strip of homes along Compo Beach back then, and the only restaurants were a bakery famous for eat-in blueberry muffins and a single Italian emporium best known for *gnocchi bolognese* prepared by the chef's maternal aunt. Even in winter, most everyone walked on the beach, and gulls sang a particular song to announce marine storms. Neighbors knew each other, there was a farmer's street market every Tuesday, and artwork was sold streetside on weekends.

The post-war economy changed everything. Jobs in New York paid enough to warrant the commute, and the boundaries of the city grew, making Westport seem closer. A new breed moved in, still creative, but with more of an eye to a dollar. Graphic artists, industrial designers, even advertising copywriters began to call Westport home. Beach shacks were replaced with solid Cape Cod style construction. Widow's walks appeared on some houses. There was a brief spurt of Bohemianism during the 1960s, but it faded, and the yuppies descended en masse. The town grew quickly. Mansions cropped up. Volkswagens and pickup trucks gave way to Studebakers and later to Cadillacs, Volvos, BMWs, and Benzes. The waters of Long Island Sound became so dirty that the ubiquitous diamondback terrapin all but disappeared. Shelling grew spotty, and eating local clams became occasionally perilous. The real artists moved to nearby Easton and Redding and South Norwalk. The local high school became noted for its drug trade, Main Street for its abundance of overpriced boutiques. Money wound up tearing the town's character asunder.

As I drove in that day, the clouds looked about to burst, and the sad winter trees glistened with ice. I cracked the window in hopes of catching the warning gullsong, but heard only the car horns of impatient commuters trying to get home before the storm hit. I circled downtown and headed east toward the beach, turning down one of the smaller side streets near the old Boston Post Road, a section where some of the original cottages still stood — a last bastion of affordability in what had long ago become an utterly unaffordable town.

Taylor, my mother, was waiting for me in the driveway. No doubt she had been peering out the window for at least an hour, her face hidden behind the drapes so as to conjure an air of mystery and imply some arcane prescience. Tall with thinning hair— she'd passed me the latter gene— she gave me a quick hug when I stepped out of the car.

"Look what I have," I sang, waving a large manilla envelope in the air, the contents making a sound like a baby's rattle.

"An envelope?"

"A present!"

"For me?" she clasped her chest.

Such are the games that span the fjords of generations. With my grandmother, the routine centered around whom I had shot dead that day. With my mother it centered around seeds. I held them aloft, just out of her reach, and she swiped for them, pretending to give up, then jumping slyly and catching the bottom of the envelope. She tore the envelope open, and plunged her hand in, coming out with several little packages. I had bought them from a Palm Beach mail-order outfit that I'd helped to recover merchandise stolen from the mail.

"Aloe vera," she read happily. "This needs cactus soil to grow properly, you know. I just happen to have some."

She reached in again, this time coming out with milk thistle and cumin, then Saint-John's-wort, goldenseal, black elderberry, feverfew and mountain laurel.

"Saint-John's-wort is just the thing for your father's depressions! Oh, thank you, thank you. They're all fabulous!" she crowed.

"Have seeds, will travel," I grinned. "And they're all organic. I made sure of it."

My mother created therapeutic folk-medicine concoctions for her friends and for her own varicose veins and my father's sundry ills. She took up the practice after what happened to Rachel, after she lost her faith in Western medicine. She believed in homeopathy and chiropractic, understood the value of Chinese preparations—it was her interest in Oriental medicine that had led to my first martial arts lessons—and had long been a skilled herbologist, preferring to grow her own plants whenever possible.

"How long can you stay?" she asked, taking me by the elbow and guiding me toward the front door.

"Just overnight. I'm in the middle of a big case."

"Can you tell me about it?"

"I wouldn't do that to you."

We stepped inside. The home, light and airy primarily because of the plants, had been purchased with money left to my mother by her parents. As always, the interior was heavy with a distinctly earthy odor, and the combined fragrances of perhaps a hundred different wild plants grew in window boxes in every room. If they could have afforded it, I knew my mother would have loved a greenhouse, but they were living off the interest from funds my father had stashed away when he knew the Bureau was onto him years before—foreign currency deals, part ownership in a small textile mill in Brussels, an account he had on the Isle of Skye—things that the IRS suspected, but never could prove. The ongoing subterfuge—more precisely, the need to avoid the paper trail generated by bank accounts and credit cards—necessitated a cash existence, exacerbating the paranoia my father had suffered since his arrest.

"He's waiting for you in the den," she said. "Go say hello."

"I flew thirteen hundred miles and he couldn't walk from the other room?"

"Please don't start, Max."

The ten foot hallway to my father's study seemed a mile long and my feet felt like lead. When I entered the room, my father was sitting behind his desk, his fingers on the keys of a computer. There was nothing else on his desk but an ashtray and a tiny faded color picture of Rachel.

"You net surf much?" he asked without preamble. His skin was pallid in the glow of the monitor, but he seemed more energetic than the last time I had seen him, flushed with excitement at the discovery of the on-line universe.

"When I need to."

He tapped the side of his computer with his finger. "Trust me, you need to, boy! This here is the wave of the future. Want to know my prediction? Electronic mail puts you out of a job within five years. No more mail to protect, you see?"

"It sounds as if that would please you."

"Don't be silly. It's just a matter of seeing what's going on and getting there soon enough. There's a whole new culture emerging. A nation of smart guys with money and time who are questioning everything, including authority. They're not too keen on law enforcement either, by the way. I only wish I were young enough to join them — my God, the way they communicate! No intermediaries, no press, no media, no politicos, just man-to-man, over these wired-up little boxes. They fight, but they're polite; they have problems, but they solve them; they're materially oriented, but they spend hours, days, discussing metaphysics, the why-are-we-here, the what-should-we-do. It's incredibly energizing to be in their company."

I could see it energized *him* anyway. He rose from his seat as if lifted by an Atlas booster and his grip was firm and dry.

"Good to see you, Dad."

"And you." We stared at each other for a long moment.

"Hey, does the name Itaipú ring a bell?" I asked at last.

"The big South American hydroelectric project?" he frowned.

"That's the one," I answered, thinking that everyone seemed to know of the dam except me.

"I know it could light up California. There's a waterfall there, one of the biggest in the world."

"Iguaçu."

"That's right. Beautiful place. I went there once, working on an ad campaign for Volkswagen Brazil. Don't imagine it's so pretty now, though, with locks and sluice gates and that great big concrete wall. Shame what we're doing to the world. Costa Rica's still good, though. Your mother and I just might retire there."

"Why?" I asked carefully.

"Switzerland of Central America. Stable government. Low cost of living. Tropical paradise."

And no IRS, I thought. "You're already retired," I ventured.

He waved his hand impatiently. "I'm just in a quiet phase right now, looking for the right thing to sink my teeth into. The Internet helps, you know. I've always been good at keeping my finger on the pulse of industry. When I was famous, people used to come to me for predictions of future market trends. Why, I could . . ."

"How are you fixed for money?" I interrupted. I'd heard the speech a thousand times before, and somehow he always managed to leave out the part about embezzlement and fraud.

"We're fine, Max."

"You sure you couldn't use a little help?"

"From you? On your government salary? I guess not."

"Just offering," I said evenly.

He shook his head, reached for a meerschaum pipe sculpted into the head of a goat, and scraped the bowl with his thumbnail. We stood there in uncomfortable silence until my mother came in.

"Chinese dinner?" she suggested brightly. "I know how you like it. There's a new place in town. The atmosphere isn't much, but the food is good."

"Let's phone in an order and have Max pick it up," my father replied.

"Let them deliver. I've been traveling all day."

"Fine. I'll have the orange beef," my father declared.

"Forget the beef, Ernst," my mother replied. "Have the Hunan eggplant. It's better for your plumbing."

"I'll have the eggplant, you have the spinach. The calcium will keep your brittle bones from breaking."

"My bones are just fine," she said. "I'm having chow mein."

"And I'm having beef."

"The beef has a sesame seed garnish. It gives you colitis."

While they glowered at each other, I went to the kitchen, called the restaurant, and ordered a completely different selection that covered all the bases; wonton soup, tofu with vegetables, cashew chicken, cold noodles with Szechuan sauce, and beef with snow pea pods. When I came back, they were sitting together on the couch, watching television as if nothing had happened.

"Food's on the way," I announced.

"So when are you due for a promotion?" my father inquired.

"Bad question."

"Are you dating?" asked my mother.

"I've met somebody," I said.

"What does she do?" asked my father.

I allowed myself a brief but vivid fantasy of me and Guiomary O'Burke alone in a private hospital room. "She's a doctor."

"Good boy!" Ernst exclaimed. "What's her specialty?"

"Internal medicine."

"Then get started already! I want grandchildren, god-damnit!"

"Stop it right now, Ernst. Max, Phayle Tollard called here. I gave her your number. I hope that was all right."

"Now *she* was a looker," my father nodded enthusiastically. "Do you remember when we walked in on the two of you having sex in the family room?"

My mother pinched him hard on the arm, and he jumped back. "She was a lovely girl, Ernst," she said.

"The world is full of lovely girls! Why do you want him to go backwards? A man needs new challenges. A man needs new frontiers. High school sweethearts are for high school."

"I was in high school when I met *you*," my mother said mildly.

"I met Phayle in college, not high school," I said.

"College," my father snorted. "A Yale degree to become a postal cop."

"I'm not a postal cop. Postal cops are almost extinct, and they serve only to protect post offices. I'm a postal inspector. Besides, maybe I would have studied harder at Yale if I hadn't counted on entering your advertising business when I got out."

"Maximillian, don't," my mother warned.

My father glared at me. I scanned a copy of *TV Guide* and wondered why the hell I had come. I heard the clock on the mantel ticking.

"You can go back to pharmaceutical sales, you know," my father said at last. "This inspector thing doesn't have to be forever. Whatever you may think of me, I've still got a few contacts."

"I'm happy where I am, but thanks for the offer."

His disappointment showed. He wanted nothing more

than to get me out of law enforcement. He thought of my badge as a wedge between us. He was probably right.

We watched the television for a while; a program on brushes with death. A man fell out of a canoe in class five rapids and tumbled end-over-end through sharp rocks, frequently disappearing in the churn. A race car driver slammed into a concrete wall, raining car parts on a terrified crowd as he slid along the roadway like a gravity-bound comet. A sky diver's parachute failed to open, and she hit the ground feet-first, sinking so deep into a marsh that only her head protruded from the muck. A motorcycle stuntman soared off a ski jump and flew straight into a tree.

"Anybody who rides a motorcycle has a death wish," my father grumbled. He didn't know about the R90S. That was my secret with Sara.

"It's amazing what they put on television screens these days," my mother shook her head.

"You have no idea," I muttered.

The doorbell rang. Dinner at last.

Nobody ate it but me.

TWELVE

The Coral Gables law offices of Grayson, Boatwright and Hughes smelled like the inside of a clean airplane. While I was waiting to see Clifton, a secretary explained that the odor was ozone. The whole place was wired for negative ion generators — machines that charged dust particles and caused them to fall from the air. The generators — in combination with the oft-dusted work surfaces of rosewood and glass — apparently spared Cliff's highly allergic throat and nose.

The secretary was in her late fifties, with legs like ship cannons and a beehive hairdo in which she stored implements; a red magic marker, a plastic mechanical pencil, a thin rolling ball pen of avant-garde design, and a little penlight.

"I know he's sorry to keep you waiting," she told me, talking while she typed rapidly on her word processor. "He's grateful that you've come. He thinks very highly of you. The world is really on poor Mr. Hughes's shoulders these days. The world, and, of course, the firm."

"It's been a tragic time," I said.

"It certainly has. Awful. There's a cloud over every-thing we do. Still, Mr. Hughes is doing his best to rise to the occasion."

I picked up a copy of *National Geographic* while I waited and skimmed a story about Mexican cave bats. Their ears were the most sensitive of any animal in the world. I wished that my own ears had done more for me lately. Despite all my eavesdropping I had no idea what was going on between my old friends, but the Diamond equivalent of bat sonar told me there was some tangled web there. This seemed a good time to try and unravel it. Rudy Schlimmer needed at least one more day to work on the tapes, and Wacona—responding to John Clarke's di-rection—was no longer pressuring me to move on to other cases.

Cliff finally emerged from his inner sanctum. He looked beleaguered and exhausted, but he tried to buck up for me.

"Thanks for coming, M. D. I'm awfully sorry about the wait."

"It's okay," I said as I followed him into his office. "I got to read about bats."

His digs looked like they had sustained hurricane dam-age. The top of his desk was awash in briefs, orders and other legal documents. Scores of yellow sticky-pads grew out of the telephone like dandelions, and even extended to the sides of a three foot scale model of the *Hindenburg* suspended by wires from the ceiling in the middle of the room. It was a beautiful toy. The miniature guy wires sus-pended from the gondola were elegantly braided, like the brake lines on a racing motorcycle, and the passenger win-dows were of precision cut glass, revealing miniature state rooms and dining facilities. The girders of the airframe were welded to perfection, and the balloon itself was of finely woven silk.

"It's not usually this much of a mess in here," he said, steering me past it to a seat in front of his desk. "But this pace and pressure are tough on me. I'm trying my best to hold it all together. It's hard to cope when I'm so scared, M. D. I count myself as lucky every minute I don't get a bullet in the head or poison in my coffee. Have you been to see Nora Boatwright?"

"No," I said slowly. "Seems to me, you and Jeff and Twy were mostly about work, so I figure you're a better source of information than she is. Besides, I don't know her at all, and Metro-Dade is working on the case."

"But they're not getting anywhere, are they? They'd have told me if they were, and I haven't heard word one from Steiner." He looked around the room, desperation on his face. "Honestly, I don't know how much longer I can keep this up."

"Maybe you should consider a vacation," I said carefully.

"Oh, that's rich, Max," he gave an ugly laugh. "Just walk away from a couple hundred ongoing cases? Send all the secretaries, researchers, and paralegals home, give the courts a buzz and tell them I'm off on holiday? That'll go over *real* well."

"How about hiring more help?"

He sighed and nodded. "I've already held three interviews. Got another one tomorrow, a smart young guy from the University of Miami. I sit here and I look at these kids and I think about when we were that young and hungry. I try and guess what Twy would say about each candidate, what Jeff would think. I was always the impulsive one, Twy the generous, positive influence, Jeff the tactician. We balanced each other, the three of us did. That's why the firm was so successful."

"I'm sure you're right," I said, remembering Jeff Grayson's blind-to-the-world focus and Twy Boatwright's bland, alcoholic generosity. "But you're at the helm now. The firm will become whatever you want it to be."

"True," Cliff responded, looking as if he'd just awakened from a fog. "Look, I'm considering a bodyguard. Whaddya think?"

"Hire one if it makes you feel better, but you can't glue him to your chest. Whoever got to Jeff and Twy did so privately, in an intimate place. I'd get a good home security system instead, and I'd think carefully about my daily routine. Write things down—where you go at what time, what route you take, and then deliberately vary it all. Change health clubs, if you go to one. If you don't, you might consider starting. Exercise is a great natural tranquilizer. Sell your car and buy a totally different model. Choose a new route home from work. Don't go back to your favorite bar. Find someplace new."

Cliff stared at me for a long moment, as if surprised to find I really was a law-enforcement professional, then jotted down a few notes. "My first legal position was as a public prosecutor," he said. "I know that cases that aren't solved in the first few days get filed under 'chicken shit' in a hurry. You gotta help me keep the steam on this guy Steiner."

"I've been off on inspection service business," I said guiltily. "I'll check with him soon. Have you thought about the Lyre and Stone angle?"

"I've thought about it, but I've thrown it right out. It's such a long shot. We might as well look at the country club where we all played golf, or the restaurant where we all ate lunch."

"What have you given Steiner to work with?"

"I sent a few dozen case files over his way yesterday, stuff I pulled from the records of the last two years."

"A few *dozen?*" I repeated.

He nodded, lifted a cardboard box from beside the desk, cleared a space with the edge of it, set it down on the desk. "Clients that were unhappy, clients whose *spouses* were unhappy, a handful of Jeff's real estate deals that went south and stung investors, three or four of Twy's corporate cases not decided in the company's favor. Here, I've made you copies." He pushed the box toward me.

"I'll look them over," I told him.

"Thanks. You can't know how much this means to me."

"I have a pretty good idea."

"Maybe," he leaned back, made a temple of his fingers on his chest. "So what's with *your* life, Max? Forget my problems."

"It's been ten years, Cliff. I don't know where to start, and if I did, I'm not sure I'd want to."

"Fine, fine. Have you seen Phayle Tollard?"

"Not since the funeral," I said quickly. "You?"

"No," he lied.

"Hell of a coincidence, her showing up just when Twy died," I ventured.

"She's got some kind of work here, isn't that right?"

"Computer software for Burdine's."

"There you go," he smiled.

"You're married, aren't you, Cliff?"

His expression didn't change. It was obvious he'd had practice when it came to Memphis. "Sure, you know that, M.D."

"I missed your wife at the funeral. What's her name?"

"Memphis."

"Got a picture?"

That brought a shadow to his face. He rustled through his papers, came up with a small silver frame, and thrust it at me. Memphis was wearing a white bikini, and al-

211

though she was clearly a large woman, she was curvaceous and toned, with very little evidence of fat. Her breasts were full and round and close enough together for a knockout cleavage. Her belly was nearly flat, her thighs muscular.

But it was her face that was most dramatic—high cheekbones, sculpted features, and full lips framed in thick raven hair. Her chin was clear and strong and there was a provocative insouciance in the way she gazed at the camera. She was absolutely stunning. If she hadn't had the same challenging eyes I'd seen at the pool, I would never have believed she was the same woman.

"What's a babe like this doing with a chump like you?" I managed.

"Something I ask myself on a daily basis." He smiled weakly.

"Must be love."

He didn't seem to hear.

Burdine's is a South Florida department store chain whose general mien is somewhere between Neiman Marcus and Macy's; its stuff is a little high, but it goes on sale a lot. I'd been in the store a few times, mostly to pick up perfume for a date or to check its sport coats near the turn of a season, but I had never paid any special attention to its checkout computers, or the way stock was handled.

Nor, apparently, had the receptionist who answered the phone at the chain's corporate office. The phrase "inventory management software" did nothing more than get me bounced from department to department for ten minutes. Finally, I reached the Data Processing Division.

"Roland Dreyfuss," said a stiff, formal voice. "How can I help you."

"I'd like to speak to the manager."

"You got him."

"Wonderful. The name is Max Diamond. I'm a friend of Phayle Tollard, and I just thought you might know where she is."

"Who?"

"Phayle Tollard," I repeated. "I called her hotel and she wasn't in. I thought I might catch her there."

"This is the Data Processing Division at Burdine's," Dreyfuss said slowly. "There's nobody named Tollard here."

"Sure there is," I persisted with growing suspicion. "She's doing your inventory management software."

"That function is handled in-house," Dreyfuss said guardedly.

"By Phayle Tollard."

"I told you I don't know any Phayle Tollard."

"But she said she was developing a new program for you. Said you needed one badly."

"Is this a new business solicitation? Because if it is, I can tell you that all you've done is succeeded in getting my back up. I don't like cold calls. If you've got a software program to sell then you need to follow the proper channels, to send an information package, along with references. If I'm interested, I'll call you."

"So you're not working with Phayle Tollard?"

"That's it for you, Mr. Diamond. Good-bye."

I set the phone down carefully, then I picked up the phone again, got the area code for Santa Barbara, California, and called directory assistance. Phayle was in the computer, but her number was unlisted. I called directory assistance again, and asked for the number for Inventory Management Software.

"Nothing by that name," the operator informed me.

"Anything close?"

"You have to be more specific, sir."

"Try Tollard Software." I was stabbing in the dark now, but I was curious.

"I have Tollard Systems," she said impatiently.

"That's the one."

She gave me the number, and I dialed it. A machine responded. It spoke in Phayle's voice and suggested leaving a message or sending a fax. I did neither. The instant I hung up the phone, it rang, and Rudy Schlimmer was on the other end.

"We matched the print," he announced without preamble.

"Matched it!"

"Cleaned it, and ran it through A.F.I.S.," he said, referring to the central computerized fingerprint database. "The Bureau came back to us with a positive I.D. The guy's a Shining Path guerrilla. You know, the Maoist group that's been blowing up everything in Peru for years now."

"Peru," I muttered.

"The good news is he's in custody."

"What?" I rose from my chair.

"That's right," Schlimmer's voice got about as close to gleeful as I imagined it could. "He was apprehended about five months ago by Paraguayan immigration in a transit lounge, headed for Miami."

I ran the calendar in my head. Five months ago seemed about the time Cruz was picked up with the package of tapes. "What's the bad news?"

"He's in lockup in Paraguay."

"What's his name?"

"Abel Lopez."

"Abel Lopez," I repeated. "Listen, Rudy, I'm sorry you had to see that tape, but I'm grateful as hell for your help. You're a fucking genius."

"Thank you. You going to go down and talk to him?"

"You bet."

"Good luck. And don't worry about me. I'm fine."

"I know you are, Rudy."

I ran straight to Wacona's office.

"Yes?" she looked up from her desk.

Her voice was icy and so was her look. She was dressed in the power black of a mortician—tight-fitting black jeans, a black silk blouse, her trademark vest, also black, black boots and matching silver-and-onyx earrings and necklace. Her Smith rode high on her hip, looking bright and shiny.

"Someone's tone of voice tells me I'm in the dog-house."

"What can I do for you?" she said neutrally.

"Look, Wacona, I'm sorry about going over your head to the I.N.C."

"You didn't go over my head, Max. You talked to him in my presence. If there's anything to say about heads, it's that you've cost me a lot of time trying to spare yours."

"I figured that, and I appreciate it."

She took a deep breath, looked like she was about to launch into a tirade, then exhaled slowly. "Good," she said.

"Listen. Dulles just called. The guy who torched the little girl? He's the same piece of shit who knifed the kid on the boat. This tech Rudy Schlimmer matched his prints from the videotapes on a closeup. A.F.I.S. had him. He's a South American terrorist, and he's in custody in Paraguay. I want to extradite him."

"I hear the words 'I want' from you an awful lot, Max, do you know that?"

I sat down in the chair across from her desk. "I'm sorry about that."

"Something else I hear too often."

"So? Would you rather that I didn't care? I didn't do

anything so wrong, Wacona. I went after the shooters on my bike because I thought I could catch them."

"After I told you not to."

"I didn't hear you," I said.

"Like you didn't hear me on Potrero's radio? Look, Max, you're not a private investigator. You're not a marshal in the old west, you're a federal agent and you're part of a team."

"A team that thought those tapes were fake."

"We may have been wrong. Are you going to hold it against us forever? The truth about those tapes is still far from clear, and even if they *are* genuine, horrible as that possibility admittedly is, they are not the only case in our basket."

"John Clark seems pretty interested in seeing it solved."

"Goddamnit, Max!" she exploded, slamming both hands down on the desk so hard the motion picked her right out of her chair. "How dare you rub my nose in your secret society bullshit!"

"Clark's not interested in the case because he's a Stoneman," I said angrily. "He's interested in it because children are the first and last of us. Because if we don't help them, nobody will. Because every inch of those videotapes pulls us all a little closer to hell."

Breathing hard, she rolled her eyes. She looked sexy as hell with her face all flushed, but I certainly wasn't about to tell her. "Do you want a transfer, is that it? Are you uncomfortable working for a woman?"

"I'm not uncomfortable at all! I think you're an awesome postal inspector and an even better boss."

"So then why the obsessive brooding?" she demanded. "Ever since this whole mess began you've become unreliable and egocentric. I've got stacks of reports due from you, I've got half a dozen cases I need your help on. I've had three meetings with Chunny and Potrero in the last ten days and you haven't been in the office for any of them."

I got up and closed the door behind me. "In the last few weeks, I've seen children raped and tortured," I began. "I've seen one little girl forced to have sex with a farm animal, another burned with a blow torch, another killed and tossed into the sea like bait."

"I'm not arguing that it's not horrible, Max, but violence is part of the job."

"I signed to be a postal inspector, not a homicide dick. I can't handle this kiddie stuff."

"Then let Sea take it over."

"No, I have to finish it."

"Why?"

"Because it's invaded my bedroom, Wacona."

She blinked. "What?"

"I can't function."

"Jesus, Max," she said, growing pale.

"I'm sorry I had to tell you that. I've never crossed the line with you before and I'm not trying to now. Don't let this case ruin our great working relationship. Don't let it end my career. I'll try to cooperate more, okay? I'll try to keep you up to date. But you have to let me finish this thing."

The ensuing silence seemed to last an hour.

"I know about the Paraguay connection," she said finally. "Schlimmer called Clark before he called you, and we've already tried for extradition. No luck. He's a communist terrorist, and Paraguay apparently doesn't think much of such folks. Besides, we don't have any jurisdiction there."

"Then let me go down there and squeeze him," I implored.

She reached into her drawer and handed me a manila

217

envelope. Inside was background information on Paraguay, a file on Lopez, and a red, official United States passport issued in my name. "We do function in your absence, Inspector," she said dryly, "so stop gaping. Clark has secured country clearance for you from the State Department, and they've cabled the ambassador down there. The resident security officer at the embassy is expecting you. Your ticket is waiting for you at the airport and your flight leaves in three hours from MIA. You'll probably want to move along."

I started to say something, but she pointed at the door. "Just go, will you, Max?"

I packed two changes of clothes, an extra sport jacket, a sweater, a travel slicker, a pair of water-resistant Timberland loafers, and my usual personal effects. I secured Picard in the shower stall, threw in some broccoli and kale, tossed the copies of the videotapes I kept at home into my flight bag, along with the Lopez file and Clifton Hughes's client information, and headed out for the airport. I heard the telephone ring just as I locked the door behind me, but I didn't go back in to answer it. If it was Phayle, I wasn't ready to talk to her, and if it was the office, well they had my mobile number.

Special Agent Ron Dryden of the Federal Bureau of Investigation was waiting for me at the gate. A nun waving a collection can stood right beside him.

"You gotta be kidding," I said.

"Thought you could slip outta the country without me?"

"What are you, my shadow?"

"Word is you have a woody for the Don's daughter."

"Fuck you." The nun cringed and hurried away.

"So it's true," the FBI man said with satisfaction. "I thought you might be smarter than that."

"What are you doing here, Dryden?"

"I came to ask you personally for a full report when you get back."

"Do I look like your coon hound? You want a report, *you* fly down and talk to the guy."

"I'm allergic to the tropics," he sniffed. "Bad food, mosquitoes, diarrhea."

"So you let good old Diamond do the work."

"I've put in plenty of hours on this," he shrugged. "The Bureau's had O'Burke connected to the Shining Path for years. There's a drug pipeline between them that keeps the guerrillas in guns and Cuco in yachts. Whatever you get from this Lopez, I gotta get it too."

They announced my flight. The gate agent came over to remind me not to change seats, that the captain had to know where I was sitting because I was carrying a handgun.

"When I get on an airplane, *my* piece goes in my luggage," said Dryden.

Recently I'd heard that an FBI Special Agent had shot his own finger off. I chose that moment to mention it.

"Just call me when you get back," Dryden reddened.

I got on board without promising anything. During the takeoff, I read the background info on Paraguay, learning that it was a landlocked nation the size of California, and shared borders with Argentina, Bolivia, and Brazil. I found out that the western two-thirds of the country was a thorn jungle called the *Chaco Boreal*. Jaguars were still plentiful there, and the Guarani Indians living in the bush subsisted on cassava and a caffeine-rich tea they called máte. Apparently these natives were a stubborn bunch, proud of their music and historically resistant to the conversion efforts of Jesuit missionaries.

I learned that Paraguay's primary industries were contraband—I figured that meant drugs—meatpacking, soybeans, cotton, animal hides, and brewing; and that despite recent moves toward democracy, a long succession of xenophobic dictators had made the country the kind of place Josef Mengele, Martin Bormann, and other notorious former Nazis could feel comfortable.

The file was colorful, but not as colorful as the one on Abel Lopez and the *"Sendero Luminoso,"* the Shining Path. The organization was described by Departments of State and Defense documents as Peru's largest subversive organization, and among the world's most ruthless and dangerous terrorist outfits. Formed in the late '60s by a university professor named Abimael Guzman Reynoso—incarcerated since 1992—the Shining Path's goal was to rid Peru of foreign influences and replace existing institutions with an ethnic Indian state, a revolutionary peasant regime patterned after Maoist principles. At its height, the movement claimed as many as five thousand guerrilla soldiers, and targeted United States, Russian, and Chinese interests in attempts to embarrass the Peruvian government. According to the file, terrorist actions didn't begin until 1980 and had tapered off of late, despite an ample budget courtesy of friendly, mostly Colombian, narco-producers and -traffickers. Still, the group's misdeeds were particularly gruesome. In addition to bank robberies and extortions, there were mass murders and executions in which mutilated corpses were left on public display, a reflection of an aboriginal belief that only the spirits of intact victims can reveal their killers.

Abel Lopez, 38, was a *mestizo* known to be a head of one of Sendero Luminoso's "cells." He spoke flawless English, with a British accent that reflected his European education. The file on him included mug shots that unquestionably revealed him to be the killer in the videotapes, as well as black-and-white CIA spy satellite photos showing him in action in one of SL's training camps. In the first image he was running through sparse forest carrying an AK-47. In the second he was aiming a shoulder-launched antiaircraft missile aloft, and in the third he was standing in front of an assembled crew, reading aloud from a piece of paper. The last photo showed him at a card table in the jungle, surrounded by his compatriots, demonstrating the construction of a pipe bomb. The psychological profile prepared by State's antiterrorist specialists, folks who had interviewed him since his arrest, revealed him to be intelligent, secretive, sadistic, opportunistic, and sexually deviant. Surprise, surprise.

There were two pages of typed text attached to the back of the report. The first page was a list of Shining Path actions that Lopez was certain to have masterminded. These included an attack on a series of power-line towers, the burning of an evangelical church run by U.S. missionaries, the bombing of a school bus outside Lima, the murder of four provincial mayors, the bombing of a tourist train, a nerve gas attack on the Pakistani embassy in Peru, the assassination of a Bank of Israel manager, and an attack on an exclusive restaurant in Lima's Monterrico district.

The second page detailed actions in which Lopez was suspected of having simply participated. These included an assault on the Korean mission in Lima, the assassination of a ranking Peruvian narcotics officer, the bombing of a hospital and a USDEA helicopter base, the murders of an Australian journalist and two French mammalogists, and last but not least, the murder of five village schoolteachers in front of their students.

I found myself wondering what aspect of blowing up a school bus and murdering teachers in front of children might have sparked Lopez's interest in kiddie porn. I closed my eyes, put my head against the cold airplane bulkhead and dreamed an egomaniacal adventure in which I swung from vines like Tarzan, shrieked like a Kurdish rebel, and rescued Lopez's young victims one after another.

I awoke when the flight touched down for a brief stop in San Salvador. It was nighttime, but bright lights from the tower illuminated soldiers and jeeps milling about the field. Most of the passengers went to the transit lounge, and the copilot retired to the lavatory with the lead flight attendant. I got a glimpse of the captain through the open cockpit door and took some coffee up to her.

Her name was Phyllis, and she was a sharp-faced redhead, about thirty-five, with fine lines around her eyes. Her enthusiasm for her work shone through as she showed me the video game that was the Airbus's on-board computer, a device capable of evaluating weather and nearby air traffic, making automatic course corrections, monitoring the complex flight systems, and calculating fuel reserves on a minute-by-minute basis.

"All I have to do is sit here and look good," she asserted.

"They picked the right pilot for the job," I declared.

"That's nice of you," she smiled. "Tell me, what are you and your gun going to do in Asunción?"

"Attend a bald cop convention."

"Ah, come on. You know the shaved head suits you. Seriously, what's a postal inspector got to do down there?"

"Interrogate a suspect."

"Now doesn't that sound like fun. How long will it take?"

"Depends on what he has to say."

"Do you know where you're staying?"

"Accommodations are handled by the embassy."

"Maybe I'll find you."

Passengers began to trickle back aboard just then, and the copilot emerged from the lavatory. "How about paying me a visit in fourteen-A?" I suggested. "Later, when everyone's asleep."

"People will talk," she winked.

"Let's hope so."

Back in my seat, I began reading Clifton Hughes' client files. They began with a litany of predatory adulteries and hostile divorces, including photographs of a man in a hotel room with a prostitute, a babysitter in purple bra and panties, a teenager in a gay bar Frenching his middle-aged lover. But the bulk of the material pertained to a real-estate developer named Dennis Reilly. According to the documents, Reilly had tried to purchase several Miami Beach lots in order to erect a string of porn cinemas. I remembered the story, as it had been featured on several evening news segments. The community had banded together to prevent construction of the emporia, despite the fact that local zoning and commercial laws did not specifically prohibit them. Jeff Grayson had aggressively sued the city on Reilly's behalf, but lost in the end. The file contained furious letters from the client, in which he ranted and raved homicidally. I marveled that Cliff had taken so long to bring Reilly to my attention, and, feeling a sudden ray of hope about Phayle, made myself a note to drop by and see Steiner about the guy the instant I got back to West Palm. Just as I stowed the file in my case, Phyllis appeared in the aisle beside me.

"Come along," she beckoned. The cabin lights were dim and most all the other travelers were asleep. Nobody seemed to notice as the two of us made our way forward.

"Where are we?" I asked, as we stepped together into the cockpit. A dark blanket enveloped the nose of the jet. I couldn't see the wing lights.

"Over Brazil, flying through smoke forty five thousand feet up."

Suddenly we broke into the clear. Below us, the ground was eerily lit up by brilliant orange lines. "I thought you'd want to see this," she said.

"What am I looking at?"

"They're burning the Mato Grasso rain forest," the co-pilot explained.

It looked like we were crossing the boundaries of hell.

THIRTEEN

Joe Tucker, the resident security officer at the American embassy, met me at the gate upon my arrival at Asunción International. He was lanky and tall, with steel bones, a square jaw and hands the size of watermelons. When he stared, there was something of the fighting bull in him, evoking stampedes in the pasturelands of Wyoming or Nebraska, where spaces were unlimited and male rage could run its course. When he smiled, however, he looked like a delivery boy from a neighborhood grocery, all creases and innocence, optimistically hoping to find a neglected young wife in a negligee at the door.

"Paraguay has a strange history of isolationism and despots," he explained as we left the airport in his jeep. "The official language is Spanish, but everyone speaks the Guarani Indian dialect. The most recent evil dictator is dead, and there's a constitution in place now. Still, the economy remains agrarian, the vast majority of the population is Indian, education and sophistication are low, and the power stays in a few elite hands. If you want to get things done, you have to know people. That, or you have to work for the American embassy."

He chuckled over that, and asked me about Lopez. As we drove, I told him what I knew. By the time we hit downtown, it was close to 8 P.M. What I could see of the city looked like a hodgepodge of new, eclectic buildings and squatter settlements along the river.

"Hardly Florence," I observed.

"Not Rio or Buenos Aires either," Tucker agreed. "There's little sense of tradition here, except where it makes colonial Europeans look good. Still, the people are incredibly warm, and the thorn jungle they call the Chaco has its own brand of beauty."

"You live on the embassy grounds?"

"Most of the personnel do. It's a sixteen-acre compound, the largest in the world. Unless I have a special guest like you, I rarely leave. I'm in charge of intelligence-gathering, the marine garrison, all embassy security. I've got a pretty good relationship with the locals, but even I can't get you into Tacumbú at night."

"That's the prison where they're holding Lopez?"

"Yep. He was at the maximum-security facility at Emboscada, but that's out of town, so they brought him around for you. We can go over there first thing in the morning, but right now I thought we'd drop by your hotel. I picked the Guarani for you, it's the best place in town. We can have a drink and something to eat after you're checked in."

The jeep rumbled over the cobblestones as Tucker threaded his way through town, finally coming to a stop in front of a tall, pale building that looked to have been built in the '60s. I went inside and signed the register, gave the desk clerk my credit card, and deposited my suitcase in my room, taking out only a gift I'd picked up for Tucker.

When I came down, the big security man had already gotten himself most of the way through a local brew. "Dinner?" he proposed brightly.

"I'm in your hands."

He proposed an open-air café close by, and as I had spent nearly half a day off my feet, I proposed that we walk. We left the jeep by the front of the hotel and set off into the most desirable shopping and dining area in town—a square bounded by *avenida* Colón in the west, *calle* Haedo in the south, *calle* Estados Unidos to the east, and to the north, the Rio Paraguay. The dinner crowd was just starting to trickle in, eating late, as they do in Miami, and I was surprised by the cosmopolitan look of the patrons. The men were nattily dressed in dark clothes, mostly with ties, and the women were done up like shoppers in a Dallas mall. Tucker had a whole bevy of local dishes he seemed eager to introduce me to; a maize stew called *locro*, a mush of corn meal known as *mazamorra*, a hot pudding with meat chunks called *mbaipy so-ó*, and more. Within ten minutes the plates were piled three deep on the table.

"Uncle!" I held up my hands.

"What say we retire the beer glasses and order up some *caña*? That's the local rum."

I drew the paper bag up from where I'd stashed it under the table and plopped it down in front of him. "Here's a better idea. Happy days."

He pulled the bottle of Lagavulin out of the bag. "And to you!" he grinned.

"Best of the best," I told him. "The pride of the Isle of Islay, pearl of the Hebrides. Open it, and smell the peat, smell the malt, smell the ocean."

"You're a goddamn poet, Diamond."

"Nope. Just a guy who loves a good single malt Scotch."

He virtually tackled the waiter for a couple of clean glasses, and then did the honors. "Never tasted anything like that, man," he said, exhaling long and loud.

"Work through it slowly. Who knows when I'll be down here again."

"I come up to Miami a couple of times a year."

"I'll have another bottle waiting. How long you been in Paraguay?"

"Two and a half years. This is my fourth D.S.S. posting. Before that I was in Guatemala, Venezuela, B.A., and Honduras."

He was referring to the Diplomatic Security Service, a small branch of the State Department created by Admiral Bobby Inman in response to attacks on embassies during the Reagan years.

"Much of a terrorist problem down here?"

"There's no Shining Path, although some Arab operatives — Sons of Hisbollah — that pulled off a hit in Argentina were captured here. Also, we had a scare in October of ninety-six. That's what brought me to the embassy."

"You start in the military?"

Tucker shook his head and poured another himself another half a glass. I figured the bottle would be gone in two days.

"I was the youngest Jersey state trooper in history, recruited right into D.S.S. at the beginning. While I was in D.C., I got to protect a few heads of state — Boris Yeltsin, Prince Charles. Even Princess Diana. That was fine, but I never really knew how much I loved to travel until I got this gig. Truth is, I crave change in perspective, in social scene, the challenge of new tactical problems."

"Marines at the embassy have any problem taking the lead from you?"

He shook his head. "They have their own chain of command. They only report to me operationally. It works out okay. How about you? There's a guy who shows up and advises the local mail service on security from time to time, otherwise I rarely see a postal inspector down here. The job good to you?"

I matched his tall glass of Scotch with my own. "As a matter of fact it is. Been a bit more than I bargained for lately, though."

"This snuff film thing?"

"Some sad and ugly shit."

He nodded. We drank. After a while, he produced a couple of genuine Cuban Cohibas. I almost started to tell him that despite the cachet of contraband, Cuban tobacco wasn't what it used to be, but I lit up instead and found the cigar pretty good.

"You ever been out to Itaipú?" I asked him.

"The dam? No. All I know about it is that the President down here has caught flack for some shady biz dealings with the hydroelectric project. Lot of money sunk in that thing. It's a cash cow for the state. Why do you ask?"

"One of the videos was filmed there."

Tucker had been leaning forward, his huge hands wrapped around his glass, but he slowly straightened up. "That implies local contacts. A network. Not good. If I had known, I would have put you up at the embassy," he said, glancing around.

"I'll be fine."

He nodded and signalled the waiter for the check.

The streets smelled of distant fire, and we walked loose and easy from the booze. We made it halfway back to the hotel before I noticed the gray Toyota. It was cruising down the darkened street with its headlights off, and the passenger window open.

"Somebody you know?" I asked lightly.

"I'm afraid it isn't. You got your piece?"

I tapped my fanny pack.

"How many rounds?"

"Ten."

"Extra clips?"

"Just one."

"Okay, you see that coffee shop up ahead on the right?"

"I see it."

"They're going to expect us to turn and run. Instead, when we get to the coffee shop, we're going to split up. You double back the way we came. Do it fast, serpentine, take another street, meet me back at the hotel. I'll cross to the other side."

It didn't go down exactly as Tucker planned, because as soon as we were finished talking, the shooting started. Body language must have sent the message, I guess. In any case, it wasn't a good tactical setup, because we had absolutely no cover. Everything happened in slow motion, as it tends to when you're moving at warp speed. I remember crashing through the window of a small grocery store and sending imitation Oreos, Nestle's Quik, and one-pound bags of detergent flying. I heard Tucker shouting, and I heard automatic weapon fire. I ducked down behind the store counter, near an old black and gold cash register, and felt a mousetrap close hard on the toes of the same foot I'd cut under the R90S.

Someone entered the shop. The dim light from the street outlined him. I peeked through a wooden slat, saw a goatee, confirmed it wasn't Tucker, and opened fire with my Glock. There was a scream, and the man went down.

Bullets sprayed the ceiling. A piece of plaster moving at a hateful velocity bounced off my neck. I picked up the metallic odor of blood, and emerged carefully from cover. The man was on his back in the middle of the store, a spent Mac-10 machine pistol beside him, his chest a bloody salad of cotton and connective tissue. He stared at me. I kicked the pistol away. He groaned.

I crossed the store on tiptoes and looked outside. The Toyota was stopped only five feet away, its wheels on the sidewalk at a crazy angle. Both front doors were open, which told me I was probably dealing with at least one more guy. Using the car for cover, I crawled around to the trunk and looked across the street. Tucker was in a world of hurt. A small, dark figure had another Mac-10 to his temple, and was demanding things in a Spanish too guttural and idiomatic for me to understand. It wouldn't have mattered if he were asking for directions to the nearest whorehouse — the pistol said it all.

Some lights went on in the buildings above. Curious apartment dwellers. Not one was brave enough to look out a window, a consequence, no doubt, of decades of ruthless dictatorship. I crawled along the curb, using the line of parked cars for cover. My Glock was empty, and my fanny pack and spare magazine were gone. I wished I had picked up the Mac-10.

"Fuck your mother!" I heard Tucker say clearly.

I shook my head. Brave man. Stupid, too. I peered between the bumper of a Ford pickup truck and the nose of a Mitsubishi Pajero. I was directly across the street from them now, not more than fifteen feet away. Tucker was on his knees, the bottle of Lagavulin broken beside him, spilling into the gutter. Things didn't look good. I cupped my hands over my mouth so as to throw my voice.

"Maricón," I yelled out from behind the car.

The response was a deafening hail of bullets which

turned the side of the pickup into a steel drum. I wanted to call out to Tucker, but instead I wriggled down into the cave of muffler, tranny, suspension, and tires that was the Pajero's undercarriage. I inched my way slowly toward the street until I caught sight of Tucker rocking on the ground, his hands at his groin. A pair of combat boots came toward me in a deliberate "L" step that bespoke martial training. They stopped. The street was quiet. My heart pounded like a rock band drummer.

An eternity went by. I thought of Phayle. I thought of my grandmother and Sea, tried to imagine what they might look like at the altar. I thought of Wacona at the gun range and Guiomary stitching my foot. I thought about the little blue-eyed girl. Silently, I cursed the kind of Third World police force that would ignore a gunfight in the street, then realized that I wasn't being quite fair. The whole shooting match had taken place in less than three minutes.

The boots started moving again. They were almost beside me. I had an idea, played it through in my mind, decided to risk it. Anything was better than waiting until he bent down and plugged me with the Mac-10. I held my breath. The feet got closer. When they were within reach, I grabbed and yanked as hard as I could.

The man teetered and went down, squeezing off a volley. The Pajero's windows exploded above me. A tire blew, and the truck sank dangerously onto my pelvis, pinning me. I met the gaze of the gunner, both our cheeks to the road. He reached for his pistol, but in one desperate yank I broke free of the chassis and beat him to it. I got up, but he yanked at my shoe, working my own trick on me. My balance was better than his though, and I stayed up. He scrambled to his feet and we faced each other. Tucker yelled something, but by the time the word "knife" registered, the blade was already moving toward me.

Critics of t'ai chi ch'uan argue that it has no specific techniques and fails to offer the kind of repetitive training required to make self-defense moves automatic. They don't understand that from the t'ai chi point of view, having a plan is a sure way to lose. They don't understand that cultivating the kind of body that can instantly sense where the opponent is going and get there first is a far better, and ultimately safer, strategy. I followed the inward course of his stab by touching him lightly on the wrist, then helped him continue the movement right past me. His arm went up and away from me, bending his body backward, and when he was close enough, I delivered a vibrating palm strike to his chest, accomplishing precisely the kind of *dim mak* organ damage I had described to Mozart. The energy from my hand went through his denim jacket, through his cotton shirt, through the outer layers of his skin and fascia, through his rib cage and right to his pericardium, shocking the heart into stillness.

The man looked at me with the same expression of incredulity I had seen on the face of the little girl as she fell overboard with the fillet knife in her ribs. He tipped slowly forward, following his own momentum and loosing his bowels. The knife clattered to the ground.

Tucker hobbled over. His eyes were wide and he was staring at me. "Are you all right?"

"Fine. How about you?"

"I will be," he grimaced, still holding his groin. He gestured at the man in the middle of the street. "What did you do to him?"

"I hit him."

"I guess so."

I looked down at the human being I had turned into a slab of meat, and I felt my stomach turn. I thought about watching Greg Hunter, my friend and partner die, and I remembered watching something light and airy flit upwards out of his body like a butterfly. I saw no such escape here. All I saw was a feast for bacteria, a smorgasbord for worms. A dish I had personally served up.

"What say we pretend this mess never happened," I said as the sound of sirens grew in the distance.

"Some chance," he replied.

FOURTEEN

Were it not for Tucker's incredible calm and finesse, the experience of dealing with the Paraguayan police — revealing who I was and why I was toting a Glock semiautomatic around, explaining one dead man in the middle of the street and another one nearly dead on the floor of a grocery store — could have been the stuff of nightmares. Despite the obvious pain of a roundly kicked groin, the D.S.S. chief managed to smooth everything over in much the same way I imagined a heartland farmer might convince the cows to come home. He drawled, he winked, he laid his massive palms on shoulders and he made the most of the powerful position the American delegation down there enjoyed.

An impromptu interrogation was held in the back of a police car, with about five cops talking very intently to the man with my bullets in his chest. In that brief conversation, a finger was applied directly to a wound, and in addition to blood, the truth bubbled out. Although he denied any association with the Shining Path, the man admitted that he and his deceased partner had been sympathetic associates of one Abel Lopez, and they had set out to make sure that whatever the United States government had in store for Lopez did not come to pass. Before an ambulance could be summoned, the shooter died in agony.

As I watched the cops remove the bodies, the last of my adrenaline drained away and I was overcome by a sense of terrible despair; the fear that this case was like a terrible disease, daily and irreversibly changing me from the man I wanted to be into something else. During my childhood, during my schooling, during my years as a salesman and even during my love affairs, I had always fancied myself immune to the hooks and drags of life that seemed to attach themselves to others. I was the one everybody came to in times of need, the man who could always find an elegant solution, the man who could find the minutes between the minutes even when time had obviously run out. Yet here I had gone and done the worst, most base thing a human being could do; I had shot one man dead and killed another with my bare palm. I had taken lives, and a part of me feared what the karmic consequences might be, if indeed there was a cycle to things. More, I feared my dreams in the years to come.

Worried about me, Tucker suggested I take refuge in the embassy. I wanted time alone, so I refused. He said the hotel might be dangerous. I pointed out that since we were dealing with local thugs rather than trained terrorists—the latter would never have let us off with our lives, nor for that matter, have lost theirs—the worst was doubtless over. We went back and forth over it—I was his charge, after all—but in the end he grudgingly arranged for armed cops to escort me back to the Guarani hotel, there to stand guard outside my room. After that, he went off to the hospital, trying bravely to walk like a man.

The trio that drove me back to the hotel were pleasant, even if their torture of the dead shooter showed me they were shy on compassion. I made small talk with them in my best Spanish, even getting them to laugh by outlining the link between baldness and virility. In the end I convinced them to set me free at the badly decorated hotel bar for a nightcap where the bartender, a roly-poly man with a slicked-down cowlick that seemed to point straight at the spot where his belly broke through his shirt buttons, served me a Johnny Walker Black, which, being blended, was nowhere near as fine an offering as the late and lamented bottle of Lagavulin. I was nursing it along anyway, gradually quelling my shakes and contemplating having stopped a man's heart with my hand, when the pretty, red-haired airline pilot who had flown me down wandered into the joint. She was wearing tight black pants, and a classy blouse of royal blue.

"Inspector," she smiled.

"Phyllis," I raised my glass. "You look stunning."

"Thank you. *You* look awful."

"Really? I was just thinking that dirt and blood enhanced my image as a stalwart protector of the mails."

"Is that really blood?" she frowned.

"Not mine. I was having dinner with the embassy's resident security officer. Some friends of the guy I'm down to interview waylaid us after our meal. Shots were fired."

"But you're okay?"

"Fine and dandy."

"And your friend?"

"Singing soprano but bound for a complete recovery. How about a drink?"

"Whatever you're having." I made a sign at the bartender. She slid in beside me.

237

"I knew a girl named Phyllis in high school. I broke her heart."

"Well you're not going to break mine."

"I figured that. You strike me as the predatory pilot of legend."

"That's me."

"Tell me something: does having all those levers and buttons at your fingertips actually lend you the illusion that you have some control of your life?"

"I stay aloft," she said. "I'm good at it."

"And when the time comes to go down?"

"I make a graceful landing."

"And when you can't? When your time is up?"

"Here I am hoping for a nice layover and you start talking like that."

I downed the rest of my drink, tapped the bar with the glass for another. "Sorry. I'll change the subject and give you the good news. I committed murder tonight. Never done that before. Shot one guy in the chest, and used my hand to stop another's heart. Don't feel too good about it, so I sure could use some company tonight."

She evaluated me for a moment's time, side to side, head to toe. Then she stood up and backed away. "You're out of luck, killer," she said.

Alone in my bed, I sat up and watched the sun rise over the rooftops of Asunción. It was a pale orb, diminished in clarity somewhat by the trash fires along the river, but dramatic nonetheless because the angle of incidence was shallow and the shadows long. Soaked in sweat and with a throbbing head, I prepared myself to see Lopez. I got up and had a long shower in a stall big enough for a horse, but under a trickle that wouldn't have drowned a flea. When I was finished I put the towel on the floor and I performed the Eight Pieces of Brocade, a *qigong*, or breath-directed exercise routine, which I did daily. I concentrated on my breathing, smelling the alcohol on my own breath, trying to sweat and breathe and otherwise force out the toxins. It was to be an important day. I had high hopes that it would hold answers to riddles that had plagued me for weeks.

When I got downstairs, intending to take a cab to Tacumbú, Joe Tucker was waiting in his jeep.

"I can't possibly feel worse than you look," he declared.

"It was the wild sex I had last night."

"You've got a real mean streak," he said, unconsciously touching his groin.

"Yow. I didn't mean that the way you heard it. Sarcasm. That's what I had in mind."

"I'll let it slide. You saved my life, after all."

We drove a little bit. At a stoplight he turned to me. "Last night your first time?"

"What?"

"First time you killed anybody."

I swallowed hard and nodded.

"And you feel like you'll never be the same," he said matter-of-factly.

"Something like that. You remember those little winter wonderlands in a plastic bubble?" I replied.

"The ones where you shake 'em and fake snow swirls around?"

"Yeah. Those. I feel like I was living in one and the bubble broke."

"That's okay," Tucker smiled. "The real world has its challenges, but it has its compensations too."

"Here's to 'em. Are you on morphine?"

"Just aspirin and an ice pack."

"And no worries about those dead jokers having friends?"

"Behold the Max Diamond marine honor guard," Tucker pointed at the rearview mirror. "I told the ambassador you could handle the whole Shining Path army with a flick of your finger, but he didn't believe me."

"One has to be smart to make ambassador."

Tucker grinned, the light changed, and we motored off. The city seemed far less fearsome in the daylight, the sidewalks seething with urchins pedaling tourmalines as sapphires, women with trays of baked goods, and everywhere people sipping caffeine-laden máte through tin straws. Gradually, however, the neighborhoods got seamier and seamier, and the air turned acrid with the smell of burning trash.

"The prison is near a military base in the southwest quarter," Tucker explained. "There's a dump nearby, too. Waste management isn't Asunción's forte. The elevation is low and the facility floods a lot. Makes the filth even worse."

"Lovely."

"Yeah, well don't feel too bad for the inmates. At least there's some semblance of a judicial system here now. Under the dictator, Stroessner, there wasn't even any pretense. If you were rich, smart, and politically dissatisfied, you were permanently deported as soon as you opened your mouth. If you were poor and dishonest you just disappeared. Judges belonged to the drug cartels, so no connected dope-runners ever did time. The country's got four prisons, and in some respects Tacumbú is the best of them. It was built for six hundred, but there are fourteen hundred in there now, all unclassified, everyone dumped together in the yard. Locals call the place *La Universidad de la Delinquencia,*" but as prisons go, things inside are really pretty lax. There's a new warden in charge, and they say he's trying to tighten things up."

"I don't want them to be lax where Abel Lopez is concerned."

"If he were in the good graces of the Shining Path, they would have sprung him already."

"Really," I mused. "You just gave me an idea."

The nauseating stench of the place smacked me in the face like a wet mackerel, making me glad there had been no time for breakfast. It was a riot of odors, not just the aroma of countless unwashed armpits and groins, but the smell of spoiled food and scores of illegal fires ignited in the yard at night—it was still cold in these low reaches of the Southern Hemisphere—mixed with the faint musky bouquet of sex. This last puzzled me until Tucker explained that there was a hotel on the premises, with rooms available for conjugal visits.

Superficially, the faces I saw were slightly different from those that I had seen in U.S. prisons, the features broader in the Indian way, the skin closer to coffee. But the expressions were as I had expected, divided approximately between total resignation and a kind of animal cunning that sought out chinks in the armor of my intention the way a rising sea looks for a hole in a dike.

"Not exactly your run-of-the-mill pen, huh?" said Tucker as we passed through security at the front gate. The area of the compound was only about five acres, and there were a couple of old buildings with an alley between them, abutted by several newer, low structures.

An academic-looking man with a shaved head, a herringbone suit, and gold rimmed glasses approached, ringed by guards.

"Warden Ballejos," Tucker said under his breath.

"Doesn't usually come out of his office. Hates being around inmates. The ambassador must have called him."

Ballejos drew close, shook my hand, introduced himself.

"Handsome hairstyle," I ventured.

He pointed at my own bald head and laughed. "I do it for the lice," he said. "No matter how much you wash, they find you. I'm afraid you've caught me with my pants somewhere just above my ankles, Inspector. I fired forty guards last week, and have replaced them with an inexperienced crew from the south. They're still deciding whether to work for me or the convicts. The clever ones will do both. The sad truth is that there is no way I can match what they get paid under the table. The cartels are richer than our government. Still, your man Lopez isn't going anywhere. Especially after what happened last night."

A drag queen in paisley approached. His lipstick was deep maroon, his eye shadow overdone, but he had nice, shaved legs and a push-up bra. "*Ola*, warden! You were wonderful last night," he cooed.

"Thank you," Ballejos answered formally.

"I've told *all* the girls how big you are," the queen went on. "You're becoming *muy* desirable!"

One of the guards moved toward him with a nightstick, but the warden held him back. "My apologies, Inspector," said Ballejos, passing a hand over his face in a gesture of great weariness. "It would appear that I am popular with the men, wouldn't it? We have a large transvestite population in the prison. They are some of our most colorful inmates."

When we reached the other side of the courtyard, we came across a group of men quietly clustered around a smooth-skinned, round-bodied middle-aged Indian woman clad in colorful Guarani garb, her thick black hair pulled back tightly in a long pony tail. I looked questioningly at Ballejos.

"Katerina," he said, as if that explained everything.

"She's a local witch," Tucker elaborated. "The Indians think she has healing powers. They say she can rid you of evil spirits."

I broke from the crew and stepped up for a closer look. "She has red eyes," I murmured.

"Caña will do it to you every time," Tucker put in.

But it wasn't her blood vessels, but her irises that appeared burgundy. I stepped in for a better look, and as I did, a man knelt on the ground at her feet. She put her hands on his face tenderly, and stroked him. He relaxed. I moved closer. She cupped his chin with a hand I could now see was rough in the way of the vegetable farmer, a palm accustomed to dirt and stones, fingers accomplished at tousling roots. She pried open his mouth and suddenly plunged her fingers straight in, rowing around in his oral cavity like a dentist run amok. His cheeks bulged to accommodate her. His face tightened and his chest began to heave. He strained to get away from her but she held him in place, trembling with the effort, until she suddenly shrieked and fell back. In her hand, the hand that had been in his mouth, a slimy black eel wriggled in her grasp. The group gasped aloud as if with one voice, and Katerina dropped whatever it was into a tin bucket beside her and covered it with a lid. Still shaking, the man got up, slowly straightened his back, smiled his thanks, and shuffled off.

I know I held my breath for a time, because when I finally remembered to breathe, I was starving for air. I turned to Tucker for an explanation, but the crowd had closed around me, driving me forward. For some reason, some instinct lodged in my primitive hindbrain, I didn't fight them. More than that, I fought my way through them to the front of the line, pushing and shoving. This witch had something, I just knew she did, and I wanted her to help me. *"Por favor,"* I said when I reached her.

She gave a tight-lipped smile and gestured for me to kneel. I did, and I felt her take my head in her hands. Her fingers explored my ears and my cheeks and pressed on my temples. When they pushed up into my nostrils, I smelled the loam trapped beneath her nails. I shut my eyes. Abruptly she was out of my nose and up to my eyelids. Her fingers fluttered there like curious butterflies, dancing on the thin skin and making shadows appear in the darkness. For a moment I felt a mad rush of terror, wondering what could possibly have led me here, to bend my knee to a red-eyed witch wrapped in a poncho. Had she put a spell on me? Was that it? Had some deft and subtle cosmic forces been at work since I left Miami, all aimed at bringing me into Katerina's hands? She pressed down on my eyeballs and I grew hot, then cold; light, then heavy. I saw tiny stars, and had the excruciating sensation of something huge squeezing through my tiny, delicate tear ducts. I reached up in self-defense, and found Katerina's thick wrists there. I gripped them, and opened my eyes.

At first the light was blinding. It was as if I had been seeing everything through a soiled and bloody shroud, which had been suddenly pulled back to reveal the sky-blue tinge of life, the vibrancy, the colors. I felt lighter and stronger and clearer than I had in months, maybe in years. I blinked. Katerina was piercing me with a cabernet gaze, directing me to her hands. There, nestled in her brown palms, were five black, shell-less snails — twisted creatures emitting a foul smell. I had a good look at them before she tossed them into the bucket with the eel. She smiled at me, this time showing her worn teeth and tired gums, and uttered something in Guarani.

"She says you can get up now," Joe Tucker's voice came booming into my head. "She says your soul was poisoned through your eyes but she has taken the poison and you will recover. She says you should pray for the children."

I got up as if in a daze. Ballejos and the guards were watching me intently. I had the distinct feeling that what had happened was no great surprise to anybody but me.

FIFTEEN

I waited for Lopez at a green steel chair before a green steel card table, alone in a little room. The smell of sweat and piss was overpowering, but I felt strong, sure of myself. By the time Tucker finally dragged Lopez in by the scruff of the neck and forced him into the chair across from me, I was sure I could leap a tall building in a single bound. Katerina had probably put some kind of spell on me.

"You need anything, just holler. I'll be right outside," the embassy R.S.O. told me.

Lopez and I examined each other for a long time. He was defiant, his eyes ablaze, the nostrils of his all-too-familiar hooked nose aflare.

I began by asking him if he had ever driven a twelve-cylinder Mercedes Benz.

"No, huh? Fantastic power. Smooth, like a turbine. How about champagne? You look like the kind of guy who likes Roederer. Wow. Just thinking about it makes me thirsty. I'm sure a guy with your contacts could pull off a six of beer in here, maybe even something up-market like Corona, but I doubt you could score champagne. If you did, you'd become so popular you wouldn't be able to sit down for a month, am I right? Well, I'm going to arrange a spot of the bubbly right now."

I banged on the door. Tucker opened it instantly.

"I need a good bottle of champagne in here," I said. "Dom Perignon in a pinch, Mumms if you absolutely must, The real thing would be Roederer, though. Roederer would really do it for Mister Lopez."

"You want *champagne?*" Tucker repeated, looking at me as if I were crazy.

"Way I look at it, denying a doomed man's last request is cruel and unusual punishment."

"I'll see what I can do," he said.

"You're what, a thirty-eight regular?" I asked, turning back to Lopez. "I'm thinking you'd look good in Hugo Boss. That square cut would make you look bulkier. You're the wiry type. I know you're strong, I've seen what you can do with a knife, but guys like you tend to get lost in your clothes. Never fear, Abe. We'll get it tailored just right."

"Don't call me 'Abe'," Lopez said tensely. His voice was low, his accent British.

"Do you have a sweet tooth, Abe? I figure you might, spending so much time around kids. Godiva and Teuscher make good chocolate. Even See's isn't bad. But the really exquisite stuff comes from this little chocolatier in New York City. They've got a shop near Fifty-first and Park. A cultured, urbane world traveler like you has obviously been to the Big Apple, right? Anyway, the presentation is half the fun, because each of their little hand-made chocolates has a different design on the top; wavy lines on a pale background means hazelnut—the fillings are different inside, too, it's not *all* show—red lines on dark chocolate mean cherry. You get the idea. Fantastic. A hell of a good-bye present."

"I'm not going anywhere," Lopez said calmly.

"Of course you are! Now let's get back to the details. We've got the transportation, we've got the clothes, the drink, the dessert. Shit, I guess we kind of skipped over the main meal. My guess would be seafood. How am I doing?"

"You can't extradite me."

I laughed. I clapped my hands with delight. Lopez frowned.

"Extradite you! Ha ha! That's a good one. I bet you wish I could, although I have to tell you that there was a big flap over the last execution in Florida probably you didn't read about it down here, but the guy's face caught on fire inside the mask they put on him. Those masks, they're a relatively new thing. There are holes so the victim can see out—cute how they call him 'the victim' isn't it?—but really the mask is for the benefit of the audience. Audience—there's another funny term, huh? Like it's a vaudeville act? Anyway, the guy's asshole caught fire too. Hell of an ending, if you'll pardon the pun! Well anyway, whatever the excesses of voltage, none of that is anything compared to what will happen to you when Peru gets you back."

"Peru?" Lopez unconsciously gripped the arms of the little metal chair.

"Sure, Abe. We're sending you home. I guess you know the government isn't actually in love with you guerrillas. Something about hating to see women cut down in restaurants and kids killed by school bus bombs? But forget that. Let's get back to the meal. I'm thinking health-conscious eating is probably a low priority for you, so we can dispense with low-fat sauces. What's it going to matter, right? I figure you'll be choking to death on your own dick maybe thirty years before your arteries can start to clog, so I say go for the gusto! Lobster bisque! How would that be for starters? Thick and creamy, enriched with some fine sherry?"

"Stop it," said Lopez, standing up.

"Already? We haven't gotten to soufflé! I'm thinking maybe something with oysters. Oops, I guess that was in bad taste. Libido isn't exactly your problem and sex isn't exactly on your calendar. At least not with women or kids. I can do a lot of things for you, Abel, but I can't do that. Oh, what the hell! Let's go ahead with the little shelled devils! Now, we've got lobster bisque with sherry, oysters Rockefeller just for the sheer perversity of it, and then something with a Portuguese flavor, say a sauteed sea bass with capers and tomatoes and garlic? All fresh, of course. Nothing but the best for you."

"I'm not going back to Peru. I have a life sentence here," Lopez's eyes flashed.

"A life sentence? Uh, yeah, you sure do. But Paraguay doesn't particularly care if you serve it here or you serve it there, especially if I ask them really nicely to send you back. They like me, see. In fact, they like Americans in general. They even like Joe Tucker, he's the head of embassy security, the guy your friend kicked in the balls last night. Nobody's pleased about that, Abel. Not Warden Ballejos, not me, not Mister Tucker."

"I don't know what you're talking about," Lopez hissed.

"Sure you do! I killed both of your pals last night, even those fancy machine pistols didn't help them, but one of them squealed on you before he died. The confession was taped by the local cops. It's amazing what a man with a hole in his chest will do for the promise of some immediate medical attention. Anyway, the warden feels that even though the Shining Path doesn't love you enough to spring you from here, you're obviously sufficiently well-connected to make trouble here in Asunción. Nobody likes trouble, Abe, so we're going to send you home."

Twin spots of froth appeared at the corner of his lips. "You can't! I'll appeal! I'll write letters!"

"Letters? That's a good one, and right up my alley, too! Who you going to write, Abe?" I asked, my voice dripping with sarcastic warmth. "Amnesty International? You think a bunch of liberals are going to pressure the government down here? You think they'll *want* to after they hear about the tapes, after we show them you knifing the little girl, after we show them how good you are with a welding torch? Think, Abe. Think about what you're saying. Even if some misguided idiot listened to your plea, nothing would happen for months or years. These things take time. I work with the mails, so I can tell you myself how long some letters take to get delivered, especially if they receive, ah, special attention? A paradox, don't you think? In the meantime, you'll be back with your friends in Lima. They're so excited! I think it's the school bus, Abe. Yes, that's what I think really heats them up."

Lopez started to quiver like a tuning fork. It looked like he was going to launch at me. As much as I hated violence, I found myself hoping he did. Nobody's perfect.

"Go fuck yourself," he said.

"What's the matter? You look unhappy. Here I am, trying to think of every last thing to make your final day on Earth luxurious and happy — Roederer champagne, man, chosen just for you — and you tell me to go fuck myself."

Keeping my eye on him, remembering his enormous capacity for sadistic violence, I edged toward the door and rapped hard for the second time. Once again, Tucker appeared in an instant.

"You working on that champagne, Joe?"

"Having trouble finding Roederer. So far we've come up with Moët and Chandon White Star. Will that work?"

"White Star? For a man like Abel Lopez on his last day? I think that's crass, Joe. We need something that will complement a truly gourmet last supper."

"I'll keep looking," Tucker assured me, his tone gratifyingly serious.

I closed the door. "Now where were we?"

"What are you doing here?" Lopez demanded.

"Just making sure you get the sendoff you deserve."

"Stop playing games with me, you bastard!" The way he said "bastard," he might have been an English country schoolmaster.

"So you don't want a good last meal and a fine suit?"

"Go to hell."

"After you, Abe."

"I go back to Peru, I'm a dead man."

"*Now* you're talking!" I enthused.

He sat back down, put his head in his hands. I stared at those hands, the muscles in them, the black hair on the tanned fingers, the veins. I thought about the girl on the boat, the surprise in her eyes. The plop her dying body made as it hit the water. I realized that I hated this piece of human garbage. "What is it that you want?" he finally asked.

"Want? I don't want anything, Abe. I've already got it all. The snuff videotapes, the kiddie porn, all of it. And we've positively identified you from your thumb print. The miracles of computer imaging! You'd be amazed."

His whole body contracted in on itself. It was as if he's suddenly lost twenty pounds and five inches.

"But even with technology being what it is today," I continued, "even with tripods and remotes and Steadi-cams, someone has to operate the camera. So tell me, who shot the films, Abe?"

Lopez shook his head.

"Let me tell you how I've got it figured. The man in the restaurant, the guy in the nice suit who came in with the young woman and the girl? I figure he worked with you on these masterpieces. I figure you took turns behind the viewfinder. Am I onto something here, Abe? I think I am! Tell me, which one of you called yourself the direc-tor?"

"The films were mine," he said dully.

"Meaning you were the creative force behind them, right? Tell me, where might I find this partner of yours?"

"He's dead," Lopez said dully.

"Dead, huh? Now that's convenient."

"*Sendero Luminoso* killed him."

"Why, because they don't care for snuff films and don't think little girls should fuck goats?"

"Because he wouldn't share the profits," Lopez hissed.

"He wouldn't but you would, huh? So how come you're still locked up here?"

"Because there are no profits. Because you bastards have the tapes."

"What was this genius film director's name?"

"I don't mind telling you. It was Raúl Nuñez. He died in Quito. You can verify it with the Ecuadorian police."

There was a noise at the door, and the lock turned. Tucker came in with a bottle of champagne. There was a red stripe across the white label. Mumms Cordon Rouge. He set it down on the table, then pulled a couple of glass flutes out of the deep pockets of his jacket. "Courtesy of Warden Ballejos," he said. "From his private wine closet."

"Mumms. It's not Roederer, but it sure is appropriate seeing as Abe here isn't talking much."

Tucker grinned at me, and ducked out. As soon as the door shut behind him, Lopez made his move. I should have seen it coming, should have sensed that his breaking point was near. His hand snaked out, grabbed the bottle, broke it over his chair and came at me. I dropped low, almost into a split, my left foot way out, my right knee bent, and blocked the bottle with my right hand while I put my knee into his groin.

He went down, and I followed him, my right arm wrapping around his neck. He struggled, and I tightened up on him. His face turned red, and he grabbed about wildly, dropping the bottle. I squeezed harder. He gagged, and being the trained fighter that he was, tried to angle his chin into the soft flesh on the inside of my elbow so as to keep his airway open. I wouldn't let him. I banged his head against the top of the steel table, hard. Then again, harder. A little bit of the spilled champagne made a damp spot in the middle of his forehead. A lump showed right away.

"He worked the camera at Itaipú, you worked it at the restaurant. Am I right?" I demanded.

"Tell me you won't send me back to Peru," he gasped.

"Worry about breathing, first, Abe," I advised, tightening my grip until his carotids pulsed wildly.

"No Peru," he repeated.

I could see he was about to pass out, and I didn't want that, so I eased up a bit. "You give me what I want, you'll stay right here in beautiful downtown Asunción. Now am I right? Was he the one that did the woman in the restaurant?"

"Sí," Lopez answered faintly.

"Speaking of that young woman, what kind of bullet did you use on her? Was it an expansion round, Abe?

Looked like an expansion round to me. Something solid and jacketed wouldn't have made that much mess."

"Maybe it was notched at the tip."

"Very nice! And who was the young woman?"

"Some *puta* we picked up on the street in Rio."

"What was her name, Abe? Do you remember that?"

"No. Raúl offered her clothes. She accepted. Raúl could be very persuasive. He wanted to fuck her. The snuff was his idea. He hid the gun on me. I didn't even know it was coming."

"Maybe I was wrong," I said. "Maybe *Raúl* was the creative one! He was the voice at the barn, right? Telling the girl what to do with the goat?"

"*Sí*. That was him. Now let me go. I can't breathe."

"It was just the two of you?"

"Yes!"

"How do I know you're telling the truth!"

"I can't go back to Peru! It's a death sentence!"

I thought about this for a second, and must have re-laxed my grip ever-so-slightly, because he suddenly convulsed, a huge effort, and nearly managed to push me off him. He had a hard, external strength, the kind of strength it takes to shove a knife between a young girl's ribs. I responded by smashing his head against the table a third time. Blood dripped down his face, mixing with the champagne.

"Why did you send the tapes to Cuco O'Burke? You're far too small time for Cuco."

"He was a conduit," Lopez said faintly. The stream of blood grew thicker. It covered half his right cheek. I felt good about it.

"A conduit to whom?"

He shook his head.

"Tell me about Twilight Enterprises!"

His eyes went wide. "How do you know about that?"

"Never mind what I know, let's talk about what you know."

"It's a business run by a slaver in Miami."

"A slaver," I repeated.

"He brings in children, sends them out again. I can get kids. I wanted to be his supplier, to work with him."

"What does he do with the kids?"

"Sells them."

"For what? Porno flicks? Prostitution?"

"The customer pays, you don't ask."

I took a deep breath, tried to stay focused. "Why the snuff film?"

"A freebie. A bonus for Mister Twilight."

My stomach did a hop. "And the kids lined up at the power plant?"

"A small sample," Lopez smiled faintly. His teeth were red.

A small sample. "Does O'Burke know this Mister Twilight?" I forged on.

"O'Burke knows everybody, and everybody knows O'Burke. We told him we had something for this Twilight. A present. An offering. Asked him to forward it along."

"Did he know what he was forwarding?"

Lopez shook his head, dripping blood onto his shirt.

"Why would he do that for you?"

"He did it for *Sendero Luminoso*. They are one of his drug connections. His business helps fund the cause. Now I've talked enough. You talk some. What are you going to tell the warden?"

"Give me the name of the slaver."

"I can't."

"Lima, Lima, here you come. Right back where you started from," I sang softly.

"I don't *know* his name," Lopez whined desperately. "If I did, I wouldn't have gone through O'Burke. A *cabrón* like that, there's always a price for a favor. Later, when you least expect it."

"The name," I repeated.

"Fuck you, postal man."

I yanked him to his feet, bent him backwards over the table. I put my hand on his face and pressed down and twisted so shards of glass bit into his scalp and neck. He struggled, but he didn't scream. He was tough, in his way, Abel Lopez was. Twisted and sick and tough as a golem.

"The name!" I hollered.

"I tell you I don't *know*! Get it from O'Burke!"

I pushed his head around some more. A fine stream started at the base of his neck. "Your carotid artery is bleeding. If I let go, you die."

"If you send me back to Peru I die too. I'm telling you I don't know who he is!" I believed him. There was nothing left for him to lose.

"Where are the children?" I demanded, covering his artery with my thumb.

"What children?"

"The children in the films."

Lopez glared up at me, genuinely puzzled. "We let those children go."

"You mean you killed them?"

"No, we just put them out on the street."

"Where?"

"In Bolivia. In Colombia. In Ecuador."

"Which cities?"

"Why do you care? They're street children. They're probably dead from AIDS now, or from starvation."

"Which cities!"

"Guayaquil, La Paz, Bogotá."

"You're not lying to me, are you Abe?"

"Why would I lie now?" he asked bitterly.

"The girl who danced on the table. The one you

257

burned with the torch. What did she do to you? Why did you single her out?"

He looked up at me. "Get me a doctor!" he pleaded.

"Why her!" I roared.

"I liked her blue eyes," he whispered.

I remained like that for what seemed like an eternity, pressing on his artery, while I tried to integrate the simple, animal cruelty of his admission. Then, gradually, I grew disgusted with the link between me and Lopez, a link formed by my own violence. "Where is she now?" I asked softly.

"I told you, I don't know!" he said furiously. "There was no reason to keep her. My life is finished. I am here forever. What more do you want from me?"

I had an answer to that, but I couldn't quite bring myself to say it. Instead, I replaced my thumb with his, and called out for Tucker. He opened the door, took a long look at what I had wrought, called casually for a doctor and followed me out of the room.

"Now what?" he asked.

"Now nothing. It was him and one other guy. They were bidding for a supply deal with a slaver when the tapes were intercepted."

"And the partner?"

"He's says he's dead. I believe him. We can check it."

"So I guess that's it, then. You've got your man."

"One of them. I still want the slaver."

"But there was no deal, right? I mean the tapes never got to the guy."

"He's still selling children. Bringing them in, and selling them. I want him."

"Then you'll get him. Can I tell you something, Max?

"Sure."

"There's three kinds of cops. Those who have lost their cool, those who are going to lose it, and those who are going to lose it again. Now what about the kids?"

"The kids?" I repeated, looking at Tucker. "The kids are gone. Swallowed by the hopeless, hungry maw of life. We don't even know their names."

"The woman shot in the restaurant?"

"A Rio de Janeiro streetwalker. If anyone misses her, it'll probably be a regular john. And me, Joe. I'll miss her." Tucker must have seen something in my eyes, because he put his hand lightly on my shoulder.

"You can't fix it all, you know. No one can. It's a whirl-pool. It'll suck you right down if you let it."

"There's one thing I *can* fix," I said, "but it requires a special favor."

"Name it," Tucker sighed.

"Send that prick Lopez back to Peru."

Sixteen

During my second year of life, while my parents were making love in our apartment in New York, my father's prophylactic ruptured. It was a small break, beginning as a microscopic defect in the latex, but it spread like an earthquake along a fault line until it bisected the rubber and let spill seed that was never intended for egg.

The result, nine months later, was my sister Rachel. I remember going to the hospital to see her, pushing in the door to my mother's private room, a door that appeared as tall as the Empire State Building and as vast as the Great Wall of China. I remember seeing my mother, sunken deep into the pillows, with a rosy, joyous look on her face that transcended her mortal exhaustion. I remember too, the tiny, swaddled girl in her arms. Babies are supposed to be born with their eyes closed, and those eyes are wont to change color over the course of time, but neither was true for

Rachel. From her earliest moments until her dying day, her eyes were the clear and brilliant blue of the coastal Mediterranean in summer, holding a promise that would never be realized and questions nobody could answer.

She stared up at me and wrapped her tiny hand around my finger at once, precociously, because developmentally speaking, grasping is supposed to come later. Nobody before or since has ever entranced me as much as my baby sister did. I wanted to move into the hospital, to stay with her, comfort her when she cried, hold her when she smiled — even, later, change her diapers, which is something most little boys (and most men) are loath to do.

After a time my mother brought her home, thus beginning a magical period of my childhood that stands alone in the temple of my memory as an interval of security, joy, discovery, and love. Rachel's first four years of life coincided with a renaissance in my parents' marriage, a period when their outward displays of affection, always the ultimate determinant of a family's health, were frequent and tender. Those were also years during which my father was happy and successful at work, a time when the apartment was filled with positive energy and change. I did well academically during those days too, but more important, the presence of Rachel gave me a new inquisitiveness and patience with my classmates and friends. The result was a mini–golden age of socializing for me. I had a friend named Matthew who had no arms, and I loved to help him pick up pencils in his feet. I had another friend named Philippe, a fantastic runner, and always first to be picked for the dodgeball team, though I myself was ponderous and always chosen last. I even had a friend named Helen with whom I played doctor. But best of all, I had Rachel, who loved me unconditionally, who wanted to bring her junior bed into my room, who wanted to watch whatever

I watched on TV, who wanted to read my books even before she could distinguish a word.

I thought about Rachel a lot on the flight back to Miami, alone in my seat by the window, staring out at the clouds. In particular, I remembered her fourth birthday. My parents threw a party for her. There were balloons and mocha cake because Rachel loved the taste of coffee, and a bunch of Rachel's friends from the apartment building were there, and so were some of my schoolmates and my mother's cousins.

I remember that I played the clown, with my face all painted. I did little magic tricks my Grandpa Isaac taught me, and Rachel figured most of them out. At one point I tickled her, and as she ran from me, she tripped over a balloon string. Her reflexes were good, and she put out her arm to stop her chin from hitting the kitchen floor. She cried a little bit, but within minutes was up and laughing again. She drew in as if to give me a kiss, but smeared icing across my cheek instead. She giggled, I growled, and we all played a round of pin the tail on Ernst, who was dressed as a donkey.

But late that afternoon, after all the children had gone home, Rachel complained that her elbow hurt. She had been wearing a little red dress over a white, long-sleeved blouse, and when my mother rolled her sleeve up, we all saw the most grotesque bruise imaginable. The years since then, and my guilt and sadness, have no doubt made it worse, but I recall that during the days that followed the bruise grew as long as a winter squash, and turned the colors of a depressed rainbow — navy blue, shameful red, burnt orange, dead-moth yellow.

There were, of course, other bruises, but it was the rash of tiny cracked blood vessels that spread over her entire body that finally moved my parents to take her to the pediatrician — thus bringing about the end of life as it might have been. The visit to the doctor turned immediately into a visit to the hospital, and my mother and Rachel were gone a long time. They came home just in time for dinner. Rachel seemed sad, my mother and father didn't speak one word to each other, and nobody wanted to hear about my baseball game. Later, after dinner, I wanted to play with Rachel, but my mother wouldn't let me wake her. Long past midnight, sensing something dire in the air, I awakened and heard voices and crept down the hall to my parents' bedroom and stood outside the door.

It was there, alone in the dark, that I first heard uttered the word "leukemia."

Great strides have been made in the treatment of childhood leukemia. Life expectancy is longer, and remission is now possible. Current treatments include sophisticated combinations of drugs and precisely targeted radiation, but back then, Rachel was dosed heavily with X rays and treated with an alkylating agent called Myleran, which inhibited DNA replication, making it more difficult for tumor cells to grow. She suffered from terrible diarrhea, and all her hair fell out. Her mucous membranes, in particular her nose and her mouth, grew raw with sores, and her appetite was poor because it hurt her so much to eat.

Rachel's suffering, and our collective frustration at being unable to ease it, was rendering tempers short. Patience was in short supply, all the more because Grandpa Isaac and Grandma Sara came to live with us for a while to help out with things, crowding our little apartment. My mother in particular seemed stressed by the lack of privacy, sighing in relief every morning when Isaac, who was still stubbornly working his garment district pushcart at the time, left for work with my father. The two of them

wore greatcoats and hats and stood in the hallway waiting
for the elevator side by side, their heads bowed low, looking like funeral directors.

Usually my grandmother stayed home with me while
my mother took Rachel to the hospital for treatments, but
there was one day when Isaac desperately needed her help
with the business — Sara had a mind for books and Isaac
didn't — and thus she couldn't babysit. This meant that I
had to go with my mother to the hospital, and remain quietly in the antiseptic waiting room while men in white
coats irradiated my sister. I did a pretty good job of amus-
ing myself with old *Life* magazines until I heard Rachel
scream in terror. Nobody was more in tune with Rachel
than I was, no one knew her intimate tones as well. I leapt
from the blue plastic chair that held me and ran through
the hospital corridor, and when another scream came, I
found the right door and burst in.

What I saw was Rachel, naked except for little lead
packs on her chest, neck, and genitals, lying on an X-ray
table. She was strapped in place by leather bands at her
midsection, ankles and wrists, and there was a sheet of
tissue under her. Above her loomed a device of armatures
and linkages and levers and knobs, culminating in a cone.
The cone was down low over her fragile little white body.
She was completely alone in the room, as everyone, even
my mother, had retreated to the protection of a lead-lined
antechamber.

They were watching though, through a specially
treated pane of glass, and they saw me enter. Rachel had
been crying, but she stopped at the sight of me, at least
until my mother burst in and grabbed my hand and
dragged me back out into the hall. She started to yell and
ask me what the hell I thought I was doing, but the look
on my face must have stopped her because suddenly she
hugged me and stroked my hair. That night my father

came home from work late, and he avoided me. During the night, I heard him go into Rachel's room. I heard him sobbing, and I heard my mother come in and drag him away. Someone must have left a window open in the apartment that night, because sometime before dawn, hope flew away.

Toward the end, they had Rachel on morphine, and she dozed most of the time. To my seven-year-old eye, she seemed never fully awake, and her thinking seemed dull. Years later I came to understand that her brain was being damaged by the regular barrage of electrons, but back then I thought she was getting dumb. Once I told her so. My mother overheard, and slapped me. There was a lot of slapping in those final days.

I went to the hospital one last time to see my sister. She weighed twenty-one pounds, and looked like a bed-bug, diminutive and skeletal and chitinous and frail. As I later reconstructed it, the chemotherapy had wiped out her bone marrow and the doctors were unable to control the series of infections that beset her, including a fungal infection that looked like snowflakes on the radiograph hung on the lightbox behind her bed. She was on a ventilator, and there were needles as big as fingers in her tiny shrunken arms. Her doctor explained — as if focusing on facts utterly meaningless to a seven-year-old would help avoid the larger news that Rachel was poised to die — that the needles were delivering three different antibiotics, epinephrine to keep her blood pressure up, and saline and dopamine to keep her hydrated and calm. There was a feeding tube in her nose, and a ventilator tube down her throat. The day she died, I fought to try and pull that tube out so that I could kiss her goodbye deeply, the way I'd seen grownups do. It took five nurses to pull me away.

It was morning when I landed at Miami International. The sun was shining, and through the leaks in the imperfect seal between the jetway door and fuselage, I could feel that the mercury was up. Florida is like that in the spring and fall. Weather fronts go through like blinks in the eyes of God, transporting the peninsula tens of degrees of latitude in moments. I sailed through customs and immigration with my little red passport, but got lost for twenty minutes in the parking structure—whoever designed MIA was smoking something, and it wasn't cigarettes—before I found my Porsche. The frustrating search did nothing but enhance my conviction that there was only one place I needed to go, and one person I needed to talk to, so when I finally found the car, I laid rubber for Mercy Hospital.

The place was a labyrinth of buildings in a wealthy section of coastline between Coral Gables and Coconut Grove. It took me a while to find the information desk, and when I did, the old man behind the counter was completely unimpressed by my shield. He made it clear that over the years many rich and powerful luminaries had been treated at Mercy, and that many had come in with their own security guards or police escorts. In all fairness to him, I looked nervous and haggard—hospitals still do that to me—and exuded the odor of cheap cigarettes from the international flight.

"We've had the FBI here," he sniffed. "We've had the Secret Service. But a postal inspector?"

"I'm not asking for the moon," I said, irritated, "I'd just like to know where I can find Dr. O'Burke."

"And I told you I would be happy to page her," he repeated.

"I am a federal officer, and this is a law-enforcement matter," I said evenly.

"A postal inspector is a federal officer?"

"Yes," I said, gritting my teeth.

"Then just let me page her."

"I don't wish to discuss official business in the lobby."

"Then I'm going to call hospital security. Maybe they can help you."

The information kiosk was a self-contained gazebo with a little round roof. As the old man picked up the phone, I vaulted smoothly over the counter, landed beside his chair, and trapped his hand on the telephone receiver. "Call nobody," I hissed.

He rocked back, his legs, in bright pink slacks, flailing about for balance. I grabbed the chair and rolled him forward so my face was next to his. "What's your name?" I demanded.

"Chaim Moscowitz," he answered, his voice trembling.

"Okay, Chaim," I whispered conspiratorially. "I've just flown in from South America with information relating to a major crime investigation. I know that you're being cautious because you know Dr. O'Burke's father is the biggest crime boss in Miami. I am really taking you into my confidence when I tell you that Dr. O'Burke has information that could save lives. Now tell me what ward she works on so that I can go to her nicely and quietly and ask what I need to ask and be out of here without causing her an embarrassing stir."

"Fifth floor," he whispered. "Internal Medicine."

"You're my man," I patted his hand.

Everything went much more smoothly at the fifth floor nursing station, probably because I didn't flash any I.D. It seemed like the desk crew was accustomed to guys calling on Guiomary; an idea that gave me a jealous twinge in my stomach.

"I've got a special little romantic surprise for her," I said, taking advantage of their suspicions by playing the nervous suitor to the hilt. "A video of us together. Do you think you could help me find a VCR and a TV, then page her to the room without telling her anything?"

It was such an outrageous request, it worked. The nurses winked at each other, rolled their eyes, even gig- gled. They found me a conference room, the kind of place doctors use to discuss patients who are not doing well, the type of room in which, a quarter century ago, a doctor had explained respirators and intravenous therapy to a seven-year-old boy.

I tried not to think about Rachel as I pulled the videos out of my travel bag, loaded the one of the little girl mak- ing love to the goat, and organized the rest in a stack by the player. I checked my look in the mute, dark television screen and prepared myself for Guiomary's arrival. As it turned out, I didn't have long to wait. She came in slowly, turning the door handle and peering cautiously into the room. When she saw me, her face lit up like a comet. "Maximillian!" she exclaimed. "What a nice surprise!"

She was wearing an open white coat with a photo name tag clipped to the collar, navy slacks and a white blouse, a drug company penlight protruding from the pocket. A stethoscope hung loosely around her neck, par- tially obscuring a lavish emerald and gold necklace far be- yond a young doctor's salary. Someone was keeping her in style. I hoped it was her father.

I told her she was the only person in the world who used my full name.

"But it's a wonderful name," she protested. "A distin- guished name."

"Still, most people just call me Max."

"I prefer Maximillian. Tell me, how is your foot?"

"Almost all better. I have the best doctor in town."

"You charmed the nurses, you know," she blushed. "They refused to tell me who was in here."

"It was mesmerism. I use the light reflecting off my bald head like an old-time hypnotist might use a watch. Tick, tock, back and forth. They go under my spell. They can't resist me."

"That last part I believe. When did you get back? My father told me that he heard you were out of the country." Cuco O'Burke was keeping track of my whereabouts. I felt a momentary panic, like maybe my parachute wasn't going to open, and this plunge I had taken, a plunge of the heart, was going to end in a high-velocity splat.

"Guiomary," I said. "Will you have dinner with me a week from Saturday?"

"Is that why you came here?" she asked coquettishly. "To ask me out?"

"It's one reason."

"Why do we have to wait so long? Are you traveling again?"

"No, but you're going to need time to forgive me."

"Forgive you?" she frowned.

Before I could explain, the door burst open. Two burly boys in blue uniforms came in, the Mercy hospital logo on their shoulders. Security. Thank you, Chaim, you old bastard.

"What's this?" demanded Guiomary, confused.

"The front desk called, Doctor," one of the men replied. "Said you might have trouble."

"I don't have any trouble, thank you. This gentleman is a friend of mine."

They looked me up and down. I could see the doubt in their eyes. Obviously they knew about Cuco. Any security director smarter than a granite slab would recognize the risk of having a crime boss's daughter on staff. "You're sure everything's all right?"

"I'm sure," Guiomary said firmly.

They departed reluctantly, leaving us alone in the room.

Guiomary's trusting gaze nearly drove me into her arms. I wanted to cry my aching heart out, to do what I had never done with anyone—tell her about Rachel. I wanted to confess to her how difficult it was for me to enter a hospital, how the white halls forced upon me my oldest, darkest memories. Instead—because I was a law-enforcement professional—I asked her to sit, and when she did, I turned on the television. Snow danced across the screen, accompanied by the loud sound of static.

"I hate like hell to do this, but I've got to show you a few short tapes."

She looked at me expectantly. I started the VCR playing. The little girl wandered into the barn. The goat made grunting noises as she stimulated its penis. "What is this?" Guiomary whispered, shrinking down in her chair.

I replaced the barn scene with the tape of the Itaipú maiming, cued to begin at the unforgettable naked lineup. "My God!" Guiomary's hand flew to her mouth.

I closed my eyes because I couldn't watch her anymore, and listened to the sound of the clinking of handcuffs, the sound of metal striking flint, the roar of the blowtorch bursting to life.

"You need to leave," said Guiomary. It wasn't clear whether she was talking to me, or to herself, but she seemed paralyzed, her eyes glued to the screen.

I loaded the restaurant sequence. The little blue-eyed Rachel danced to a few notes of violin music, and then the late and unlamented Raúl Nuñez pulled the trigger of his competition Colt Gold Cup, spattering the young hooker's brains everywhere.

All the color drained from Guiomary's face. She rose and headed for the door. I intercepted her, forcing her to turn around and sit down again. I put the last tape in. She hid her face in her hands. I grabbed her wrists and pulled them down. She turned her head away. I turned it back. The boat scene came up on the screen: the naked teenage girl emerged from the cabin, Abel Lopez led her to the gunwale. Guiomary twisted and bucked.

"Watch!" I commanded hoarsely.

Abel penetrated the girl. Guiomary struck out wildly, pummeling my arms, my sides, my hips. Abel produced the knife, and using the tip of his blade, found the soft spot he was looking for. Guiomary shrieked and burst into sobs.

I let her go.

"You made me watch," she said finally as if she still couldn't believe it. We were still sitting together in that room. Ten minutes of silence had passed.

"I'm sorry. You could have closed your eyes."

"Why did you do it?"

"Those tapes were intercepted in the hands of your father's courier."

"My father has nothing to do with those tapes!" she said dully. "He runs a nightclub. He owns condominiums. He doesn't film murders with children dancing naked."

"You may be right about that, but I still need your help."

"My help?" She seemed suddenly exhausted. "Do you know how many FBI men have tried to get to Cuco through my bed, Maximillian? How many undercover cops and agents of the Drug Enforcement Agency? What makes you think you're special? What makes you think I would betray my own father for you?"

Her disappointment in me hurt. No more Cervantes romance. No more Dulcinea. No more tilting at windmills. Here we were, back in the cold cruel world where she was the daughter of a crime boss and I was a cop.

"Your father was going to pass the tapes on to someone, Guiomary. A slaver. A man who sells children into prostitution, maybe into death. I'm not sure your father ever saw these tapes, or knew what was on them. He was a link in the chain, that's all. I'm not after him. I'm after the other guy. As for what makes me special, that's an easy one. The cops, the FBI, the DEA, those men weren't in love with you."

"And you are, huh? Well, I have news for you, Maximillian. You don't know what love is. Nobody who loved me could do what you just did. Nobody who loved me could have shown me those tapes! You're just a cop willing to go one step further than most, that's all. If I told my father you'd be dead by the end of the day." That last declaration spilled out of her, sounding so juvenile and terrifying and spoiled and sad that it left both of us wild-eyed and breathless.

"Guiomary," I said, reaching out to her.

Her hand flew to her mouth. "My God. Did you hear what I said?"

"You're angry. You have a right to be."

"I can't stand this," she said, curling up like a conch. I don't want anything to do with murder and torture and porn and policemen. Why can't everyone just leave me alone?"

"You're brave," I said, taking her hand. She tried to pull away, but I held tight. "You stayed around Miami, which is more than I could do. When my dad got in trouble with the law, I ran as far away as I could." That got a flicker of interest from her, but it faded. "Ever since I saw you in that green dress at the New Havana, I've been thinking of you night and day," I went on. "I should be afraid of your father, but I'm not. But you're right. I am just a cop willing to go one step further, and I'm sorry for what you had to see, but I need your help desperately."

"Just forget about me," she said, sounding old and tired.

"I've tried. I can't. Will you help me find the slaver's name?"

"Go away."

"Please?"

"Go before I call those guards back here."

I handed her my card. "Ring me day or night," I said.

"Don't count on it."

"I *am* counting on it."

She straightened her blouse and her coat, and adjusted her name tag, as if reminding herself who she was. Then she walked out.

I don't know what I had been expecting, but Metro-Dade Detective Todd Steiner wasn't it. He looked like a refugee from *Miami Vice*; shirt of mauve silk, slightly pleated tan pants, a wethead haircut, maroon tie, Bruno Magli shoes. His face was faintly pockmarked, as if he had suffered from acne as a child, but had scrubbed his face every day since with fine sandpaper.

"Max Diamond," I introduced myself.

"Todd Steiner, like it says on the door," he shook my hand.

"Nice shoes."

"I was wearing Maglis when O. J. Simpson was still in diapers," he said defensively. "Anyway you're not a fashion plate. Looks to me like you're wearing *clogs*!"

"They're good on airplanes. Let the feet swell. I just landed at MIA. International case."

274

"Big man."

"The biggest. Look, I thought I'd stop by while I was down here and check up on the Boatwright-Grayson killings. Cliff Hughes gave me the same files he gave you, and I read them on the flight. What do you make of this guy Reilly?"

Steiner leaned forward on his desk and made a temple of his hands. "I think he's too loud to be a killer."

"Unless the homicidal urge just washed over him one day."

"I don't think so. I've gone over his business operations, checked out the deal he tried to pull off in South Beach. He's not a bad guy, just a business man who knew those theaters would make money down there."

"He's willing to set up porno houses for a buck, that's gotta say something about him."

Steiner shrugged. "Owning a blue-movie theater in this day and age isn't the worst thing in the world. This is Miami-Dade, Diamond. You wouldn't believe the stuff I see. Anyway, I'm not a morality dick—I'm only interested in whether he killed your friends."

A morality dick. That was a good one. "And you don't think he did?"

He shook his head. "Too methodical a customer. A planner. Careful. The forms he filled out, the way he went after the city council for those permits. Calculating."

"The letters I saw were pretty inflammatory."

"That much is true. He lost his temper. Still, a nasty letter is a long way from murder."

"You'd be surprised how many times I see the two come together in my line of work."

"I probably would. Anyway, he's got an alibi for Boatwright."

"What about for Grayson?"

"He was eating out alone. That's what he says, anyway.

Got a restaurant manager who remembers seeing him, but won't swear to the time."

"So tell me what you're thinking."

"I've toyed with the idea that we have two killers, a copycat if you will, but I've decided that's wrong. The way I'm leaning right now, Grayson's death was a diversion. A way of covering up Boatwright's, of drawing us off the mark, making us think they're linked so we'll look in the wrong place for the killer."

"How do you get that?"

"Those three attorneys were involved in totally different things. Their outfit is set up to be three practices under one roof. They didn't work together on cases or even share secretaries or paralegals. Nobody with a grudge against one of those lawyers would have any reason to have a grudge against another."

"The killer might not know how the firm works."

"True. And in that case, your friend Hughes is in a world of shit."

"And what about Hughes himself?" I asked slowly.

"You mean as the killer?" Steiner looked surprised at that one. "Why don't you tell me? You're the one who's known him since college. To me the guy seems scared shitless. Rising to the professional challenge of being alone in that firm, but scared shitless nonetheless. Plus, he's a timid little guy, and there's no motive."

"I don't disagree," I nodded. "I just wanted to make sure we both had our cards on the table."

"One more thing that supports my theory about one murder clouding the reason for the other," Steiner added. "If this were a raging vendetta against the firm, I'd expect to see some physical damage by now. A fire, vandalism to the building, carefully planted libel that costs the firm its reputation, a financial attack on its investments or holdings. I haven't found anything like that. Then there's the fact that your buddy Boatwright liked the horses a little too much."

"Gambling debts?" Somehow, the news didn't surprise me.

"Big time."

"You're thinking some bookie did him and then tried to cover his tracks with Grayson?"

"Just a thought. Trouble is I've got no hard motive. He gambled, he lost, but he seems to have paid."

My cell phone rang. "Max, it's Wacona. Your plane arrived two hours ago. Where are you?"

"I'm in Coral Gables, meeting with Detective Steiner."

"Coral Gables, huh? Well quit slumming, get on the freeway, put your foot to the floor, and don't let up until you get here. Regina Diaz's brother is holed up in the West Palm G.M.F. Somehow he got into the administrative offices with a weapon. He's holding hostages, and he's demanding to see you."

SEVENTEEN

The West Palm Beach General Mail Facility on Summit Boulevard is a large facility, relatively modern as post offices go, with an enormous work floor, big rear loading area, up-to-date sorting equipment, teller window computers and the U.S.P.S. video network wired in so that customers can watch TV while they wait in line. When I arrived, the Palm Beach County Sheriff's Office had established a perimeter, and customers and employees were being efficiently shepherded out through the front door and to their vehicles in the parking lot. A couple of uniforms in pressed tans tried to stop me from getting in, and shook their heads in disapproval when I flashed my I.D., but let me pass. I couldn't blame them. I still hadn't been home to clean up, I was exhausted and propped up on coffee, and my five o'clock shadow was halfway to a short beard.

I went through the double doors labeled ADMINISTRATIVE OFFICES and found

279

Wacona standing in the front hallway, conferring with Mozart.

"This looking-like-shit is getting to be a regular thing with you, Max," Wacona said dryly.

"Nice to see you too. Where's Chunny?"

"A fraud workshop in Atlanta," Mozart replied. I could tell Wacona wished that wasn't so. Hotshot though she was, it would have been good to have the old man at a crisis scene like this one.

"Who's taking the lead?"

"I am. There's a sheriff S.W.A.T. leader outside, but I'm holding him off."

"What exactly went down?"

She pointed to a door with a circular window labeled CONSUMER AFFAIRS at the end of the hall. "From what we can piece together, Diaz's brother came over here looking for you. There was a line of people, and apparently he got tired of waiting. When one of the floor employees slipped out to take a break, he caught the security door before it could close and slipped inside. He must have gone down the hallway, seen the sign for the administrative offices. Anyhow, he ended up inside there, and he's got the postmaster and Fred Groom hostage, as well as secretaries and we're not sure who else."

Fred Groom was the district manager. He'd been running postal operations in Palm Beach county for years—a chain-smoking, coffee-swizzling bureaucrat, but a guy who surprisingly enough shared my love of motorcycles. We'd gone riding a couple of times. He had a big Harley dresser. It was his pride and joy.

"How did you find out?" I asked.

"He let Groom ring us. We came right over."

"Do you want me to go inside?" I asked Waco.

She shook her head, pointed to a desk phone. "I'm not putting you in the line of fire. You can reach Diaz from here. Don't promise him anything, but find out what he wants and how many people are in there. Try to get him to put Fred on the line." I called.

"This better be Diamond," said the voice on the other end of the phone.

"This is Inspector Diamond," I said carefully. "Who are you?"

"Diamond, you *hijo de puta!*" he swore. "You killed my sister!"

"Who's speaking?"

"You had to go after her, huh? Getting your jollies off tailing a beautiful woman around. Like it was going to break you to pay her a lousy couple of grand a month. Two little kids are orphans now, just because you stuck your nose in her business."

"What happened to your sister was tragic, but it didn't have anything to do with me personally or the United States Postal Inspection Service."

"I wanted to adopt her kids," he said, his voice suddenly sad. "But I have a sheet, and they won't let me. I thought maybe you could help."

"That's why you came looking for me?" I asked, incredulous.

"That's right," he said, furious again. "And nobody would even talk to me!"

"What's your name," I asked quietly.

"José."

"All right, José. Let's see if we can get this straightened out. Put one of the hostages on the phone."

I heard a shuffling sound, and then someone picked up the receiver. "Max?" a hoarse voice came across the line. "It's Fred."

"You all right?"

"For the moment. This guy's wound pretty tight. Don't fuck with him, okay? Give him what he wants."

"What happened, exactly?"

"He came in asking for you, got agitated when we told him you didn't work here, insisted that you come to him."

"Where are you, exactly?"

"My office."

"How many in there with you?"

Regina's brother came back on the line before he could answer. "Enough talk. Now get in here, before I have to start killing people."

"I wish you hadn't said that," I sighed. "It changes everything."

Small-town police departments assemble their Special Weapons and Tactics team from regular officers who have other duties. Larger communities, and many county sheriff departments, have dedicated S.W.A.T. teams that train together full time to stay sharp. The Palm Beach County Sheriff's Office was headquartered only a few blocks from the G.M.F. and although technically they would coordinate with the U.S.P.I.S.'s own team if the situation dragged out, they were eager to go in quickly. This put pressure on Wacona, and it showed.

"Don't worry. Nothing bad is going to happen on your watch," Mozart soothed her. She seemed to accept this assurance from him, and I found that astonishing. If I had said it, or, worse, if Chunny had, she would have flared with a self-righteous tirade about her own competence. There was something in Mozart's manner, however, that seemed not to raise her hackles. Maybe it was just that the little guy was gay.

"I need to go in, but I need to know something about the layout first," I said.

"I'll call a tech. We'll get microphones and a camera

ASAP," Wacona said briskly. She seemed back in charge now.

"Why not let Palm Beach S.W.A.T. do it?" I suggested.

"Forget that. Let *me* do it," Mozart urged. "I was on a surveillance this morning. I've still got the shit in the car." Before Wacona could even answer, he had scampered out of the station. We both watched him go.

"He was a marine," she said distantly.

"He was more than that. He was a tunnel rat in Vietnam. I assume you realize what that means?"

"Titanium testicles," Wacona said wryly. We looked at each other and we laughed. It was nice, especially considering the circumstances. While we waited for Mozart to return, I filled her in on the last couple of days, omitting, of course, my visit to Guiomary.

"How are you going to identify this Twilight guy?" she asked.

"I've got a couple of leads," I said vaguely.

Mozart reappeared with his equipment in a briefcase, and the three of us pored over the station blueprints together, finally deciding that the wall shared by the D.M.'s office and the work floor was the best place to put in the fiber-optic viewer.

"A distraction would buy us some time to set up," I mused.

"So we order a pizza," Waco suggested.

"A pizza?" Mozart and I chorused.

"Sure. It'll keep Diaz from thinking about what else we might be doing."

There was something amazing about Wacona when she got cocky; almost a Jekyll and Hyde thing. She went from officious and serious to radiant and magnetic. She beckoned to one of the uniformed deputies in the atrium, and he came over at a trot. "We have hungry hostages.

Which do you think is better, Dominos or Pizza Hut?" she asked the cop.

"Papa John's," the kid replied instantly. He looked about the right age to know. "Get one vegetarian and one pepperoni, that way everyone will be happy."

"You're going to go far in the department, deputy. Remember that I said that. Now go outside for me and tell your pals to let the delivery truck through when it shows up."

"Yes ma'am!" he saluted smartly.

Equipped with two-way radios, Mozart and I rushed off to install the viewer. The last thing I heard was Wacona on the phone with the pizza parlor, demanding the very next pies out of the oven. I couldn't imagine anyone saying no to her.

Normally, the giant post office would be humming with activity in the middle of the afternoon, sorting machines running, workers pushing carts of flats and bundles here and there, the distant roar of trucks coming and going at the loading docks out back. Instead, there was a science-fiction-like silence to it; the aftermath of a neutron bomb attack maybe, or the consequence of some vaporizing laser beam from space.

"I've heard more noise in a funeral parlor," Mozart whispered.

"It'll be a funeral parlor if those S.W.A.T. yahoos rush in here while we're skulking around."

"You ought to trust Wacona more by now, Max. She has everything under control. She's a Gemini, you know. She wears great perfume, but don't doubt she can kick ass."

"What are you, the Wacona Smith expert all of a sudden? You're brown-nosing her, aren't you, you bastard?"

He cuffed me on the side of the head.

We found the wall we were looking for, and knelt down beside it together. Mozart put a masonry bit in the little hand drill and laid out the eyepiece, the bug, and a piece of fiber-optic cable attached to a small video screen. I called Wacona on the two-way and told her we were in position.

"Good," she said. "Pizza's here. Some mid-day stoners with the munchies are going to have to eat the carpet instead. And Diaz is asking for you again. He said he's sick of waiting. I told him I wouldn't send you in there and let you shoot him. He says he just wants to talk."

I left Mozart to the business of drilling through the wall, and hustled back out to the atrium. The S.W.A.T. presence was growing, young guys milling about with glinting eyes. Wacona was juggling two pizza pies back and forth in her hands. I rang Diaz and told him I had pizza.

"Pizza?" he said incredulously.

"Come on, José, I'm trying to help you here. Those people are innocent, and I'm betting they're hungry. I've got two pies waiting."

"Keep the pizza and offer me immunity instead. And while you're at it, fix it so I can adopt my sister's kids."

"Free some hostages, then we can talk."

"You want me to trust you? You're the guy who got my sister's head shot off! I wanna know how come I don't hear about no investigation on the news, nothing about finding her killer. I want you to stop covering up the truth of what happened, that you were harassing her for making a few extra bucks for her kids and you got her murdered by some gangster."

"I'm working hard to find her killer, Diaz," I said carefully. "A big news story wouldn't make our job any easier."

"Fuck you and fuck your job. I want television cameras here. I want the world to know what happened to Regina. I want you to tell them."

"Television cameras," I repeated.

Wacona rolled her eyes and shrugged her way into a bulletproof vest, fastening the Velcro tabs snugly over her breasts. It was an incredibly sexy gesture, and by the looks on the faces of the cops, I wasn't the only one who thought so. She picked up the pies, preparing to take them in.

"Let me," said one of the S.W.A.T. officers. Wacona brushed him aside.

"She's going in," I told Mozart over the two-way. "Wait about forty-five seconds and then drill."

"Here comes the pizza," I told Diaz.

"Forget the pizza! Get that reporter!"

Wacona headed in. I watched through the little glass window in the door. She made one heck of a delivery girl, her hips swinging, the pies balancing on her shoulder. She put them down by the door to the administrative offices, and made a big business of shouting and knocking. Nobody opened the door. Finally, she backed out.

"I told him I had one with olives and peppers and extra cheese, and one with pepperoni," she informed me when she was safely with us again. "He just kept yelling your name."

"I've got video," Mozart informed us over the two-way. "Diaz is thin and nervous. Hyperactive, like maybe he's speeding. He keeps drinking from the fountain. He's got seven in the D.M.'s office, three women, four men. They seem unhurt, but he's got a wondernine in his belt. Could be a Baretta, I can't quite tell. Some of the hostages are eating the pizza. Amazing, huh? Look, there's an air-conditioning grille right behind the D.M.'s desk. I'm thinking I can go down the duct and get in there. How about rounding me up some flash grenades?"

The S.W.A.T. leader rocked forward on his feet like a sprinter. There were tiny beads of sweat under his black baseball cap, and his nostrils were flared. He was ready. "Those ducts are about two feet square," he snorted. "He doesn't have a prayer of climbing through it."

"Just get the grenades," Wacona said.

Sheriff's deputies had been holding a few news teams at the parking lot perimeter, and I instructed them to admit one reporter and one cameraman. Then I called Diaz and told him that if he wanted that interview, he'd have to free a couple of women. He said *coño* a few times.

"You can curse me out all you want, José, but you're still going to have to cooperate. At least if you want out of there alive."

"Fuck you," he said.

"The vest makes the going slow," Mozart told me over the radio. "Didn't wear one in the Nam. I'm going to need a diversion when I get to that grille. Don't call me again, sound travels in these chutes. I'll tap the mike three times with my finger when I'm ready. You tap it back three times when you want me to break through."

The reporter came in then, an auburn haired beauty with the arrogant, invulnerable swagger of youth. "Were you responsible for the sister's death?" she asked me without preamble.

"Of course not," I answered amicably. "I was investigating her for worker's compensation fraud when I rescued her from being beaten to death by her boyfriend."

"She's dead though, right? So you didn't really save her?"

"Can we go off the record here for a second?"

She made a sign with her finger and the cameraman put his lens down.

"Regina Diaz was accidentally hit when her boyfriend — who beat her deaf, by the way — was shot down gangland-style on the courthouse steps. No doubt you remember the story. This guy José is holding hostages at gunpoint in the administrative offices. He wants to talk to you. We'll only allow that if he releases the hostages, or comes out alone."

She nodded. Mozart made my radio click. I called Diaz and told him the reporter was here, and that I was bringing her in.

Postal inspectors are trained for this sort of action, but unlike riding a bicycle, one has to keep current if one wants to survive. The reflexes required, the tried and true techniques that have been developed and observed at the cost of lives and over a period of many years, need to be honed and practiced. That was why there were S.W.A.T. teams. I wasn't current, I hadn't practiced, and I wasn't honed. In fact, as I led the reporter in, I was scared as hell. "Talk to him," I urged her.

"Mister Diaz, this is Karen Lazarus from the local news You need to free some hostages before they'll let me in!" she yelled down the hall.

The door at the end of the corridor suddenly swung open and a middle-aged woman in a cocoa-colored dress came dashing out. She shoved past me and Lazarus without even looking at us, heading for the outdoors like a sun-starved iguana.

"All right! I'm waiting!" Diaz called out.

"Come talk to her in the hall," I called back.

"And give your snipers a shot at me? I don't think so!"

"Let me go," Lazarus implored.

"No chance."

But she was a glory hound, and that wasn't the answer she wanted. Winking to her cameraman, she bolted for the office. I tried to grab her, but I tripped on her microphone cable and went down. Desperately, I sent Mozart the signal on the two-way, and before my thumb had even come off the button, there was a series of flashes so bright I was sure my eyeballs would melt. I heard Lazarus scream. Still blind from the flash grenade, I felt oiled steel jammed roughly between my teeth. I blinked, I gagged. I tried to pull away.

"You took my sister," Diaz said into my ear. "She was all I had."

I tried to focus, but got only starbursts and the faintest outline of movement. When my sight finally returned, it was piecemeal, but enough to see that I was on the floor in the hallway with Diaz. Shapes rushed by me; presumably the news team and hostages. They couldn't see any better than I could, and they bumped into each other in a panicked frenzy, falling, getting up again, using their hands to guide them along the wall.

"Take the gun out of Inspector Diamond's mouth," I heard Mozart say.

Not words I ever thought I'd hear. I looked up and saw vaguely that he was wearing dark goggles. He looked like a raccoon. His service Baretta was against Diaz's temple.

"I'll kill him," Diaz said faintly.

"And I'll kill you," Mozart hissed. "And you know what? I'll enjoy the hell out of it. You're chicken shit to me, see? And if you don't take that gun away from my partner's head, I'm going to wipe the floor with your tongue and put ten rounds straight up your ass."

Diaz's expression was incredulous.

"Do it now," said Mozart.

Diaz eased the gun out of my mouth and let it clatter to the floor. Mozart had the cuffs on him in an instant. He waved his little good luck Zuni frog at me and grinned.

"Sorry it didn't go down smoother," he said. "The fucker saw me throw the grenade and he covered his head before it went off. He didn't get it full in the eyes. It happens."

"Help my niece and nephew," Diaz implored.

"I'll see what I can do," I said, but as Mozart hustled him away, I was thinking that there was nothing I could do about the Diaz children, or any of the others who had so sadly and obliquely entered my life.

EIGHTEEN

As I departed the crime scene, I ran my tongue over the roof of my mouth. The front sight blade on Diaz's pistol had torn up the skin there. One quick glance into the Porsche's rearview mirror showed blood on my tongue. The pain wasn't mediated at all by the fact that I had just helped free seven hostages. I was going around in circles and I knew it. All the resources of the United States Postal Inspection Service, all the fancy video analysis, my own investigative persistence, even an international foray, and I was no closer to stopping the murderers and child pornographers from operating in South Florida.

My cell phone rang. It was Guiomary. "I just saw you on a news flash," she said. "Are you all right?"

"I'm fine."

"You don't sound fine. What happened to the hostages? The story was a little sketchy."

"They're all right."

"And José Diaz?" Karen Lazarus had sure let it all hang out.

"Nobody shot him full of holes, if that's what you're asking."

"I'm glad. Look, Maximillian, I need to see you."

"Wasn't it just a few hours ago that you threw me out of a conference room?"

"Please don't make this any more difficult than it already is."

"All right, I'm southbound on I-95 right now. Just north of Lake Worth. Do you want me to come to Miami?"

"I'll meet you halfway. Do you know Young's Circle in Hollywood?"

"It's a park, right? At Federal and Hollywood Boulevard? I was down there for a street fair once. Not a place to park a Bentley."

"I'm not worried about my car," she said, and hung up.

For a long moment, incredible weariness did battle with a spark of hope somewhere in my marrow. Then I put on the dome light and drove straight and fast. When I got to Hollywood, I stopped along the boulevard just long enough to pick up some antiseptic gel for my mouth, then went down to Federal Highway. The park was empty except for a few homeless men asleep on benches, and one crazy old woman who affectionately called the squirrels "cocksuckers" as she threw them their daily bread. Just to be sure we would be alone, I poked my head in both johns and had a gander around the pavilion at the east side of the circle. Guiomary showed up about ten minutes later.

"Your mouth is bleeding," she said as she came up to meet me beneath a parade of palms.

"Diaz shoved his gun in there."

"Why?"

"He had his reasons."

"What were they?"

"It was his sister that your father had killed. He blamed me for it. He wasn't entirely wrong. I've been dragging everybody into my own private quest, even that poor woman."

"The children quest?"

"That's right."

"Maximillian, explain to me why you care so much about these children."

Exhausted, I leaned against a palm tree and ended up sliding heavily to the ground. "I find that a strange question."

"Tell me anyway."

"Do you know the song 'Southern Cross' by Crosby, Stills, Nash, and Young?"

She shook her head.

"What about 'These Dreams' by Heart?"

"I know that one."

"How does it make you feel when you listen to it?"

"Wistful, I suppose."

"Why?"

"What does this have to do with the children, Maximillian?"

"Bear with me for a minute. Why wisftul?"

"I'm not sure."

"Could it be because not realizing our dreams is the worst thing that can happen to us? Our dreams are what we are. They separate us from each other, they bind us *to* each other, they make life something more than eating and screwing and breathing and shitting. Those poor helpless kids had their dreams taken away. Ripped from them. Do you understand? Someone stole their dreams, their futures, and their hope and I think that's about the worst crime in the world." I was flushed when I finished, and Guiomary stared down at me.

"What makes you feel that you're the one who needs to make that right?" she asked quietly.

Two pigeons postured over a few kernels of Cracker Jack. A drunken man spun in a balletic pirouette. I heard grasshoppers, the last ones out before winter. Maybe they were just crickets. I heard the quickening of my heart. Something was coming up out of me, something I didn't want her to see. I tried to move away, but she stopped me.

"Maximillian?" she prompted.

"I had a little sister named Rachel," I said at last. "She had blue eyes just like that kid dancing on the tabletop, the kid who was burned by the torch. She died of leukemia when she was four and I was seven. I loved her more than anything in the world. More than anybody before or since."

Guiomary took a step closer to me.

"Max," she said.

"You asked. You had to go and ask."

She took a deep breath. "My father didn't know what was on the films," she said at last. "He agreed to pass them on, that's all. He won't say to whom, and I pushed him as hard as I could. He says to speak a name would ruin his reputation. He did tell me that he absolutely did not order the hit on Cruz."

The hit on Cruz. I looked at her. Slinging the lingo cost her. She looked older. There were new lines on her face. I felt sad for her. I wanted to hold her. She was a stranger, but somehow our lives had become inextricably intertwined. "You believe that?" I asked.

"Oh yes. I know when he lies to me, Maximillian. I've known for years. When he lies, he says 'Goodness, Guiomary, what a thing to say.' When you came to the house that day, when your ankle was bleeding, I asked him whether what you were saying was true, and he looked me straight in the eye and he simply said no. That was the truth."

294

I nodded. She was making sense. My own father had speech patterns too. So did my mother. Family foibles. My poor dear Rachel had been a foot shuffler. Ask her something and if she wasn't being truthful, she had shuffled like a soft-shoe queen.

"What I told you about my sister, that's a family secret," I looked up at Guiomary. "I've never told anyone about her before."

"That's okay. What I did for you this afternoon, asking my father about his work, I've never done for anyone before either."

She slid down next to me. Slowly, I inched my body toward her. Closer. Closer. She smelled very faintly of baby powder deodorant activated by nervous perspiration. It was a lovely smell. We touched, generating a thousand little static shocks. I know she felt them too, because she shivered. I took her head in my hands, and I kissed her. She tasted of Cinnamon Tic Tacs. Her tongue was on fire.

Then she was gone.

I stumbled bleary-eyed out of the elevator, suitcase in hand, and headed down the walkway to my apartment thinking about Guiomary's kiss. A bat zoomed by, chasing a huge white moth. I turned the corner, and suddenly a man leapt out of the shadows and hurled himself at me.

"*Haiiiyaa!*" he screamed, aiming a karate chop at the base of my neck.

My adrenal glands squeezed off a volley, and I dropped under the blow, spiralling to trap his hand and pull him off balance.

"Almost got you!" Rigoberto the produce boy cried, looking up at me from the ground.

"Rigoberto," I said, keeping my temper — and with it,

the desire to drive my heel through his cheek—in check. "I am not Inspector Clouseau, you are not Cato. This is not a Pink Panther movie. I am exhausted, it's late, I haven't been home in days. Because I am so nice, I am going to let you live."

He jumped up, grinning. He was a handsome kid, and his smile transformed his face into a palace of shining white teeth. "You gotta admit that was a good one, huh?"

"Brilliant," I said wearily.

"Am I a t'ai chi master yet?"

"Not yet."

"But keep practicing, right? That's what you always say. Do everything two thousand times and then I'll understand."

"Ten thousand," I said, opening the door.

He followed me in, toting a box of produce.

"The turtle's sick," I said. "I'm not sure if he'll eat right now, but we can try. I left him in the bathroom with a heat lamp. I haven't seen him in a few days."

We went in and let him out. He looked better. I cleaned the floor. Rigoberto ran through his form once, in my living room, and I gave him some pointers, which were mostly about relaxation—the most challenging aspect of the internal martial arts. We live in a culture that generates pushing hard and working all the time. T'ai chi can't be beaten into submission like some things in life, it has to be finessed. It has to be seduced. Like love, it has to be given time.

I sent Rigoberto packing and ran a hot bath. I lathered my head for a shave and was about to set razor to flesh, when the doorbell rang. I closed my eyes and pretended I hadn't heard it, but whoever was out there was insistent. At length, I rinsed and went to the door in a towel.

"Open up, M.D. It's Phayle."

I hesitated. "I just got back into town from some over-seas travel, Phayle, and I'm bone tired. Would it be okay if I called you tomorrow?"

The silence that followed was so long, I thought she'd left. I used the peephole. She was still standing there, and the look on her face was a one-act play.

"You ask if it's okay to leave me standing outside your door? What's happened to you, Max? What's happened to us?"

I opened the door. Phayle looked me up and down, then swept past me. "We need to talk."

"Listen . . ." I began.

She held up her hand.

"No, *you* listen. I don't see you for something like eight years, it seems like some of the old magic is still there, but you've got a problem in bed. Even though I'm horny as hell for you, I tell you that's okay, and am as nice as anyone could be about it. Are you too embarrassed even to talk to me? Is that what this is all about?"

"Not at all. I was out of town."

"Was it talking about kids at Monkey Jungle, Max? Was that it? Did I scare you?"

"Of course not. It was a business trip."

She nodded, relaxing a little, and asked for a drink. I came up with a Hurricane Reef. She winced when she read the label.

"Sometimes I'm just in the mood for raspberry-flavored beer," I explained.

"Jesus, M.D., you really have gotten weird. Look, you better tell me right now, is there somebody else?"

"Not really."

"Not really," she repeated. "So you lied to me?"

"Since you've been in Florida, I've met somebody. But it's a dead-end relationship. It can't go anywhere."

"My good luck at work again," she said bitterly. "And all the while, I was thinking you suspected me of killing Jeff and Twy."

She said it so offhandedly, the same way she had brought up Lyre and Stone in the bar in South Beach that night, that it rocked me backwards.

"So you do then, don't you," she said, narrowing her eyes.

"Phayle," I said.

"Don't 'Phayle' me, Max Diamond. You think I killed your friends, isn't that true?"

I sat down on the back of my couch, the strains of "Lucky Man" flooding my head.

"Quite frankly, there are a few things bothering me," I said carefully.

She drained the Reef. Pretty stoic for someone who didn't like berries with her brew. "Why don't you share them with me, Max? My bet is we'll both feel better. And while you're at it, how about another beer?"

I went to the refrigerator for the second time in two minutes, thinking all the while how tired I was and how badly I had wanted to avoid this. I gave her the beer and plunged in. "I find it one hell of a coincidence that you just happened to be in South Florida when these guys started dying," I said.

"A coincidence?"

"That's right. You say you haven't been in touch with any of us for years. Suddenly, a business opportunity arises and you come to South Florida. Boom, Jeff and Twy are dead."

"The Burdine's account is a plum, Max. I'm sorry if my being close enough to service it intrudes on your space!"

"Cut the shit, Phayle. I called Burdine's. They've never heard of you."

Her arms fell to her sides, and she gaped at me. "You called them?"

"I'm a cop, Phayle."

"And you think it's your job to check up on me?"

"Just routine. Just trying to clarify things."

Her gaze was boring into me like a dentistry tool. I felt naked in my towel. Vulnerable. "Well, maybe I can clarify things for you, *Inspector*. The truth of the matter, as you've discovered, is that I didn't come down here for Burdine's at all. I came to adopt a baby."

"A baby?"

"Is that a word you don't understand? B-A-B-Y. Like little tiny human?"

"Why adopt?" I asked faintly.

"I'm not right inside, if you must know. I can't have a child of my own."

That caught me off guard, and I made apologetic noises. She waved them aside. "We're a little past saying we're sorry, Max. We're into heavy truth, here. I came to Miami because Cliff Hughes offered to help me. Getting past the rat-bastard adoption screeners is tough for someone like me, a single parent who's been treated for depression, had a couple of two-night stays in the loony bin, a dose of Thorazine. 'A woman of the world,' that's what one agency called me. I've tried to make it easier on myself, to have my medical records sealed, to find a worthwhile man."

She paused to laugh. It wasn't a happy sound. I saw that her second beer was gone, and I went to get her a third without being asked. She followed me into the kitchen.

"For a while there I thought you might even be the one, Max. Isn't it amazing, the games we play with ourselves? It was a childhood fantasy, that's all. I knew you were a quality person. I even thought you were honest."

"Phayle . . ." I interrupted.

"Shut up, okay, Max? This isn't your fault, it's mine. It doesn't really matter at this point if your new relationship is going anywhere. The way I feel right now, I couldn't care less."

"Cliff said he would help you?"

"Cliff would go to the ends of the earth for me, Max. Twy and Jeff, too, and not because they're true blue, but because they all had so much to lose."

"What are you talking about?"

"I know all about them, see? I read the alumni magazines year after year, following their careers, the notes on their marriages, their children, their professional reputations, their lives."

"What are you saying here?"

She took another long pull on the Hurricane and looked at the bottle. "This raspberry really is repulsive. Look, Max, let me see if I can help you understand, okay? You know who ruined me inside? You know who tore up my uterus so that it had to be removed when I was only twenty-one years old? Your *buddies*, that's who," she spat, nearly choking on the word. "Your macho, secret society friends."

I felt my legs go weak. I leaned against the little table.

"Aw, what's wrong? Does this news shock you? Are you sure you haven't known all along? Haven't at least suspected?"

I knew in that moment that I *had* suspected, at least I had sensed a tension underneath the looks, the glances, the uncomfortable silences. I realized I had been avoiding prying into it out of fear of what I might find.

"I see that you have. Well, let me confirm it for you. They *gang-raped* me Max."

"No!" I felt the last tiny vestige of my innocence seeping away, and I stamped my foot on the floor like a child having a tantrum.

"Yes," she said, her voice finally beginning to slur from the alcohol. "In the clubhouse. In the sacred, male, Lyre and Stone clubhouse; that brick-walled building that holds in everything, even screams. And I did scream, Max. Loudly. At least until Twyman Boatwright the third shoved his shirttail into my mouth. He broke one of my teeth with a hard button. I had to have it crowned. Of course, that was the least of my worries."

"When?" I managed, trying to make my dry tongue function inside my cotton mouth.

"It was in the middle of that freak April blizzard senior year," she answered. "You probably remember the one. The snow outside made a huge white blanket, keeping anyone from hearing or seeing a thing. While they were on top of me, I remember looking up at the stained-glass window of the clubhouse, at an image of the Virgin Mary, her chin crooked, wearing a robe like the Mona Lisa. She was glowing from the street lamp outside."

"Where was I?" I croaked. The voice didn't sound like mine.

"We were in the middle of one of our broken-up periods. Remember those? I was one commitment-shy girl, wasn't I, M.D.? We hadn't been together for a few months, you showed up at my dorm room, we had a huge fight, and you stormed out. I came looking for you at the clubhouse. I knew I wasn't supposed to, but I did anyway. I figured you would want to hear that I thought you were right, that I was sorry, that I wanted to be with you again. You weren't there, but the three of them were. Smoking cigars. I still hate that smell because of it. And they were drunk. Not too drunk to know what they were doing, but drunk enough."

I felt like a statue, unable to move. Phayle polished off

the last of the Hurricane Reef. "Why didn't you tell me?" I whispered.

"Oh God, how I wanted to! I wanted you to fly into a fit of macho rage and geld them. But what exactly could I have told you? That your best friends had gang-banged me drunk? What would you have thought of me? That I was a whore? That maybe I wanted it? They would have said that, you know, and who would you have believed? You knew my sex drive was high—good God, you marveled at it often enough. We weren't on the best terms that year, in case you've forgotten. They would have denied it was rape, told you I wanted it, told you I was only angling to break up your friendship because I was jealous. Those guys had the gift of the gab, all three of them. They could probably have convinced you that *I* had seduced *them*. Think about it. Three words against one."

"That doesn't give me very much credit."

"Oh, come on, Max. You're wounded, now?"

"You could have gone to the police."

"And had it play out the same way? Their words against mine, my name all over the papers right before graduation? Would have looked great on job applications, don't you think? Promiscuous co-ed in secret society rape scandal?"

"I have to hear every detail. Everything they did," I said mechanically.

"Why? Out of prurient interest? So you can make it all right, somehow? It's way too late for that, and anyway, there's no *mail* involved. Nothing for you to solve, nothing I need from you, nothing I want you to do. I only came to South Florida because Cliff promised he would get me a baby. A girl child. That's the only thing I care about now. That's the only thing that can set any of this right."

"So you arranged something with Cliff?" I asked. I was

trying to recover, trying to quell my growing rage with cool cogitation.

"I'm barren, Max. Can you understand that? I endured a trauma-induced hysterectomy. Even if I could never prove who caused that trauma, do you think your three buddies would want me gabbing to the papers, would want interviews with my doctor? You think their wives would stick around through a shitstorm like that? Their clients? You think they would risk everything when all I wanted was a baby girl? Cliff handles adoptions. It's a piece of cake for him! He's already agreed to do it, he's working on it right now. We're just waiting for the right kid, the best kid, the perfect kid."

"Cliff handles adoptions?"

"It's a service the firm offers," she explained. "They bring in children from South America."

An emotional wrecking ball made contact with my solar plexus. I wanted to pass out so I wouldn't feel that feeling any more. *A service the firm offers.*

I sat down hard. Right on the floor.

The creatures Katerina the witch had taken out of my tear ducts were back, and this time they were feasting on my guts.

"I have to ask you something," I managed, looking up at her.

"I've told you enough," she said with finality.

"It's about Cliff."

"Go to hell, Max."

"That night at the clubhouse, did he do what the others did?"

She looked at me strangely. "Why are you doing this?"

"Tell me, Phayle. Did Cliff Hughes do the same thing the other two did?" I had to ask it, but even as I did, I knew that the last, tiny hope for me and Phayle fled with the question, fled just as surely as if I had beaten it straight to death.

"Go to hell, Max Diamond," she headed for the door.

I leapt up and stood in front of her, blocking her way out. "Please tell me. I have to know."

She tried to get around me. I put my arms around her, but she shoved me away.

"Please Phayle. If you ever loved me. It's incredibly important."

"He held me down. He touched me."

"But did he . . ."

"No, goddamnit, he didn't join in. What he seemed to want most was to watch."

NINETEEN

During South Florida's tourist season — which begins at Thanksgiving and extends through Easter — the cafes of Coconut Grove and South Beach draw people away from the Coral Gables Miracle Mile at night. Accordingly, nobody saw me park the R90S in an alley, under the moonlight, not far from the offices of Grayson, Boatwright, and Hughes, and nobody saw me stand in the shadow of the back door and attack the heavy security lock with my pick gun. The unit was built for business, and the cotton gloves I was wearing didn't make feeling the tumblers any easier, so it took time and much fussing before it fell.

Breaking and entering was a serious breach of every professional oath I had taken, and if I had possessed even one shred of evidence to support my suspicions, I might have gone for a judge's document — even if it was just a "sneak and peak" warrant. But as it was, I was flying pumped and vibrating and blind, on the wings of intuition, which had given me, in my four years with the postal inspection service, the reputation of being a man of unerring instinct, if not great professional restraint. I knew I was risking my shield as the lock gave way, and I worried about it, but I pushed the door open anyway.

The instant I was through, I was sprinting for the staircase, under which, during my last visit, I had noticed the alarm control box on the wall. I figured I had between thirty and sixty seconds to disarm the mechanism, but either my watch was running on island time or there was an unusually short delay built in, because while I was still working the lock on the outside of the box, red lights starting flashing throughout the two-story building.

I took the stairs two at a time, heading straight for Cliff's office. I didn't even try the knob, but hit the door running, bursting the latch. I sat down in Cliff's chair and looked about desperately. The telephone rang, no doubt the alarm company calling for the password in case of user error. I ignored it, and after a time the ringing stopped. A moment later, the office was filled with a wail as earsplitting as a WWII air raid siren. I shoved in my motorcycling earplugs and continued my frantic search. If my terrible suspicion was true, Clifton Hughes would never put the files I was after anyplace where somebody might stumble across them. He was too controlling, and he had too much to lose. No, if those files were at the office at all, they would be someplace very, very close at hand. I tried the desk drawers, and they rolled open easily on high-quality bearings. There were the usual things inside, a bottle of Mont Blanc fountain pen ink, a dozen sharp pencils bound together by a rubber band, several heavy-duty paper clips of the sort one might use to clamp together a legal brief, a box of strong French peppermints, a roll of antacid tablets, a pair of reading glasses, a few business cards, and two face-down pictures of Memphis Hughes, the one Cliff had shown me, and another, more recent one, in which the big woman had already gained substantial heft.

In a lower drawer, equipped with a file hanger, I found a variety of loose papers and personal files — five restaurant menus, the owner's manual for an XK8 Jaguar, health insurance claim forms. I checked the drawers for false backs and bottoms, but found none. I made the round of the walls, tapping and pushing, hoping for a hollow panel. I pushed on the edges of the bookshelves and on the books themselves, hoping to activate a secret mechanism like in the movies and open a passage to a hidden room. I found nothing. I dashed to the window and looked out onto the street. There was no sign of cops yet, but I knew that the noise of the alarm would keep me from hearing any approaching sirens.

Right then I began to worry that I was crazy, and that my sudden flash of insight had been wrong. Maybe the only thing that connected Cliff Hughes to anything nefarious was the fact that I knew him. Maybe there were other lawyers in town who liked to watch sex more than have it, and who ran adoption agencies that brought in children from the Third World.

Chagrined, I headed for the door, inadvertently striking the model of the *Hindenburg* with my shoulder. The model swayed on the wire that connected it to the ceiling in the middle of the room, and tipped nose downward. I heard a clunk, and I was almost out the door before it struck me as strange that such a well-made toy should have something loose inside. I went back for another look, tried to open it, found a hinge at the rear near the rudder, and pulled it apart. A thick manila envelope fell out onto the floor.

I should have torn it open at once, what with the cops on the way, but instead I was frozen by the image of Jeff and Twy raping Phayle Tollard in a dark, cold, stone building during a blizzard, while Cliff watched. I tried to imagine wealthy and desperate couples sitting in this opulent office, desperate for a child to fill a void in their lives, never knowing that for every Third World kid they helped give a life full of promise and plenty, Cliff consigned another to hell.

I picked the envelope up off the floor, reached in and pulled out a sheaf of papers. There were copies of receipts for rent paid by Twilight Enterprises on a storefront in the Airport Industrial Complex, and there were various and sundry receipts for transport; airline tickets, bus and train tickets, rental cars. There was even a list of people I assumed were clients, names and addresses. Telephone numbers.

The burglar alarm siren ceased as suddenly as it had begun, and I heard the front door slam shut. I ran to the window and looked out. There were two patrol cars in the street, blue lights flashing, doors wide open. My pulse hammering in my head, I put the papers back into the zeppelin carefully—no way was I going to lose these papers on an illegal entry technicality—closed up the zeppelin and ran for the door. There was a copy machine alcove down the hall, between Cliff's office and the stairs, and I ducked into it, compressing myself into the tiny space beneath the feed trays and the floor. I heard cautious footsteps, voices calling back and forth to each other, agreeing that the interloper had probably fled, what with a noise like that going off. A cop walked carefully past in the hallway. I could see his shoes. He stopped, the toes pointed toward me, and I held my breath. A moment later, he moved on.

I counted to ten, figured he was at Cliff's office by now, and slid out from behind the machine. I tiptoed to the top of the stairs, peered over, saw that the way was clear and made it down. I hid behind the door in the client washroom while the second cop walked by, then dashed for the front door. I followed the edge of the building to the alley, reached my bike, raised the kickstand and pushed it silently for half a block before riding off.

Since I landed at Miami International, I had been going like the Energizer Bunny. I hadn't watched the news, I hadn't been to sleep, and I hadn't checked the Weather Channel—South Florida's weather fascinated me—for the local forecast. If I had, I might have taken the Porsche, because by the time I reached MacArthur Causeway, an autumn gale was whipping Biscayne Bay up almost to the edge of the bridge.

Harbor Drive emerged like a ghost in the driving rain, sea spray making the asphalt slick, the wind making nearby yachts bob up and down as if they were trying to punch the sky with masts. I turned into Cliff's driveway, killed the bike, got off, and rang the doorbell.

In only his trousers, Cliff looked as if he'd been yanked out of sleep, but was in the process of getting dressed. Probably the alarm company had called. "Kinda late, isn't it, M.D.?"

"Tough shit, Mister Twilight," I said, pushing roughly past him.

He gave a visible start, then tried to cover. "What did you call me?"

"Don't," I shook my head.

We stared at each other. "How did you find out?" he asked at last. His voice was high and tight.

"Your bad luck."

"Was that you at the office just now? I got a call there'd been a break-in."

Like I was going to just admit it. "Selling kids to porn freaks is not exactly what most people would consider adoption, Clifton," I answered, pulling out my little Glock. "You want to tell me what they do with them? Make movies? Keep them hidden in the basement? It all appears on the up-and-up, right? Under the umbrella of 'adoption'? But you know who these creeps are, don't you? And you make special deals."

He eyed my gun. I turned on the overhead light. The room was lovely, with green print fabrics on couch, loveseat and chair, and a French Country influence in the furnishings. A happy, rich house. "I'm an attorney, M.D. I know every deal is special. Tell me what happens now."

"Well, let's see. I'm a law enforcement officer and you run baby love slaves and sell snuff videos. How do you figure this should play?"

"Not snuff," he said. "Never snuff."

"Tell it to the judge."

"You're aiming a gun at me," he said.

"You bet I am. How long has this been going on, Cliff? How long with little girls? Or is it little boys, too?"

"Not boys," he said faintly.

"So how long?"

He waved his hand. "What does it matter?"

"It matters to me."

"As long as I can remember, then."

"Did you only like children when we were at Yale?"

"I suppose so."

"And what is it about children that appeals to you, exactly?"

"Stop it, M.D."

"Call me 'Inspector Diamond'. Now I asked you a question. What's the attraction? Is it the little titties, is that it? The little panties? Little high-heeled shoes? The fact that you're the first? Something about kids being small?

Helpless? Obedient? Do you even touch them, Cliff, or do you just watch, like you watched Phayle, at Lyre and Stone, the night of the snowstorm?"

He went down like his little *Hindenburg*, deflated, in flames. "She told you?" he whispered.

"Are you going to say you didn't participate? That you tried to stop them? That you didn't get off on it? Is that why you agreed to help her get a kid? Because you're blameless and innocent?"

He was trembling now, his lower lip out like he might cry. It was pathetic.

"Maybe you're just teaching these kids the right way," I went on. "Breaking 'em in gently. Making sure their first experience is a positive, loving one. Is that what you tell yourself, Cliff? Is that what you tell the other sick bastards you sell films to?"

"I can't stop, M.D.," he said almost inaudibly.

"Inspector."

"I can't stop, Inspector. Lord, you don't know how hard I've tried. I've been to everyone. Shrinks, ministers, even a psychic."

I held up my free hand.

"Is all this what you told Jeff and Twyman? Right before you killed them?"

His head, which had been sinking steadily toward his chest in defeated despair, jerked suddenly upward.

"You think *I* killed Jeff and Twy?"

"Don't play with me. I'm not in the mood. My guess is that you could get Phayle only an illegal kid, and that tipped them off. Am I right? And how did they react? With horror? Did they want you out of the firm? Out of their lives? Out of the country?"

"Stop it," he whined. "I swear, I didn't kill Twy and Jeff!"

He was on his feet now, and strange shadows danced

on his face. A bolt of lightning struck close by, and in the sudden brilliance, out of the corner of my eye, I saw something monolithic on the move. Thunder clapped, a great weight collided with me, and I went down.

Memphis Hughes stood over me, holding my gun. Her hand made the Glock look like a toy.

"All those years of law school, and you still don't know when to shut up?" she shook her head at Cliff.

"Your husband's a murderer, Memphis," I said, climbing slowly to my feet. "The police are on their way. Give me the gun."

She stood there like some enormous stone Amazon gone to seed, her fat quivering, her chin set, her eyes afire. "I don't think so, *Inspector*. I don't think the police even know you're here. I think you came alone on your motorcycle, in the rain. I think you're dumb enough to do that, and dumb enough to believe that my husband killed his partners, the only people who ever made him a cent in his life. Well, I've got news for you. Cliff didn't kill them. He doesn't have the balls for it. He never *has* had the balls to do what needs to be done."

The shock on Cliff's face could not possibly have been feigned. *"Memphis?"* he sputtered.

"Did you think I was going to let them take away everything you've worked for, everything we've waited for, everything we deserve?" she spat. "Maybe you've forgotten how long it has taken for that supposedly great brain of yours to come up with some version of success—the failed real estate company, your pathetic stock market business, your fish-based pet food that not even a pig would eat. Well, I remember all of it, Clifton, and I wasn't going to let them cut you out of the partnership. They were planning that. You knew I overheard them talking. They were planning to just put you on the street because you didn't pull your own weight."

My old classmate wavered unsteadily in the shadows. "You killed them," he said incredulously.

"How hard do you think it was, really?" she said bitterly. "Jeff in his bathtub, soaping his armpits, singing a song. Twyman half-drunk and playing with his expensive toys in the garage. All it took was a pair of rubber gloves."

"You're crazy," he whispered.

Something changed in her expression. "*I'm* crazy? Me? You pathetic voyeur! You think I don't know about your little secret? You think I don't know about the children you sell through your adoption agency, the tapes you send out, the pictures, the magazines, the little business you run out of the storage shed? You think that isn't the *real* reason I've never given you a baby, Clifton? Can you imagine me delivering a child into your sick hands? I leave innocent little children out of my problems, Cliff. I just knocked off a couple of sleazebag lawyers."

It struck me at that moment that Memphis was at once terrifying and tragic, a woman swallowed, digested, and spit out by the fierce worm of her love for her husband and his terrible obsession. I realized that by staying with him, she had become like him.

Cliff's expression went from incredulity to rage. He took a step forward. Even in the pale light, I could see that his face was perilously red. It occurred to me that something might burst in his brain—a vessel, a sulcus, a lobe.

"They were my friends," he declared in a dangerous voice. "I would have worked something out with them."

"Ha!" Memphis snorted, keeping the gun trained on me. "Like what? Early retirement? An oath of silence? Do you also think you can work out a deal with your cop friend here? A short prison sentence, perhaps? Something for old times' sake?"

"You ordered the hit on Cristoforo Cruz and Regina Diaz," I said suddenly.

"Anything can be had for a price. I learned that from my husband."

Cliff blinked and looked at me as if he had forgotten I was there.

"Cruz was the last link to Clifton, right?" I pursued. "The only one left who knew anything about who those tapes were coming to."

"That skinny bitch sister just got in the way of a bullet. The shooters did her a favor. She was dying slowly anyway."

At that moment there was a bark, and a fluffy little white dog came barrelling into the room, its tongue wagging, its body vibrating with excitement. It was Daniel, the bichon frise stud. Memphis glanced down, and as she did, Cliff rushed her. They clenched together for a moment in what might have been a rough embrace, and then my Glock went off.

Cliff looked up in surprise, and then he sat down hard. Blood erupted from his belly. Memphis screamed and engulfed him in her heft, cooing over him, stroking his head as the life drained out of him.

"Poor baby, sweet baby. Who loves you most? Who loves you more than infinity? Hold on for Mama, don't die on Mama," she whispered.

Quietly, I picked up the hot gun and used the phone.

TWENTY

     Jeff Grayson's wake took place on Dennis Reilly's yacht. Reilly, it turned out, had been downright mortified to have been considered a homicide suspect by Todd Steiner. The party was his way of making amends for his raving letters, and he set things right in style. The boat was a vintage, teak-decked, seventy-two feet CrisCraft, with a canvas cover over the open fishing deck shading chairs and tables brimming with champagne and hors d'oeuvres for the pleasure of the fifty-odd people on board.

     A quartet from the Florida Philharmonic—Jeff's friends and grateful recipients of his generous support—made a miniature concert hall of the lower cabin, sending the sweet strains of Corelli concerti issuing forth as the boat plied the interior waters of Biscayne Bay. A number of well-heeled couples—Donna Karan designs seemed to reign supreme, as did Ralph Lauren weave belts, chino trousers and polo shirts—danced cheek-to-cheek to the music, while other folks clustered in small numbers, sipping champagne from Baccarat flutes and talking law, real estate, corporate strategy, and stocks. There were a few lovebirds in the crowd, and they favored the narrow, covered side decks, where they circled arms to sip from each other's glasses or kissed and nuzzled, inspired by the perfect weather.

Twy's widow Nora was there, never far from friends who physically touched her constantly, seeking to imbue her with their love and support as a reminder that they had not forgotten the tragic wave of recent events in which she too had been caught up. Her two little boys hid in her puffy peasant dress a lot, covering their faces and sucking their thumbs.

Brooke Grayson was along, and she and Phayle stayed together at the bow, their legs dangling over the edge, seeming to have no use for any of the rest of us. An unlikely bond seemed to have developed between them, an ironic development Jeff Grayson would probably have found discomfiting.

The United States Postal Inspection Service was amply represented by me and Mozart and Waco and Chunny. The four of us hovered near the stern, by the crab cakes and crudités. Disguising our voices beneath the low rumble of the engines, we speculated as to whether Memphis Hughes would receive the death penalty or succeed with a "diminished capacity" plea. Wacona feared that a good attorney would use Memphis's obesity as a signpost of her mental decay, proof that her marriage to Cliff had been such a living hell that she had systematically destroyed her health and looks. I thought such a tactic would probably be tried—hell, I'd had the same thoughts myself—but felt sure the prosecution could prove to a grand jury that divorce had always been an option, as had going to the police, and that the contract killings — though the triggermen remained at large — of Cruz and Diaz cemented the premeditative quality of her homicidal nature.

We were all more certain that Clifton would see hard time. Despite the fact that the bullet Memphis fired into him with my gun had consigned him to life with a colostomy bag, the illicit material found in his garage — as well as the file recovered from the miniature *Hindenburg* — had resulted in a bevy of confessions and a spate of arrests nationwide. The FBI, postal inspectors, and local police had rescued scores and scores of kids, as Clifton had been running his show for years. Wacona was personally spearheading the effort to get the victims — including some shocked and terrified wives — into counseling, and, where required, into protective custody.

The widow Grayson seemed not the least perturbed by the purely capitalist character of our host. In fact, the two of them obviously got along so famously that at one point Gwen summoned Brooke so that she and Reilly could be introduced. Reilly tried hard, I could see that, showing Brooke the controls of the yacht and telling her how pretty she looked in her little red bikini, but Brooke's reserve bordered on outright suspicion, for which I mentally saluted her.

The meeting did bring Phayle aft, though, and she slipped her arm through mine and stole me away from Waco, Mozart and Chunny, leading me up to her favored spot at the front of the boat.

"I was wrong about you," she said.

"You were right, too," I answered, taking a Te Amo Torpedo from my pocket. "I've been oblivious to lots of things for a long, long time. Thanks for trusting me the way you did."

"Better late than never, huh?"

I nodded, bit off the end of the cigar.

317

"You going to smoke that right here, right now?"

"Actually, this one's for you."

"I told you I hate them!"

"That was the old Phayle. The new Phayle is going to love them. This one tastes like chocolate. Here, cup your hands."

She did, and I lit it for her. When I had a good round ring of fire going, I passed it over. "This one's a funny shape. Looks like a dick."

"I hadn't noticed," I said innocently. "Here. Put it in your mouth."

"You're disgusting," she rolled her eyes.

"Go ahead and try it. No inhaling. Just taste it, then blow the smoke."

She did. "Chocolate, hell," she said.

We watched the shoreline slip past. It seemed to me we were close to Cuco's place, motoring along the inland edge of the bay.

"Incredible the way you unraveled this thing." She shook her head.

"I didn't unravel anything. It came undone by itself. Even that wouldn't have happened if you hadn't come clean with me. I have one question for you, though. About an Emerson, Lake and Palmer song."

" 'Lucky Man,' right?"

"That's the one."

"What about it?"

"Jeff was listening to it in the tub when Memphis killed him."

"Oh," she shivered.

"And right after that, you whistled it at Monkey Jungle."

"That's why you got weird on me that day!"

"Yep."

"Jeez, M.D. You blot out our whole relationship, or

what? I used to sing that song to you at Yale, reminding you how lucky you were to have me. Jeff and Cliff and Twy even sang it for the two of us one time in a 'round' when we were all drunk together. Tell me you don't remember that."

"It's coming back now," I lied, marveling at how maudlin and perverse it was that the theme song of our days at Yale had been Jeff's parting selection.

Phayle took a long draw on the cigar, and blew it out. "That's okay, Max. I forgive you. And I hope you can forgive *me*, but after all this, I can't really think of you romantically anymore."

"Ouch."

"To be honest, I see you more like a brother."

"A brother," I repeated.

"Don't give me that look. You're all right with this, aren't you? I mean, you've got a new relationship, right? Even though you said it can't go anywhere? I know you, Max. Impossible relationships are your specialty. By the way, everything's back to normal now, right? In the bedroom, I mean."

"I think so," I said. "I'm not really sure."

"Well if you're not, you will be soon. I don't see you being down for long. By the way, I like this cigar, you corrupting bastard."

With the greatest sense of satisfaction, I took out one of my own, an H. Upmann Lonsdale, and lit up. We sat there together in the salty breeze, our legs touching.

"Brooke is an amazing child," Phayle announced after a while. "I think we're going to stay in touch."

"You'll have a kid of your own some day. It's not too late."

She leaned over and kissed my cheek tenderly. "Thank you for saying that, M.D."

From the stern, the faint tones of "Taps" floated

forward. We got up and made our way back, just in time to see Gwen let Jeff's ashes fall little by little from her fingers and into the warm waters of Biscayne Bay. In the distance, on a long dock, I caught a glimpse of a figure in an immaculate white suit. He gazed out at us across the water, and even at this distance I recognized his posture, his elegance, and his power.

He offered his arm to a dark-haired beauty in a sundress.

The dress was yellow, the color of my Rachel's hair.